ADVENT ROMA

A Heart for Christmas

SOPHIE JOMAIN

AUZOU
CANADA

Welcome!

Open a **sealed chapter** every day and discover the next chapter in this Christmas story set in a ski resort in the French Alps. Make sure you have a letter opener and a hot chocolate by your side!

Happy reading!

Snowflakes fall gently onto the already white surface of the highway. Mont Blanc and the surrounding mountains are blanketed in snow. Tourists from all around are driving steadily along, their skis and snowboards packed onto roof racks. No doubt the ski resorts will be rubbing their hands together in glee.

I smile as I catch sight of the safety information displayed on the overhead sign:

FEEL FREE TO USE THE RIGHT LANE, SANTA HASN'T BOOKED IT.

Not that Mom needs to worry about the message; she's driving as if the engine had been capped at a speed of 75 km/h. It's driving me nuts… At this rate, spring will have arrived before we do.

All I Want for Christmas Is You is playing on the radio for the umpteenth time, the little velvet bulldog wearing a Christmas hat is bobbing its head on the dashboard, and trucks honk furiously as they pass us, but Mom, eyes fixed on the road ahead, is completely unfazed.

A tiny sigh creeps out of me, and I concentrate on the scenery. We should get to Morzine in about an hour, where I'm staying with my dad until Christmas.

It's been ages since I was there last, almost three years. And to think that's where I spent every single winter vacation until the age of sixteen.

Until the accident.

Until my heart gave out, and I was told I couldn't do any kind of physical exercise. It was only three years ago, but it feels like centuries ago.

"Do you want me to stop at the next gas station for a bit of fresh air before we leave the highway? ... Hello? April? I'm talking to you!"

"What's that? Oh, sorry, Mom, I was dreaming."

"Do you need to stop for a bit? This is our last chance before we leave the highway."

I smile at her, and she relaxes a little.

"No, you can keep going."

"Are you sure?"

"Absolutely."

She's looking at me weirdly. She's not convinced, I can tell. I know her like the back of my hand.

"I really don't mind stopping. Truly."

"Mom, if you'd like a break, that's cool, But I'm fine."

She focuses on the road again, but her strained little smile doesn't fool me.

Her overprotectiveness isn't a new thing; she's always been like that. I was born with a defect in my left ventricle, so I've spent my whole life being careful, and she's spent her whole life protecting me. There's no such thing as coincidence – if you have parents who watch over you as closely as my mother does, then you can be sure there's a weighty medical file around somewhere.

It's not a complicated story. I had a heart attack when I was sixteen, and a pacemaker was put in. I had to be really careful and take it easy for a few months, but then, overnight, I was told I wasn't allowed to walk more than twenty steps at a time. My heart was giving up on me. I had to wait in a hospital until one became available for a transplant, which happened eight days before my seventeenth birthday.

In April it'll be two years since the operation. April, just like my name. A month that must have been predestined for big things.

I unlock my phone and start scrolling through TikTok and Instagram – anything to take my mind off the situation. If you have a heart transplant at my age, in the best-case scenario your life expectancy is around fifteen years. Then you have to get a new heart and cross your fingers it works.

I think about that every single day.

The videos I'm watching are incredibly stupid, but I can't tear myself away from them.

And then, as if expressly intended to save me from yet another culinary disaster on Chefclub, I get a beep from WhatsApp.

Have you left yet?

An hour ago. You?
Still in Grenoble?

Yeah. I'm so bummed I can't
come til the 10th. My project
summary's due in Jan and
I haven't finished taking photos
of the museum collection.
I'm stuck here...

Don't worry, I won't
miss you!

Yeah right!!

Eva is my best friend. Before my operation, we had met up in Morzine every year since we were six years old. She was born there; her parents own the biggest sports store in town.

She's in her second year of an archaeology degree, and although she's trying to make me think she's pissed off she can't come earlier, she actually loves studying all those old artifacts.

Think you'll go out?

Yeah...

Whatever! You're such a recluse!

We'll see what happens.

OK.
Anyway, I'd better go,
I have so much work to do!
Love you!

Mom takes the Nangy exit and gets in line for the toll-booth. I can see from her expression that she's managed to read some of our messages. I hate it when she does that.

"You can still change your mind, you know."

I pretend not to understand what she means.

"And stop in a gas station?"

"No. I can turn around and we can go home."

I haven't left the house much since my operation. I built a kind of protective bubble around myself to avoid infection and make sure I stayed as healthy as possible. Buying time until my next heart procedure. I did my high school diploma via correspondence and started university a year late, from home.

I'm definitely not going to win any prizes for social interaction, so three weeks in Morzine is going to be a test. And here is Mom giving me an out, so I don't have to go through with it.

It would be so easy to say yes and not take any risks, but I don't want to back down now that we're almost there.

I've decided I want to be stronger than that.

"No, it's fine, Mom."

"You don't seem fine."

"Maybe. But I want to spend time with Dad. We haven't had many opportunities over the past three years."

She purses her lips and bites back what she was going to say. She doesn't like talking about my father.

My parents separated just before my heart attack. The pressure got to them. As time passed, they had been drifting farther apart anyway. They fought all the time.

Mom has always been really overprotective, but Dad just wanted me to make the most of life. They officially got divorced two years ago, and they still have polar opposite views on things, so today Mom is stressed because while I'm with Dad, she won't be able to control anything.

I turn and look at her as she stops at the tollbooth.

"Mom?"

"Yes?"

"Everything will be OK, you'll see. I'll be really careful."

She tries to smile, briefly caresses my cheek with the tips of her fingers and lets out a big breath.

"Almost nineteen," she says as she gets out her credit card. "You've grown up so quickly."

It's half past four when we arrive, and the sun is already going down.

Morzine is only at an altitude of 1,000 metres, but there's a lot of snow here too. Everything is white, from the mountain slopes down to the roofs. There's not a square inch of grass or sidewalk to be seen. All the Christmas decorations are up, and there are so many of them! Some things never change; it's exactly how I remember it.

My father's chalet is on the Route des Nants, at the south-eastern edge of the township, just outside the main centre.

Mom stops at the bottom of the snow-covered drive and makes a face.

"Can you send a message to your father and tell him where we are? I'd rather not drive up. There's too much snow."

"Even with snow tires?"

She sighs.

"Just do it, please. I don't feel comfortable."

I pull on my wool hat and parka, and get out of the car.

I take a deep breath. The air is piercingly cold, and I can smell the pine trees. The mountains…

I've missed them so much.

My heart beats faster as I look around at the winter resort of my childhood, the wooden chalets dotted along the hillside, bunched up against each other, the cable cars, the clock tower of the Sainte-Marie-Madeleine

Church. There's something truly magical about Morzine in December.

"Hey!"

My father has already seen us and is almost running down the hill. His unruly brown hair is sticking out from under his beanie, and despite the layers of fleece-lined clothing he's wearing, he's still as trim at forty-five as he was when he was twenty.

When they were still married, Mom often said she hoped I'd inherited the same genetic make-up as him. She's blonde, not very tall, and as it's turned out, I'm kind of a mix – not too tall nor too short, well, maybe a little on the short side, I guess. But at least my feet touch the floor when I'm sitting down. I have my dad's brown hair and my mom's blue eyes. The perfect combination.

"Hi, Princess," says Dad as he pulls me in for a hug. "You look good."

"Hi, Dad."

I can hear the emotion in his voice.

It's been so long since we spent a vacation together. It makes my head spin just thinking about everything he must have done to make sure I'm happy.

"Hello, Etienne," says my mother. "Thank you for coming to meet us."

"Hi, Amélie. Of course, no worries."

As he leans over to give Mom a quick kiss on the cheek, she politely avoids it. She likes to be formal. She doesn't think there should be too much familiarity between her and Dad. But you can tell it's not natural for her. For example, she never wears make-up, except when she knows she's going to see him. As if it was still important. Sometimes I wonder if she really is as indifferent as she makes out.

"So, what do we have here!" he says as he checks the open trunk. "Is that all?!"

He looks at the lone, medium-sized suitcase I brought with me, in addition to the bag I have slung over my shoulder.

He's either disappointed or surprised, I'm not sure which.

"I'm only staying three weeks."

"I know, but you need more than usual in the mountains. Did you bring waterproof clothing?"

I shrug my shoulders. I hadn't planned on going skiing anyway.

"Never mind," he says. "Maybe the gear you wore three years ago still fits. And if worst comes to worst, we'll just buy something."

"April needs to study for her exams," says Mom, as if to shut down any adventurous ideas he might have. Me scrambling through snow isn't really what she has in mind. "And can I remind you that she has just had a major operation."

Here we go again…

"As if that's something I could forget," Dad replies. "And actually she hasn't just had her operation, it was over a year and a half ago. Can I remind *you* that we've been told it's important for April to get back to a normal level of physical activity?"

"Normal, yes. But for you 'normal' seems to mean endless treks, extreme skiing and athletic warm-ups in the snow. Everything that April should avoid."

"And who decided that? You, not the doctors."

"April is on immunosuppressants to protect her transplanted heart, which means that her immune system is compromised and that she needs to be monitored on a daily basis. Etienne, I don't want to..."

Oh, come on. They're already starting up?

"Hey! I do have a brain, you know. So, if you both don't mind, I'll decide what I do each day."

"April..." says Mom.

But that's not going to work anymore, I'm too old for this now!

"Dad, as Mom says, I have exams in January that I need to study for, which will keep me busy for a few hours every day. Mom, if I feel like going outside, I will dress warmly, but I will not fill out three copies of an authorization form for you to sign."

My parents look at each other a bit sheepishly, while I scowl. It's unbelievable how they much they bicker, as if I wasn't there, as if I haven't already had a hard time, as if I wasn't able to think or make decisions by myself.

I grab my suitcase, push past them and start walking to the chalet at a speed that is bound to bring Mom out in a rash. Even five minutes is too much to hope for before the two of them get started. It goes off the rails in no time, and frankly, I'm over it.

"Sweetheart, wait!"

Dad rushes up to take my baggage. But I don't stop.

"Go and help Mom instead. She has a huge bag of food in the trunk."

"Food?"

"Yes. You know, for the girl with the lousy immune system who might die if she eats a square of chocolate. Or has one gram of salt too many, who knows?"

Stunned, my father comes to a stop in the snow, but I keep going.

I've had enough, damn it!

Even though for the past twenty months I've been walking and breathing normally, my life could be summarized by the words "caution" and "restriction." I'm careful about everything, absolutely everything. So, I would really like my parents to stop adding to it and not ruin my Christmas vacation with their own fears.

As I reach my father's old Savoyard chalet, my bad mood starts to fade. The façade is decorated with a row of cow bells that belonged to my grandfather, and on the first floor, the carved balcony and windows with wooden latticework give a 360° view across the village and the neighbouring mountains. It's one of the biggest chalets in Morzine, and to be honest, I've always thought it was one of the prettiest too.

Dad almost never locks it, so all I have to do is push open the door. I hang my backpack up on the coat hook with a smile.

The entrance opens up into the living room, which has timber walls from ceiling to floor. The stone fireplace is lit, the armchairs and suede couch haven't budged, the rug is still just as worn and, in the corner, majestic and as yet unclothed, there is a tree waiting in a bucket. Dad hasn't forgotten.

He always used to wait for me to arrive before decorating the Christmas tree.

There's even the plastic container I used to rummage through and find all sorts of treasures to put on the tree when I was little.

"Its name is Norbert," says Dad as he follows me into the chalet.

"Norbert?"

"Yeah, because there are Nordmanns everywhere nowadays."

My smile grows. Dad has always had funny ideas.

"Would you like a coffee? Or tea?" he asks Mom, who has barely come more than two steps inside.

And yet when I think about the amount of time she has spent here.

"No, thank you," she says, with a look at her watch. "It's already five o'clock, and I'm going to Thonon to see Cathy. I'd better not hang around. I don't like driving at night."

My father nods. I know exactly what he's thinking. He's never really liked Cathy, he always found her too raucous. I turn to my mother, who's staying with her friend for a few days.

"OK, Mom. Be careful!"

If she says, "You too," I'll scream.

But she doesn't. She walks over, hugs me for a moment and looks at me with glistening eyes, as if she's not going to see me for months.

"I'll be back on the 25th. Don't forget to call me regularly, OK?"

"I promise!"

We give each other a last hug, and then she heaves a great sigh.

"All right, then. I'm off! Have fun."

"Shall I walk you to the car?" asks Dad.

"No, don't worry, I have the right footwear," she says, pointing to her winter boots. "See you in three weeks!"

The door closes behind her, leaving my father and me alone.

"So, now what?" he asks.

I pretend to think and look over at the passage through to the kitchen. I know exactly what to say.

"A hot chocolate and an old movie!"

His face lights up.

"I hoped you'd say that. You're on!"

The next morning, I wake to the sound of my phone beeping. Surprise, surprise, it's Mom.

So, how was last night with your dad?

We watched some movies. And you?

Perfect! What are you doing today?

Studying. Don't want to fall behind.

Good idea, all your hard work will be worth it! xxx

I put my phone on the bedside table and stretch like a cat.

My bedroom hasn't changed. There's still the same small double bed, unvarnished wooden desk, traditional wooden wardrobe and the curtains and duvet with kitsch red and green checks. The room is just the same, and I slept just as well as I always used to.

I leave my warm bed and pull on a fleece, before opening the shutters. The bay window looks out over the balcony I share with Dad, whose room is just next to mine. The incredible panorama that stretches out before me takes my breath away, as usual. Our chalet is nestled against the mountainside, slightly higher up than the others. From where I'm standing, I can see the whole village, snow-covered fields, evergreen forests and the Alps to the west, lit up by the morning sun's rays. I'm in boxer shorts, it's freezing. Mom would have a fit if she saw me. It's time to get moving! I put on some thick wool socks, put my hair up quickly in a bun and go downstairs for breakfast.

The fire is roaring, and Dad is standing at the kitchen table drinking a coffee, dressed in his winter gear ready to brave the cold.

"Ah! Hi, sweetheart! Sleep well?"

"Not bad at all."

I give him a kiss and open a cupboard to get out a mug.

"My coffee machine is being repaired, but I found the old filter machine if you want."

"Thanks, Dad, but I drink green tea in the mornings. It's better for you on an empty stomach. You should try it."

"As if! I have a big snowshoe trek that starts at 9, but I should be finished early. Mid-afternoon, I think. My clients are a bit tricky. You don't want to come, I suppose?"

I give a forced smile.

"No, no. Thanks though!"

"You'll find everything you need for lunch in the fridge, and tonight I'll take you out for dinner!"

"Oh… OK."

For someone who can't eat normally, restaurants are such an ordeal.

"What are you going to do today? See Eva?"

"No, she doesn't arrive until the 10th. I'm going to study."

Dad frowns.

"You're meant to be on vacation."

No point reminding him that law school is not an easy run, especially in first year. He has a fair idea, but Dad and school have never been the best of friends. I raise my eyebrows as I notice the time on the clock and see Dad getting another cup of coffee. It's 5 to 9.

"You sure you're going to be on time?"

He looks at his watch.

"Holy moly, I'd better go! See you later, sweetheart, and don't forget to put more wood on the fire!"

He downs his coffee in one gulp, grabs his backpack and leaves the chalet like a shot. My bedroom isn't the only thing around here that hasn't changed… Dad is still always late!

I swallow my pills – the ones I've got to take for the rest of my life to prevent my body rejecting the transplant. The same ones that trash my immune system and make me get sick more easily than everyone else. I put the kettle on, get out a teabag of green tea, two rice cakes and a clementine, and go and sit down by the fire with a banket and my laptop.

My plan for the day is simple. I'm going to stay inside and convince Dad not to go out for dinner tonight. He's bound to want to eat raclette, tartiflette, croziflette,[1] or some other cheesy "lette" business that I haven't been able to touch since my operation. We can decorate the tree instead!

I turn on my laptop and settle in for some serious studying. I'm on my third cup of tea, my head full of information about family law, youth law, divorce, marriage and civil unions, when I hear a loud knock at the door. I look at my watch. It's almost midday.

Damn, I'm still in my pyjamas, my hair is a mess, and I haven't even showered! I wrap the blanket around my shoulders and open the door.

Argh... It's Augustin Favre, Eva's brother. I'm so shocked to see him here I almost drop the blanket. But given what I'm wearing, I manage to keep a hold of it. Now's not the time to show off my amazing fashion sense.

"Hi," he says with a smile.

His voice is much deeper than I remember.

The last time we saw each other, I was about to turn fifteen. He was almost eighteen and was covered in pimples. But not anymore... The two of us never really talked much. He spent all his time on the slopes – he wanted to become a ski instructor – and I spent all my time with Eva, setting the

---

1. TN: Croziflette is a hearty baked dish made with buckwheat flour pasta, cream, lardons and topped with reblochon cheese. Tartiflette is similar but has potatoes instead of pasta.

world to rights. We had nothing in common. Then after high school he left to study sports in Grenoble, and we haven't seen each other since.

"Hi."

"Is your father around?"

"No, he's out with clients and won't be back before 3."

"Oh. Did he leave anything for me?"

Slightly puzzled, I instinctively look toward the table and the sideboard.

"I don't think so. What are you looking for?"

"An itinerary. Can I come in? He usually leaves it in his office."

"Um… I… Yeah, sure."

I step aside and close the door after him. He takes off his red beanie, revealing a mop of brown, wavy hair that's in need of a pair of scissors.

I can see that he's changed without really changing. He still has the same brown hair, the same dark eyes and the same tanned skin, but he doesn't wear glasses anymore. And he's grown at least twenty centimetres. He's really tall and is wearing an official ski instructor outfit. Obviously, Augustin has achieved his goal.

"Take a seat in the living room, I'll go and see if I can find it."

"Thanks, and… ah… you have something in your hair."

"Huh? What?"

He points to the top of his own head.

Oh, great. I have a piece of rice cake caught in my bun.

"Thanks, I'll be back in a minute!"

Oh, that is so typical…

I'm mortified and quickly go up to my room. I pull on whatever I can find, jeans and a hoodie from yesterday. I do my hair and then go straight to Dad's office. Just as Augustin thought, there's an envelope on the table with his name on it. When I get back to the living room, he's just finished lighting the fire. The large flames are already giving off heat.

"I got it going again, it's cold outside. Although now that you're dressed, you'll probably feel a bit warmer," he adds with a grin.

Kill me now!

He brushes his hands on his trousers and takes the envelope I hand him.

"It was in the office. What kind of itinerary is it?"

"My friend Jimmy and I like getting off the beaten track."

"Backcountry skiing?"

He nods.

"The ski resort doesn't mark these trails, and the guides don't go there even with more seasoned tourists, so it's really quiet. Your father knows all the best spots to snowboard safely."

"I see."

"What, you're the kind of person who gets scared?"

"No, the kind of person who is careful, especially after so much snow."

"We know what we're doing," he says with a wink. "Anyway, I'd better go, otherwise I'll be late. Thanks for the envelope."

"And thanks for lighting the fire!"

He heads to the front door and grabs the door handle, then hesitates and turns back toward me. Not that I've moved at all.

"You're looking well."

I want to smile at him because I can tell he's being genuine. "Thank you."

"How long are you here for?"

"Until the 25th. I guess you're around all winter?"

"Yep! I'll be here until mid-April. Right, this time I'm going. Eva arrives on the 10th. We might catch up before then?"

"Um… yes, maybe… Oooh, shit!"

As I step back, I knock the coffee table with the back of my leg and lose my balance. I just manage to stop myself from falling over. My face goes bright red.

"You OK?"

"Yep, I'll just see you to the door!"

Augustin smiles – the way you do when you think back on all the embarrassing things someone has done.

Come on, April, a little dignity.

I walk up, chin held high, and open the door for him.

"Goodbye, Augustin."

I can see he's holding back a laugh.

"Goodbye, April," he says, just as formally.

I close the door without further ado and lean against it with my eyes closed.

You are such a klutz, April Hamon!

When I open my eyes again, I see Augustin's beanie on the table. Damn! I grab it and rush outside. I'm not even wearing shoes.

With his long legs, Augustin is already part way up the road.

"Hey! You forgot your hat!"

He turns around, raises his arm and jogs back to get it.

"Thanks! But now you'll have to change your socks…"

I look down. Of course, I'm standing in twenty centimetres of snow.

"See you soon," he says in a warm voice, looking down at me from his not inconsiderable height.

Is he flirting?! With me? Fine, then.

I answer just like Eva would: clear, simple, cut-and-dried. "See you!"

Once Augustin has gone, and I'm sure I'm well and truly alone, I burst out laughing. I haven't experienced anything like that since… well, ever! As Eva would say, you've got to try everything once. Sure, but not with her brother… How embarrassing!

I reach for my phone and sit in the armchair.

> Your brother just stopped by.

Really? What did he want?

> An itinerary my father left him.

He's such a pain in the ass with his backcountry skiing! What are you up to?

Studying. And you?
Making progress?

Not really. Can't wait to be on vacation.

I leave it for a minute or two, hesitate, and then go for it.

Your brother has really changed.

You think so?

It's been almost four years since I last saw him, so yeah!

True, that's ages!
There's one thing that hasn't changed though, he's still totally reckless...

Reckless or brainless?

Both! Mom freaks out about him.

I can still remember how he loved doing crazy tricks and would compete in all the extreme freeriding competitions. Even though Eva and I adored skiing, it still annoyed us because it was all he thought about. Though with hindsight, I've got to admit he was super talented. And cute.

At least he is now!

> Does he have a girlfriend?

> Probably several… I pity the girls who fall for him. You'll have noticed he's quite good looking.

I reply, but not entirely truthfully.

> Sure, but he's not exactly Chris Hemsworth!

> Chris Hemsworth!

I smile, get myself a plate of pasta and then flop back into the armchair and turn on the television.

It's time for a break.

Dad gets back late afternoon, once it's already dark. I wasn't worried because that's what trekking is like. You know the departure time, but not when you'll get back. The usual story.

"Sorry, sweetheart," he says as he removes his parka and hat, which are covered in snowflakes. "My client twisted his ankle but didn't want to call the emergency services. We weren't even very far from the village, but the snow was starting to fall. It took us ages to get back. Then I had to take him to the doctor. Anyway."

"Don't worry about it!"

"How was your day?"

I point to the empty plate still on the table, my laptop and the pages I've been studying. "Less active than yours but still busy."

He collapses onto the couch. He looks exhausted.

"That guy was so draining. I've never seen anyone who talks so much. I have such a headache."

I should be ashamed of myself, but the opportunity is just too good to miss...

"What if we stayed at home tonight? We could decorate the tree and have dinner in front of the TV?"

"Are you sure? I don't want you to spend all your vacation locked up inside."

Well, I do...

"No, don't worry about me. I've only been here a day."

"OK, thank you, darling. We're just postponing dinner out. Right, I'm going to have a hot shower, and then we'll decorate Norbert! While I think about it, did Augustin Favre call in?"

"Yes, I gave him the envelope I found on your desk."

"Good work, thanks!"

Oh man, I just can't help myself. I have so many questions.

"Has he been a ski instructor for long?"

"He officially started this year, but before that he was a trainee. He's one of the very few instructors to have completed the national sports instructor certificate in only four years. That's unusual, but he's really talented."

"Is that why you give him routes for backcountry skiing?"

He can hear the tone of reproach in my voice.

"Good grief, you sound just like your mother! Sweetheart, I'm sure it's not news to you that legally, in France, backcountry skiing can't be banned because that would go against our right to the freedom of movement. However, your good old dad has been a mountain guide for twenty-five years, and the last thing I'd do is send this boy to his death."

I can tell he's annoyed.

"That's not what I meant, Dad. Eva and her mom think Augustin is a bit too reckless."

"They're not totally wrong, which is why I'd rather he come to me for advice than just set off somewhere that isn't safe."

I nod. I'm sure he's right.

"Actually, while we're on the subject, we're invited to dinner at the Favres' on Sunday night."

The day after tomorrow? At *his* house?

Augustin didn't mention it. Probably because he didn't know yet!

"Right, a shower! And then we'll decorate the tree!"

I watch my father head off, and my pulse accelerates.

So, we're having dinner at Augustin's parents' house, and he'll be there? Well, how about that. Let's hope this time I don't make a fool of myself.

Annoyed with myself, I shake my head and go into the kitchen.

Dad has a principle that he only drinks strong alcohol on special occasions. But he's still quite happy to have a glass of good cider, and he always has a bottle in the cupboard. I rummage through the fridge and prepare some taramasalata on toast, a few cherry tomatoes that are most definitely not in season, some pickles, some Tomme de Savoie cheese, a packet of veggie chips I grabbed from home, and, because Dad loves it, a few slices of dried sausage that he'll be the only one to eat.

I arrange it all on the coffee table and when Dad gets back, he is delighted.

"Hey! That's a great idea! It's so good to have you here with me, my girl."

I give him a hug and smile.

"I'm happy too, Dad."

"Shall we do the tree first? It was December 1st yesterday, so Norbert should already be dressed!"

Outside, dusk has fallen, and the snow has taken possession of the night. Inside, in front of a blazing fire and the table waiting for the two of us, Dad and I continue one of the loveliest traditions ever to exist. And even though the decorations are the same we used when I was ten, our Christmas tree is the most beautiful in the world.

In the universe even.

It is so cold there's steam coming out of my mouth.

It's -5°C out, and I would much rather have stayed inside in front of the fire, but today we're planning to buy some winter trekking clothes and shoes for me. To stop my father pestering me, I agreed to go on a walk with him for an hour or so, tomorrow morning. There's no way I'm getting out of this one.

I didn't tell Mom when we spoke on the phone this morning before I left the house, otherwise she would have made a huge deal out of it. Nor did I go into any detail about my plans for the day. Not that that stopped her from giving me the following advice: eat well, sleep well and… think carefully before doing anything with my body. She's always had a sixth sense.

"Do you mind waiting? I'll be ten minutes max!"

While Dad goes into the information centre to see what group bookings he has, I sit myself on a bench out front, pull up my neck warmer and scrunch up my face. It's so cold!

All around me the chalets are bedecked with Christmas decorations, fir tree branches hang from the balconies and lights twinkle from the roofs. Every single store is playing the game. Even the trees at the bottom of the slopes are lit up. There are lanterns hanging from facades, and it looks like an ice-skating rink is being set up in the village square, next to the old wooden merry-go-round. I can't believe it, in two weeks, there will even be an outdoor rink! Christmas is such a special time, the whole village is transformed. I love the atmosphere, and I'm not the only one. It's still the low season and the resort is already overrun with tourists.

"April?"

I turn around and frown as I see a tall guy with long brown hair smiling at me.

"Jimmy?"

"Hey, I didn't know you were here, it's been ages!"

Three years. Yep… It looks like Augustin isn't the only one to have changed since then. The last time we saw each other Jimmy had a shaved head, and I was a good twenty centimetres taller than him. I feel like I'm the only one who's still a midget.

"I got here on Friday. And you?"

"I'm staying with my folks for the season. You need a barman, I'm your man! Can I offer you a coffee?" he says, pointing to the bar behind him.

"Um… I'm waiting for my father. He'll be here in ten minutes."

I glance through the window into the information centre. Dad is deep in conversation with the manager and probably won't be finished straight away. It's true, I do tend to look for excuses.

"We have plenty of time. Come on!"

I wasn't expecting to bump into anyone so early in the season. And I hate surprises. Come on, April, make up your mind! He's not going to eat you.

I take a deep breath and glue a smile on my face.

"OK, I'll come."

The Blue Yeti is your typical ski resort bar. The walls are lined with timber planks and decorated with old wooden skis, vintage sleds and, of course, since it's December, there are Christmas decorations everywhere. There are elves in every corner – big ones, small ones, red ones, green ones – and in the middle of all this, there's a giant, two-metre-high, blue Bigfoot.

"Sugar with your coffee?" asks Jimmy.

"No, thanks, but a bit of milk if you have any."

"Your wish is my command!"

The machine does its thing, and he puts a huge mug on the counter before me.

"So, what's new?"

"A heart… and you?"

I don't know why I came straight out with it like that, but it was worth it to see his face.

Back when I used to come to Morzine regularly, Jimmy and I didn't have the same circle of friends. So, he doesn't know what happened to me. The first time Eva and I met him, we were fourteen, and it was here, in the Yeti. He was helping his dad. She got a crush on him and wanted to see him all the time, and because the Pléney chairlifts are only five minutes away from the bar, she would make sure we came and ate crepes at the end of each day skiing. Jimmy was sixteen. He wasn't interested in her at all, but that didn't stop Eva.

I look him straight in the eye and smile before explaining it to him.

"I had an operation."

"A heart operation?"

I nod.

I can see he's shocked. He takes a step back from the bar and runs his fingers through his hair. An unconscious habit apparently.

"Whoa. I didn't know. Was it serious?"

No, dude, they swap people's hearts out just for fun...

"Yeah, kind of, but I'm good now."

He stares at me as if seeing me properly for the first time. He looks a bit embarrassed.

"You look it. I mean, you look good. Augustin told me you had a few health issues, but..."

What? I'm not able to hide my surprise.

"Augustin told you about me?"

"Yeah, in passing. It was a while ago."

He rummages through a drawer and pulls out a business card for the Blue Yeti, before scribbling something on the back and handing it to me.

"Hey, tonight a few friends and I are going to the Tibetan Café, come and join us! I put my telephone number on the back."

"Oh, I... I'm not sure, I won't know anyone."

"You'll know me!"

The entrance bell chimes, and a group of about fifteen people come in looking for a table.

"I've got to leave you, sorry, but I'll see you tonight, OK? Nine o'clock?"

I finish my coffee in one go and get ready to leave.

"Don't expect too much, you'll probably be disappointed…"
Jimmy gives me a cheeky, sidelong glance.

"I have a feeling I won't be! And my feelings are never wrong!"

I leave the Blue Yeti with a sad smile. I'm going to end up disappointing him, I know.

What do you mean you're not going? Are you feeling sick?

Hey, you're the one who likes him, not me!

I know! I haven't seen him for over two years, and I want to find out what he's like!

Two years?

Every time I went back, he wasn't there or… Anyway, we never crossed paths.

And so you want me to check him out?

Exactly! I want to know if he has a girlfriend. Make sure you find a way to tell him I'm great. And take a photo of him!

Huh? You want me to send you a photo of him?

Not just one, heaps!

Girl, you're crazy!

I never said I wasn't!
So are you going to do it?

Wait, you're not serious?

Of course I am!

What the...

I'm relying on you! Right, I'd better get back to work or I'll never get there by the 10th. See you!

I don't want to do this. It feels like more than I can handle. But Eva has never let me down, not even over the tiniest thing. She was there when I couldn't imagine doing something on my own. She spent hours on the phone listening to me and so many weekends at my house because I didn't want to go out. She's always been there for me.

OK, she's been fixated on Jimmy since we were fourteen, and he's never shown the slightest interest in her. OK, what she wants me to do is pretty immature, and even the *thought* of being surrounded by people gives me the heebie-jeebies, but there's no way I'm going to be ungrateful for all she's done. I'm going to take it on the chin, it's the least I can do.

The Tibetan Café is one of the most popular bars in town. I went there once with Dad when he took me to a music concert.

I remember there was a huge wooden Shiva against one wall and a white Buddha behind the bar. The barman had tattooed arms, and it was packed. As I walk in, it feels like I've travelled three years back in time. The sculptures are still there, so is the boss, and it's still just as crowded.

I take a deep breath. I'm starting to feel a bit stressed out by all the people, so I try and control myself. I think of the many times I've been in this kind of place without it being a problem, and look around, trying to find something I can focus on. Jimmy is at the back of the bar with two friends, in an alcove that looks like a mini living room. When he sees me, he beckons me over.

"I knew it!"

I give a small smile.

"Hi."

"You made it! This is Margot and Jeff, Jeffrey. Guys, this is April."

She is petite, with a dark bob and a voluminous silver anorak. He is tall and blond with a full beard and shoulder-length hair. He looks older than the others. Twenty-three, twenty-four perhaps.

"Do I really look like a guy?" jokes the girl, slightly annoyed. "Nice to meet you, April. Don't be intimidated by these two, they're actually softies. All mouth and no..."

"Hey, hey!" interrupts Jimmy. "Move over so she can sit down."

Margot shifts to the next armchair, and I find myself between her and Jeff. It's been a long time since I had so many people around me, I feel a bit tense.

"What would you like to drink?" asks Jimmy.

Oh, great.

"A Perrier and lemon, please."

His friends look at each other. No need to guess what they're thinking. I'm always seen as the resident killjoy, the stick-in-the-mud who doesn't know how to have fun, the pain in the ass. This is *exactly* why I hate going out in groups.

"April had a heart operation," announces Jimmy, who can see I'm feeling awkward.

Well, that doesn't help the atmosphere at all. I feel obliged to play things down.

"It's fine, I feel fine. I just need to be careful."

"Yeah, of course..." stammers Jeff. "That must be so intense."

I settle for giving a nod.

"Have you just arrived in Morzine?" asks Margot.

"Two days ago. I'm on vacation with my dad."

"Her father is Etienne Hamon, the guide," adds Jimmy.

Jeff looks amazed.

"No way… I love that guy! He always has the best tips. You know you can always trust his trails."

My father, famous and he doesn't even know it.

"Do you ski?"

Ah. A sensitive subject… I try and avoid it.

"Not really anymore. And what about you, are you all from Morzine?"

I learn that Margot and Jeff are seasonal workers and have been coming to the resort for two years. I listen to them describe their love of the mountains, the people, the village. I'm quite happy not to be the main subject of conversation. Suddenly Jimmy starts waving.

"Hey, dude, come and join us!"

At the sight of Augustin arriving toward us, I turn pale.

"Sorry, guys, I'm with my coworkers tonight, they're waiting for me over there."

Margot throws a glove at him.

"Hey! What's this obsession you all have with saying 'guys' when there are girls around?"

Augustin bursts out laughing before finally noticing me.

"Oh, you're here?"

"Yep, in flesh and blood. I can't believe it myself."

"You didn't come in pyjamas, that's cool."

Thankfully the bar is dark, and no one can see me blush.

"You two know each other?" asks Margot.

"Yeah, we have for ages. April is my sister's best friend. Anyway, sorry, dude," he says to Jimmy, "I've got to go. See you Monday morning for some powder action?"

"For sure!"

"I'll be there too!" Margot adds loudly.

Augustin nods politely and heads off to find his work-mates. At our table, the conversation is becoming animated. Jimmy, Jeff and Margot are comparing the best off-piste spots, their gear, objectives they're aiming for, annoying tourists who think they can go anywhere. I learn that they meet up with Augustin on Monday mornings to go skiing, and that they all love it. Jimmy is unbelievably enthusiastic, he's waving his arms around, miming situations and barely breathing between each sentence. Once upon a time I would quite happily have let myself get caught up in it all, but not now.

Skiing is a thing of the past for me.

I sit there listening to them, nodding sometimes in word-less agreement, but I feel like I'm suffocating. They're all nice, and the atmosphere is friendly, but I just can't seem to get in the mood. I can imagine how I look.

This sucks. I pick at the skin around my nails. My eyes are roving all over the room like an animal in danger. I force myself to smile. It's hard to blend in with the crowd when the noise, the smells and the sheer number of people is practically paralyzing me. I'm finding it harder and harder to control my anxiety.

I should never have come.

"And you? What do you think?" asks Jimmy.

I have no idea what he's talking about.

"Oh, I… I'm not sure. I have to go to the washroom."

I get up, my ears ringing, and make my way to the back of the bar. Just as I'm about to open the door, I feel a hand on my shoulder.

"Hey, are you all right?"

I look at Augustin with eyes that are no doubt a bit glassy. I don't have the strength to lie.

"Not really."

"Do you want me to walk you home?"

I'm a bit short of breath, so I try to calm myself.

"Yes, that would be good."

"OK, I'll wait for you outside."

"Thank you."

When I get back to Jimmy and the others, they haven't seemed to notice that I'm not doing so well.

"I think I'm going to leave you now. I'm worn out, and tomorrow I've got to get up early to go trekking with Dad."

"Lucky," says Jeff. "That would be so cool."

"Yeah."

I have my phone in my hand, pretending I'm typing a message, but what I'm actually doing is taking a photo of Jimmy as best I can. I'm not going to forget the whole reason I came here.

"Do you want someone to walk you home?" asks Jimmy.

"No, no, don't worry. It's only ten minutes away. I'll see you at the Blue Yeti sometime?"

"Yeah, that'd be great."

"It was awesome to meet you," says Jeff with a huge smile.

I nod, then put on my coat, gloves and hat, giving them the warmest smile I can.

"Thanks for the evening, and for the drink."

"Come back whenever!" says Margot.

I wave goodbye and make for the exit. Augustin is waiting for me on the sidewalk. It's snowing and it's windy, but

I close my eyes and turn my face up to the sky to breathe in as much of the fresh mountain air as I can.

"Are you going to be OK?"

"Yeah, sorry, I just felt so hemmed in."

"I noticed. I was watching you. Did something happen?"

"I… no. Look, your friends are great, I'm the problem."

He frowns.

"You? Why?"

"Can we talk as we go?"

He nods, and we start walking through the snow. It squeaks underfoot.

"Careful, it's slippery," warns Augustin, as I lose balance slightly in a gust of wind.

"Sorry. It's just it wasn't a good idea for me to meet up with Jimmy."

"Why not?"

"Ever since my operation I struggle in crowds."

"Are you agoraphobic?"

"No, I don't think so, it's just that… I've kind of cut myself off these last three years and…"

The words get stuck in my throat. I'm having a hard time speaking.

"Don't worry, you don't need to talk about it. It's fine."

We keep walking for a few seconds in silence, then Augustin stops at the crosswalk even though there's not a single car on the road.

"Do you like Jimmy?"

I nearly choke.

"What? What kind of a question is that?"

"I'm just curious. He's my friend."

Eva would slit my throat if I told him anything. I smile at Augustin.

"Did no one ever tell you off for being too curious?"

"OK, OK, it's your business. Watch out, it's slippery here."

Oooooh! I skid and lose my balance, and only just manage to avoid falling over by grabbing on to Augustin.

"You all right?"

"Whoa! It's like doing a challenge on *Survivor*!"

He starts laughing. There's a bit of a slope to get up to my dad's place, I can tell this is going to happen again.

"Here, hold on to my arm."

I don't need to be asked twice. When we get to the chalet, he opens the gate to let me through.

"Are you going to manage?"

Dad has left the porch light on. I have five metres to go.

"I should make it."

"Well, in that case. I'll see you tomorrow at mine."

"Sure thing!"

We're going to end up joined at the hip.

"Thanks for walking me home. And thanks also for having…"

"Seen that you were struggling?"

"Yeah."

He gives me a wink and pulls the pom-pom on my woolly hat.

"See you tomorrow, April Hamon, and oh… before I forget."

"Yes?"

"Jimmy isn't single. *Bye!*"

And he lopes off as if nothing has happened.

Eva is going to be disappointed.

I have to admit that my photography skills were not outstanding. On the screen, all you can see is Jimmy's sweater, his chin and a bit of his mouth, which is all twisted because he's talking.

What is this awful photo?

It's to arouse your interest, girlfriend!

He looks like a monster!

Go and stalk his Insta then!

I couldn't find it... He must have a pseudo.
Did you have a good night?

Yeah, they're nice people.
But he has a girlfriend, sorry.

Oh? Did you see her?

No, your brother told me.

Really? He was there too?

With his workmates, but he walked me home and we chatted a bit.

Did you tell my brother I asked you to find out about Jimmy? Please say you didn't.

Who do you think I am? No, he asked me if I was interested and then said he wasn't single.

My brother asked if you were interested in Jimmy? Whoa...

I guess he was curious.

Curious? My brother doesn't give a shit about other people's lives! That is so weird.

"Sweetheart, are you ready?"

Sorry, I've got to go. Dad's waiting for me to go on this trek. Pray I break a leg so he won't ask me again.

You wish! See you!

I put on my gloves, hat and neck-warmer and think about what Eva just said. She's so harsh when she talks about her brother. I don't get the feeling he doesn't care about people. I mean, he offered to accompany me home when I didn't feel great at the Tibetan Café.

"April!" Dad calls out again. "I'd like us to be there by 9:30 at the latest!"

"Coming!"

I had forgotten how incredibly beautiful it is. It's a total change of scene. As we walk, it's as if I'm discovering the mountains all over again, the incredible expanse of white, the jagged peaks, the forests, the silence, the cold on my face. I try to settle down and relax. But I can feel my worries crowding in. They're always with me. Respiratory failure, irregular heartbeat, dizzy spells… I can't help it, but Dad knows how I'm feeling. He walks slowly, stops and looks at the view, lets me catch my breath.

"Let's go this way," he suggests. "We'll cut through the forest to the top of the cliff. It takes a quarter of an hour longer, but it's worth it for the view, and we can stop and have a rest there."

By the time we get to the top, I'm out of breath, but he was so right about the view! The Vallée de l'Abondance stretches out in front of us as far as the eye can see, with Lake Montriond, the Pointe de la Chavache, the Pointe de Nantaux, the deep blue of the sky and, just over there, about fifty metres away on the rocks, a family of ibex looking back at us.

"Oh, Dad, look! Look!"

I'm such a kid. But I always get like that when I see an ibex. I sit on a snow-covered rock and keep my eyes fixed on them.

"I'm so happy to be here with you, sweetheart."

"Me too, Dad."

He smiles at me.

"Hey, April, I… I've been watching you, and what I see just breaks my heart. I would so love for you to get your self-confidence back, and for you to live the life you deserve."

"I'm doing my best. Coming here, breaking out of my routine, trying to live normally. That's already heaps."

"But you deserve more. You can do more."

"Based on your criteria, not mine."

He makes a sound of frustration.

"For goodness' sake, April, it was a year and a half ago, almost two years now. Stop holding yourself back. Come out of your shell."

I give a deep sigh. I am not going to fight with my father.

"Dad. I want to decide for myself, without any pressure. But this is exactly what you're doing, pressuring me. I'm here now, with you, so let's just make the most of it without thinking about what more I could be doing. OK?"

I can see his expression grow stormy, but I'm not going to let him keep going on at me. It's the last thing I need.

"OK. But it suits you being free like this. Look at you," he says with a smile, "your cheeks are all pink, just like when you were a little girl."

I roll my eyes.

"Dad, it's cold. It's because of the cold."

"Yes, but it's not just that… Anyway, we've talked enough. Do you think you can walk to the Joux-Verte mountain pass? It's about an hour away. It's relatively flat, and we'll walk at your speed."

I give him a conspiratorial wink in answer.

"Only if you stop being such a chatterbox!"

He bursts out laughing, pretends to zip his mouth closed and then gives me a hug.

"I promise! Right, let's go."

I'm shattered by the time we get to the Favres'. We got back from our walk much later than planned after stopping at the snack bar at La Joux-Verte, where I ate a bowl of pumpkin soup and Dad had a sandwich. As soon as we got back home, I went and collapsed onto my bed. This could be a long night.

"Hi! Come on in!" says Elise, Eva and Augustin's mother, as she welcomes us at the door. "Oh, April, you're still just as pretty! I'm so happy to see you."

She gives me a huge kiss on the cheek and ushers us into the living room.

The Favres' chalet is set back a little from the others, further up the hill. It's modern, sleek and has large glass windows on each floor. It is as stunning inside as it is out. As you come in, the first thing you see is the huge fireplace in the middle of the room. It provides a central point for the rest of the house and is surrounded by couches and armchairs. And sitting nonchalantly on one of them is Augustin. He gets up to come and say hello. I don't think I've ever seen him dressed like this – beige chinos and a white shirt unbuttoned at the top and with the sleeves rolled up, Stan Smiths and folded up pant cuffs. You'd swear it was summer outside. It takes nerves of steel for me to remain composed. He is SO HOT.

And what effort have I gone to? None at all. Jeans, winter boots and a hoodie. Hmm… great.

"We're having croziflette tonight," Nicolas, Augustin's father, tells us. "Elise remembered how much you used to love it."

I smile politely, but the idea of it makes me want to screw up my face. Why, after a day of winter sports, do people serve dishes dripping with cheese and stuffed with bad cholesterol? I hope they've made a salad to go with it at least.

But, of course, that's not the case, and once we're at the table, I only nibble away at it like a kid with a plate of Brussels sprouts.

"You don't like it?" says Elise, with a worried look.

Is she kidding? I love it, I always have. It's just that if I start eating it, I won't be able to stop. The lie comes to my lips with surprising ease.

"Oh, yes, it's delicious. But after our big walk this morning, I was starving and ate way too much for my afternoon snack."

"You still have an afternoon snack? Like children do after school?" says Augustin, teasingly.

"Yep, that's her – snack, burp, snooze!" says Dad. I give him the death stare. All I want is for the floor to open up and swallow me.

Augustin bursts out laughing.

I've never felt so stupid.

Quick, create a diversion.

"Excuse me, I just need to go to the washroom."

I know! It's not the most subtle of excuses.

Augustin looks down and smiles, and I escape as fast as I can.

I thought I'd dodged a bullet, but when I get back, the next topic of conversation is even worse.

"So, April, would you be interested in a season's ski pass?" Nicolas asks. "I get three every year because of my partnership with the council, but with the work we have at the store, Elise and I don't have time to go skiing. Eva gets here on the 10th, I'm sure the two of you would love to get out on the slopes together. And then if you come back in February, you'll be able to use it again!"

My heart rate speeds up.

"Umm..."

I look over at Dad, hoping he'll see that I need his help, but he's not with me on this one and is focusing on the minuscule pieces of food still left on his plate.

"I... I'm not sure I'd make the most of it; it'd be a shame to waste it. You don't know anyone else that could use it?"

"My friend Jimmy would love it," says Augustin. "That would make up for all the coffees and grilled cheese sandwiches he gives me for free. As long as you're sure you wouldn't use it!"

His father looks at me.

"Are you sure, April?"

"Yes, yes!"

"Well, OK then, in that case," he says doubtfully.

"Right, how about tiramisu for dessert!" says Elise happily.

Oh, have mercy. I think my face must have gone white.

"Mom," interrupts Augustin, "would it bother you if April and I go out onto the deck first? I think the moon is still bright enough to see with the telescope, and she might like to take a look."

I look at him in surprise. I have no idea where he got the idea from – astronomy has never been my thing – but his suggestion is perfect.

"No, of course not," replies Elise. "We'll start without you!"

I leave the room with Augustin.

"That's three times in twenty-four hours that you've come to my rescue. Is my face as easy to read as that?"

"You have no idea! Wait here, I'll just grab something from the kitchen."

When he returns, he hands me an apple.

"Is that for me?"

"I'm not the one starving of hunger. Come on, it's through here," he says, pointing to the stairs that lead up to the mezzanine.

Once upstairs, he takes two thick blankets from a trunk and opens the bay window.

"You do know I've never been interested in the stars, right?"

"My parents don't know that. Nor do they know that the eyepiece has been broken for ages. Make the most of it."

And he's smart too…

An exterior light switches on as soon as we step outside. The deck is covered in snow, but my boots are just the thing. We walk over to the balcony and look out across the village lit up with its multitude of Christmas decorations. They make the roofs look even whiter. I take a bite of my apple.

"Why are you so strict on yourself?" asks Augustin without warning.

"What?"

"You know what I mean. Jimmy said that you're really careful about what you eat and drink, and I've seen you, you don't let yourself go."

"So?"

"I'm not being judgmental, it just feels like you're being a bit... hard on yourself."

I don't know whether to tell him to get lost or start crying.

"Yes, you are being judgmental. And it wasn't like I had my appendix removed."

"That's true."

I swallow.

"Look, I'm not sure I want to talk about this."

He ignores what I just said.

"Do your parents force you?"

"To restrict myself? No way!"

It's a cry from the heart.

"Well, not Dad, anyway."

"But your mom?"

"No, no... Look, I'm going to have to take pills every day for the rest of my life to prevent my body rejecting the transplant, and those pills make my body weaker. I'm not depriving myself of anything, I just want to make sure I don't get physically sick. Mom stresses about it all the time."

I pull the blanket tighter around me.

"Why do you even want to talk about this?"

"To try and understand."

"Understand what?"

He shrugs his shoulders and smiles.

"What you're going through."

Since when have he and I ever had this kind of conversation? Without meaning to, I can feel my jaw clench.

"I just don't get why people feel like they can try and change me, just to suit them. Yes, I am careful, but that's completely understandable. Everyone treats me as if nothing even happened to me, but damn it, I nearly died!"

"Hey... don't get upset. Despite what you think, I'm not judging you. OK, I get that the thing with your pills is serious, but aside from that, what I see is someone who is afraid of their own body and who doesn't seem very happy."

"How can you say that after only two days? I *am* happy. My life has started again, and anyway, you don't even know me."

He smiles.

"Of course I do, I was there when you won your first medal in a ski competition. You were six years old, and you'd just met Eva."

I don't say anything.

"Got you! See, you can't say I don't know you. For my family you're not some stranger. And even though my parents were a bit heavy-handed by suggesting things you didn't want to do or eat, it's because they want to see you as happy as you were before your operation."

I swallow again.

"I just don't want to do anything stupid, that's all."

"I can imagine. What do the doctors say?"

"They're more relaxed than me."

"Then why don't you listen to them?"

I give a snort of bitter laughter.

"It's funny you should ask that, my parents fight all the time about the same thing. Mom thinks that I have to be very careful, and Dad thinks it's time to move forward."

"Those two things aren't incompatible, you know."

"For them, they are."

"And what about for you?"

I pause before answering him.

"I don't want to disappoint them."

"There's no way that'll happen."

"Yes, it will. If I do what Dad says, I disappoint Mom. If I do what Mom says, I disappoint Dad. See?"

Augustin frowns.

"And how do *you* fit into all that?"

"I just try and get by."

"If you want my opinion, that's your problem right there. You're getting by rather than living."

This time I really do laugh.

"For you, everything seems so easy. But it isn't. Dad thinks exactly the way you do. When I was a kid, he encouraged me not to shut myself away because of my illness. He said, 'Your heart defect does not define you,' and I believed him. But then my heart gave out, and everything changed. I want him to understand that and stop pressuring me."

Augustin looks at me with genuine sympathy in his eyes.

"But you also have to learn how to let go and trust your new heart. It's your ally."

"I know it is, that's why I do what I do! Please don't act as if you know what you're talking about. It's because it's so important to me and because I won't get another that I'm so careful. It's that simple."

"Hey, wait a minute. Sure, I don't know what it's like to have a heart transplant or a liver transplant or even a toenail transplant, but I do know that half a plate of croziflette is not going to kill you."

I look down. I know he's right.

"To digest our food, we need to be active. Do you do any exercise at all?"

"Under supervision, in a rehabilitation centre. Once or twice a week. And if I exercise elsewhere, someone has to be with me at all times."

"Cool! So, here's something for nothing. If you can run on a machine, you can run outside. And ski too. So, honestly, eat a bit more of the things you like and then do just the right amount of activity to make up for it."

I lean on the edge of the railing and let out my breath. I did not see this conversation coming. Of course I'm allowed to exercise outside of the centre, up to a point and while following strict rules, but managing my fear is another story.

"I can see you're scared, and fear is healthy. As long as it doesn't paralyze you," he says, as if he's reading my thoughts.

I start laughing despite myself.

"You realize you sound like an old person?"

"What? LOL! Well, I'm older than you anyway, and I know I'm right!"

I pout.

"Admit it, deep down you want to do more, right? Get out of the rut you're in, find the sense of excitement you used to have?"

"Yes… I think so."

It's the first time in months I've been able to express anything like that.

"On Tuesday morning I have a class of primary school kids who are learning cross-country skiing. I know you can't do exercise on your own, so come with me. You'll be back on the skis, but without any pressure."

"I'm not sure I can."

"Stop thinking about it! It'll be really easy, just an hour, nice and slow. Come on. And then I'll buy you a crepe. With no sugar. It won't be that bad."

I don't say anything.

"April. Tuesday, 10 am, in front of the Super Morzine cable car."

I know it's ridiculous, but I feel like I'm about to cry. Sure, I get that what he's suggesting is not a big deal, but he doesn't realize how much it stresses me out. I fall silent. He realizes I'm not going to come.

"My sister was wrong about you," he says finally. "She told me you were brave, but she's wrong. You're just scared."

I feel mortified.

"How dare you say that!"

Augustin looks me straight in the eye, as if challenging me.

"Prove me wrong."

Then he turns around and leaves me standing in the middle of the deck on my own. I grab the snowy railing and look up at the sky.

I hate him for saying that, but I hate myself even more for having to admit that he's right.

"It's Monday, ravioli day!"

My mother used to love the film *La vie est un long fleuve tranquille*,[1] and so when I was a child I'd hear her sing out that phrase at the beginning of each week.

It became such a habit that I still think about it every Monday, even though today is going to be study day rather than ravioli day.

Before leaving for his trek this morning, Dad left a note for me on the kitchen table.

Hopefully I should be back around 1:30pm. Don't forget to tell me what you want for Christmas!

I feel like telling him I want an external hard drive I can plug into my brain.

---

1. TN: A 1988 French comedy film set in the north of France that takes a satirical look at the differences between the lives of workers and those of the bourgeoisie. The English title of the film is *Life Is a Long Quiet River*.

I haven't budged the whole morning; my laptop is on my knees, there's a Thermos of tea on the bedside table and sheets of paper are strewn over the bed. I'm the study queen... I've read and reread entire chapters on family law, memorized legal clauses and made summaries of proceedings. My head is stuffed full of information, but in one hour, tops, I know I will have forgotten everything.

When midday comes around, I'm just about to have a shower when my phone beeps.

A WhatsApp message.

> Hey, how's it going, it's been ages! How are you?

My heart starts to race. It's him.

Here I am, safe in my bedroom, two hundred kilometres from Lyon where this message probably came from, but I can feel the anxiety bearing down on me like a lead weight.

I struggle to breathe and sit down again on my bed.

Why is he suddenly coming back into my life now? What does he want? I close my eyes and remember everything that happened. There is no way I'm going to sink into another depression.

He can just get lost.

I send a message to Eva with my stomach churning.

> I just got a message from him...

> From who?

> Benoit...

> What? That bastard?
> You better not reply!

> No, but...

> April! I thought you'd
> blocked him!

> He never wrote to me
> again, so I didn't bother.

> Well, make sure you do it now! He is
> such a loser. You're blocking him, right?
> And don't answer him.

> I won't...

> Good. Sorry, I'm at uni and I have
> a meeting with my tutor in 5.
> Forget about him. Love you.

That "bastard" was my first boyfriend.

We got to know each other at the hospital while I was waiting for my transplant.

Now I wish I had never met him, and I hate thinking about him. I can't believe he had the nerve to contact me. We don't have anything in common anymore.

I don't know what he wants, and I'll never know. I read his message one more time, delete it and then block him, before writing to Eva again.

I did it.

Great, now my day's ruined. It'll take more than a shower to wash away those bad memories, but I am not going to get depressed about it.

There's only one thing to do. Make cookies. Yes! And I'll eat at least one of them. Woohoo!

I get ready in a hurry and go down to the kitchen.

I connect my phone to Dad's speaker and turn the music up loud before ransacking his cupboards. I smile as I find our old box full of Christmas cookie cutters.

When my parents were still together, we made cookies every year and hung them on the tree. There are even some ribbons in an old plastic bag and a needle to make holes. I roll up my sleeves, put on an apron and get out the butter, sugar and cinnamon. Here goes!

And the upshot is… after one hour I've made two batches of cookies in all sorts of shapes, as well as some gingerbread men.

The incredible smell wafting through the house reminds me of when I was young. My bad mood has totally evaporated, and I even find myself belting out *I Wish You a Merry Christmas* when it comes up on the playlist.

Just as I bellow, "and a happy new year," someone rings at the door. I turn off the music, wipe my hands and go open it.

"Jeff?"

"Hi."

I'm surprised, I hadn't noticed how tall and broad he is. He's even bigger than Dad. Once again, I feel like a dwarf.

With his overgrown beard and blond hair flying around his hat, he looks like a slightly freaky Scandinavian lumberjack.

"Did you know I could hear you right down the other end of the street?"

"Oh, whoops. Sorry. Did you want to talk to Dad?"

"Um… ah… yeah, that's right. Is he there?"

"No, not yet, but he won't be long. Come on in."

He knocks his shoes on the doormat to remove the snow, takes off his hat and enters the house, totally keyed up.

"We did an awesome run this morning. You should have seen it. Crazy. The conditions were perfect. It was such an adrenaline rush! At one point I did a massive trick, it felt like I was going to take off and fly! I landed on my skis, and my head was spinning. But I just did it automatically."

"Cool. You want a coffee?"

"Yes, thanks. It smells good in here. Did you make a cake? I'm starving."

"Cookies. Make yourself at home, I'll be with you in a second."

When I return with a plate of cookies, tea and a cup of coffee, Jeff is looking at the Christmas decorations. In particular, at a tiny pair of wooden skis that he's touching with the tip of his finger.

"Jimmy told me you used to ski quite a lot. Do you miss it?"

"Yeah, sometimes, but even if I wanted to start again, I'm not sure I'd still know what to do!"

Jeff joins me on the couch and picks up his cup of coffee.

"It's like riding a bike, you never forget. I broke my leg when I was eighteen, double fracture of the tibia and fibula, as well as the cruciate ligaments. It was a serious accident. I didn't ski for two years, but it all came flooding back as soon as I got on the skis again. When you're really into skiing, all your old reflexes come back in no time."

I'm listening politely, but you can't compare his broken leg to what I've been through with my heart.

If I get tachycardia, all the reflexes in the world won't help me. I know, my life seems to boil down to "if" this and "if" that, but that's exactly what's keeping me alive.

"I was thinking," he continues, as if he heard my thoughts. "I know you don't ski anymore because you're worried about your heart and all that, but if you wanted to get back into it slowly, I'd be happy to come with you. I have plenty of free time during the day and, you know... I'd like to."

His speech half makes me smile, half makes me sigh. I know he means well, but I'm not sure.

For most people, the idea of vacationing in a winter sports area if you don't ski makes no sense at all. That's what Jeff, Augustin and Dad think.

I don't want to have to argue with everyone and keep explaining that getting over what happened to me is difficult, and that right now I'm not sure I can. And that maybe I'll never be able to.

What I am good at though is avoiding the question.

"That's a nice offer, I'll think about it! Oh, but you never told me what you're doing here in Morzine."

"Ah… Margot and I work in a kind of hostel that organizes stays for students, holiday camps and groups. She works at the reception, and I'm in the maintenance department."

"And you've been doing that for two years, right?"

"Yeah, but we didn't know each other before."

He shifts closer to me and gets a serious look on his face.

"We're not together, you know."

"Um… OK."

He takes a sip of coffee and looks as if he's about to tell me something meaningful.

"She's not my type of girl."

Apart from smile politely, I don't know how to reply to that.

"She's a real pain in the ass," he continues.

"A pain in the ass?"

"No, I mean, she's cool, but you know, she kind of has a big mouth, and she never agrees with anyone."

"Oh… Right."

"At one stage, she really liked Jimmy, but nothing happened. They're too different, you know."

No, I don't know. Nor do I know why he's telling me all this. But hey, Jeff seems to love sharing secrets, so I may as well try and find out more. Eva would be stoked if I managed to get some more information for her.

"So, Jimmy has a girlfriend, I hear?"

"Yeah, he's with someone, but they don't see each other much. She's studying in Paris. I don't think their relationship will last long."

"Oh, why is that?"

"When you do seasonal work, it's way easier if you don't get attached to anyone. It's not a very stable job because you never stay in the same place. If you choose this kind of life, it's far better to avoid any extra restrictions or hassle."

"Right... so being in a couple is a hassle?"

"Too right it is! I mean, just look at Augustin. He had a girlfriend for a few months, and it was such a slog."

"Was it?"

OK, so now Jeff has my full attention. I'm not going to lie – up until five days ago, I couldn't have cared less what Augustin was up to. But now, no point denying it, I'm intrigued. So, I dig a bit.

"They didn't get on?"

"Not in the end. They both studied sports in Grenoble, and it just got so difficult. For their work placement they went to the same ski resort, and all they did was fight."

Jeff helps himself to yet another cookie.

"These are so good. Man, they don't make girls like you anymore!"

I have no idea how he thinks I'm supposed to reply to that. All I can see is the collection of crumbs slowly accumulating in his beard.

"Has Augustin been single since then?"

It's a bit of a loaded question and not particularly subtle, but I can't help myself, I really want to know.

"Yeah, it's much easier to have fun that way."

Then Jeff looks at me oddly and shuffles closer.

Um, what the hell is he doing now?

"So, April, what about you, do you like having fun?" he asks in a velvet-smooth voice.

No, what?! He's trying to hook up with me!

"Um, I don't think we have much in common," I say, as I edge back.

He looks at me, sighs and then puts on a weird voice.

"Here's the thing, Bernard. You and I have a similar problem. We can't rely on our looks, especially you. So, I have one piece of advice for you. Forget you don't have a chance, just do it, go for it! You never know, a misunderstanding might even lead to something!"

I can't imagine the expression I'm wearing on my face, but it must be memorable.

"I beg your pardon?"

"It's from the film *Les bronzés font du ski.*"[2]

"Jeff, I know the film. It's just that…"

"You're not interested. No worries, at least I tried!"

And he downs another cookie. This guy is nice, but he's completely nuts.

When Dad walks through the door, I could kiss him. It's starting to get quite awkward here.

"Come on in," he says, "it's much warmer inside."

---

2. TN: A now-cult 1979 French comedy film set in a winter resort. The English title of the film is *French Fried Vacation 2.*

Just behind him are Jimmy and Augustin. I started the day thinking of Mom's favourite film, *Life Is a Long Quiet River*, but it's never long and quiet! When Augustin notices Jeff on the couch, I can see his surprise.

"What are you doing here? You said you were leaving early because you had something to do."

Jeff seems completely caught off guard.

"Um... I had a change of plan, so I thought I could swing by and pick up an itinerary for next week."

"That's a bit hasty," points out Dad. "We don't know what the snow will be like yet."

Jeff scratches his head in embarrassment.

"Yeah, you're right, sir. It's just that our freeride this morning was so cool, I couldn't wait to do it again!"

Going by Augustin and Jimmy's faces, they aren't convinced.

And I realize that Jeff told me a big, fat fib. Just because he wanted to see me? Whoa...

"I'll be back in a minute, wait here," says Dad. As he leaves the room, Jimmy and Augustin look at Jeff, intrigued.

"So, guys, what are you doing here?" asks Jeff, trying to play it cool.

"Well, we didn't come round to eat cookies on the sly, that's for sure," says Jimmy with a laugh as he notices the state of Jeff's beard.

Jeff brushes the crumbs off like a kid caught red-handed.

"We came to get a can of oil for the snowmobile. It ran out as I was going back down," says Augustin.

When you go backcountry skiing, you don't have many options for getting out there: ski lift, helicopter or snowmobile.

And if it's the snowmobile, then the person driving it doesn't get to ski. Today it must have been Augustin.

"Ah, bummer, dude. Anyway, I'd better go. I've got to get back to the hostel. Unless you need me for anything?"

The two others shake their head.

Jeff hastily puts on his coat.

"Right then, I'm off. See you later, April, and thanks for the coffee!"

There's no point in accompanying him to the door; he's already rushing out.

The front door has barely closed when Jimmy bursts out laughing.

"I can't believe it! He came here for you!"

Oh man, cringe…

"Here you go, I found it!" says Dad, interrupting us. "I've had it for a while, but it's never been opened. Is the snow-mobile far away? Do you want me to take you?"

"No, don't worry, it's only a twenty-minute walk away," replies Augustin. "We'd better go. I have a class in an hour. Thanks, Etienne."

Then he turns toward me and gives me a wink.

"Tomorrow morning, 10 o'clock, at the top of the Super Morzine?"

I open my mouth to say something but change my mind and just smile. He's not going to give up that easily!

"OK," he says, "let's go. Thanks again, Etienne."

The boys head off, and as I'm putting the cups and plate of cookies on the tray, Dad gives me a strange look.

"Where are you going tomorrow morning?"

"Nowhere. Augustin asked me if I wanted to go with him on a kids' cross-country skiing class, but I'm not going to go."

"Why not? It could be fun."

"The skiing or the looking after kids?"

Dad smiles. He's clearly more motivated than I am.

"When you were sixteen, you and Eva did your youth leadership certificate so you could look after children on their school ski trips. This is the perfect opportunity for you to put it into practice!"

"Thanks for reminding me that I was never able to use it because just after that I had my heart attack."

As soon as the words are out of my mouth, I regret it.

"Sorry, Dad, that wasn't fair. Excuse me."

Dad comes over and grabs a hold of my hands. He looks at me lovingly.

"I'm the one who's sorry for what you had to go through, April. I wish that none of this had ever happened to you, but what's done is done. But maybe this is your chance to make up for some of that lost time? If Augustin has suggested this activity, it's because he knows there are no risks. *I* know there are no risks."

"That's where you're wrong, Dad, no one can guarantee that."

"Trust your own body and cut yourself a bit of slack. Don't push too hard, but let your body move. It needs it. How long will the walk last?"

I let out a sigh.

"An hour."

"It's just an hour. Your cross-country skis, boots and poles are still in the garage."

I don't say anything, and probably because he doesn't want to pressure me, Dad changes the subject.

He turns to the table and looks at the plate of cookies on the tray.

"Please reassure me that greedy guts didn't eat them all!"

"Ha! There are still plenty."

"It's my lucky day! Hey, have you thought about your Christmas present?" he asks, biting into one of the cookies.

"Not yet. And you? What would you like?"

Dad looks at me with a serious air. I can see the emotion in his eyes, and I know, I just know he's going to say something important.

"I want you to start living your life again."

I didn't sleep well. I was kept awake for much of the night by the wind clanging the cow bells against the chalet wall. They had never bothered me before, but last night they were like a strange accompaniment to the thoughts racing through my mind.

Dad wants me to live my life again, but where should I start? How do you get things going when you've been on stand-by for so long? I looked at the problem every which way, examined the few certainties I still have and weighed up the pros and cons. And I came to the conclusion that Dad is right. I have to start living life again.

Out of all the questions I asked and all the answers I came up with to make that start, only one thing has stuck in my mind. This morning I'm going to meet Augustin at his beginner class, and that in itself is going to be a huge leap forward.

And yet despite this, last night my stomach was in knots. I kept thinking of good reasons not to go, that I was making a mistake and that I'm actually getting weaker, that I was going to wreck everything I had done to ensure my survival, that something bad was definitely going to happen. In the morning, though, something more powerful than fear took hold of me.

Desire.

I want to spend time with him.

Why? I don't know. I'm not sure I want to ask myself that question.

My heart is pounding, and I haven't even started moving yet. I take a deep breath and go off to have a shower.

I pull my hair up into a ponytail and search through my wardrobe for my old cross-country skiing outfit. Tight black pants with a white, fitted jacket. I've lost a few kilos, but it still fits. I add a headband to keep my ears warm, a sleeveless puffer vest, and I'm ready.

"So, you've decided to go? I'm proud of you," says Dad as he sees me coming through the door. "What time do you think you'll you get back?"

"No later than midday, I'm guessing. If I manage to survive the kids, that is…"

"It'll be just fine, sweetheart. I won't be back until 3 pm at the earliest. I have a long snowshoe trek near Avoriaz."

He downs the rest of his coffee and puts on his beanie.

"Make sure you eat some breakfast before you go and take a bottle of water with you."

"Yes, Dad!"

He smiles at me, before giving me a kiss on the cheek.

"See you later and have fun!"

I make some scrambled eggs on toast and a green tea, all of which I swallow down as quickly as I can. I'm going to be late.

I've just gotten my skis out and put on my ski shoes when I get a message from my mother.

> I didn't want to harass you and thought I'd wait until you sent me a message, but I might as well believe in Santa Claus! I can see you've forgotten you still have a mother.
> Is everything going all right?

> Hi Mom. Sorry, the days are flying by. Yes, all good, and you?

> The days are flying by?
> What are you getting up to?

Red alert! She'll try and worm it out of me, but there's no way I'm going to tell her I went out the other night, or that I went trekking with Dad, ate croziflette and that I'm going cross-country skiing. I'm not completely mad.

> I've been studying, walking around Morzine, watching TV. The usual.

> How are things with your father?

> Great! Are you still at Cathy's?

> Yes, I decided to stay a few extra days.
> I'm leaving tomorrow. Having some days off has done me a world of good.

Before my cardiac arrest, Mom was a high-school English teacher. Now she's a self-employed translator for big pharmaceutical companies. She works non-stop. No one deserves a break more than she does.

I look at my watch; I need to hurry. I leave the chalet and take the road toward the Super Morzine cable car.

Cool! So you're not missing me then!

You're joking, right? I think about you all the time! You promise you're looking after yourself?

I promise, Mom! Cross my precious heart!

Idiot! Anyway, I'd better go, we're off to Geneva for the day! Love you.

It didn't snow last night, and the road is clear. The sidewalk is still icy, but my ski shoes handle it better than my other winter boots would. Plus, they're made for walking, so it's not a big deal. With my skis over my shoulder, I go down through the village toward the Super Morzine cable car. It's exactly 10 am when I get there. I quickly buy a round trip ticket and dive into a cabin with eight other people. The trip barely takes five minutes, and I can feel my tension mounting. I wonder if I'll even be able to get up on my skis without falling over.

Once we get to the top, I see groups of children in front of a chalet with an alpine restaurant in it. There are hats, goggles and skis stuck in the snow, and the kids are hollering so loudly I almost turn around and go home.

"You made it! Brilliant!"

Too late. Wearing sunglasses and his ski instructor outfit, Augustin is heading straight for me. To be honest, between his dazzling smile and his tight red pants, I can't decide where to look.

"Hi..." I answer, feeling as relaxed as if I were in a nudist colony.

"I'm so happy you made it. My colleagues and I have just put the kids into groups. I have a bunch of twelve, and there's a trainee with me. Ready?"

No, not really, but I don't let it show. And in any case, Augustin is smart enough to guess how I'm feeling. But I do appreciate that he's not making a fuss about it.

I follow him to the meeting point. There are twelve kids who are about eight years old, tops. They have skis on, fluorescent yellow ski jackets, their name written in felt pen on a label on their chest, and they're all wearing a Santa hat with a pompom. They stand out from a mile away, but I've got to admit they're pretty cute!

"Where are their supervisors?"

"They'll wait for us here," says Augustin, pointing to the seating area outside the restaurant. "Waiting while the kids are off with a ski instructor must be the only time it's worth being a teacher! Come with me, can you?"

He takes me to the guardrail next to the chalet and gathers up a funny, fur-lined red coat. He slips it on, buttons it up the front before my startled eyes, then leans down to pick up a tall wicker basket.

"Could you give me a hand, please, this thing is hard to put on."

He lifts it by the straps that are attached to each end, and I realize what it is. It's the basket Santa carries on his back! A basket full of bits and bobs.

"Ha! You're dressing up as Santa Claus!"

"Yep, a man's got to do what a man's got to do!"

I help him put the basket on.

"Can you have a rummage inside? There are a couple more things I need to add."

I do as he says and pull out a black belt that he ties around his waist, a fake beard that he attaches behind his ears, and a red hat with flashing lights that he slaps onto his head. I can feel myself starting to laugh.

"Don't get smart, Mrs. Claus, there's one for you too!"

"Huh? No way!"

He digs around in the pocket of his huge coat and hands me a hat just like his. Embarrassing! But it also catches me so much by surprise that I forget to be stressed.

"Count yourself lucky I haven't taken a photo of you! Right, let's go."

Argh, what have I gotten myself into?

"Is everyone OK?" asks Augustin, as I ski next to him. Adrien, the trainee, follows up at the rear.

"Yeeees!" yell the kids.

We've been skiing for twenty-five minutes, and up to now, the little gremlins have been so focused on their movements – push, bend, glide! – they've not said a word.

"How're you doing?" he whispers quietly to me. "You feel OK?"

The groomed trail is as flat as a frozen lake. It's cold, the sky is a deep, deep blue, and the forest around us is so quiet that the only sign of life is the swishing noise of our skis on the snow. Everything is good. I'm not out-of-breath and it's such a joy to be out in the snow again.

I look at Augustin with a smile. Ha! I just can't get used to his fake beard!

"Yes, thanks. It's doing me good."

"I told you it would!"

"Do you often dress up as Santa Claus?"

"No way, I like to mix things up! One year I came as an abominable snowman. That was fun."

I can't picture him covered in fur from head to toe!

"Do you like being with the kids?"

"They're way less complicated than adults. They have no filter at all, but they're not as draining!"

"Mister!" a child cries out unexpectedly. "I have sore legs."

"And I need to pee!"

"I'm thirsty!"

It takes just one complaint for a whole barrowload to come flooding out.

"This, however, I like a whole lot less," grumbles Augustin as he comes to a stop.

He takes off his skis and stands half-way down the line.

"Who wants to stop for a while?"

Of course, every single child raises their hand. With the help of the trainee, we remove everyone's skis, then Augustin asks them to sit down in the snow, next to the track.

"So, who needs to pee?" he asks. Now, of course, no one puts up their hand.

"And who's hungry?"

This time there's a deluge of little hands waving in the air. We should have seen that coming.

Augustin rifles through his mysterious basket and pulls out a paper bag that he shakes about in front of everyone.

"Ho, ho, ho! I've been given an important job today, children. Do you know what it is?"

"Nooooo!" they reply in unison.

"I have to feed you before you decide you need to go hunting for rabbits!"

"I'm a vegetarian!"

"I don't eat rabbit!"

"I love chocolate rabbits!"

I can't help laughing as I help Adrien hand out the snacks. The cookies and apples disappear in no time.

The kids are all full, and we're about to leave when all of a sudden, a little boy gets up and runs across the trail to the forest on the other side where he sits down.

"Hey, what are you doing?" calls out Augustin.

"I don't like it over there. It's better here."

"I know the snow is softer over there, but I'd rather you came back here with us, please. I explained everything before we left, remember? We have to stay in a group, that's the rule."

The kid crosses his arms and sticks his bottom lip out.

"I can't believe it," groans Augustin. "Hey, come on, back you come!"

But then a second child runs over to the first, and a third, and in less than a minute, everything is in complete disarray. There are kids running in all directions, laughing, shouting, rolling around in the snow and throwing snow-balls at each other. Augustin, Adrien and I just stare at them, dumbfounded. It just came over them all at once. Augustin has even pulled his beard off.

"These aren't kids I'm looking after, they're demons..."

He lets them play for a bit longer, then finally asks everyone to gather around again. Of course, no one listens, so with the help of Adrien, he tries to herd the kids back, getting hit by a few snowballs along the way. I laugh as I watch them going to and fro, until I spot a girl heading for the forest.

"Hey, munchkin, where are you off to?"

She pretends not to hear me and speeds up.

"Come back, please, it's dangerous over there!"

The cliff face is fewer than thirty metres away.

She is clearly no better at listening than the rest of the group and takes off through the trees.

Damn!

I run after her as fast as my heart will let me, but the sudden effort is too much. I'm not able to catch up with her, and I keep tripping over roots. The girl races away, unaware of the danger, and reaches the edge of the forest.

"Stop! There's a cliff right there!"

Taken by surprise, she finally stops, just three metres from the cliff face, on a flat bit of snow. I stop too, totally out-of-breath, and hold onto a tree while I gain my wits.

"That wasn't very clever of you, do you realize that..."

I break off and my heart races even more. The snow is unstable and is already starting to give way beneath her feet. It could collapse in seconds. A wave of panic comes over me.

"Don't move! Please, don't move..."

The little girl turns around to look at me with her big blue eyes.

"Why? Am I going to fall?"

"No, not if you come back toward me. But slowly."

No point in letting her know I'm scared to death.

"Just come back to me nice and quietly, OK?"

She does as I say, but suddenly lets out a cry as she sinks into the snow.

My reflexes take over. I leap up and grab the hood of her jacket to pull her toward me. Her Santa hat isn't so lucky. It slides down with the snow and ends up twenty metres below.

We're both sitting on our butts. I have my arms around her, and we're trying to get our breath back.

"Are you OK?"

"Yes. I was really scared."

"I know, darling. But it's all right. You're safe now."

"Is everything all right?" asks Augustin as he runs up to us.

"Oh, just had the living daylights scared out of me, but we're OK."

"You won't tell my teacher, will you?" asks the girl. "I'll get in trouble if you do."

Augustin and I look at each other, then he reads her name on the label stuck to her coat.

"Melina, we have to go back and join the others. But don't run this time."

He helps us both up, and as we follow our tracks back to the group with Melina ahead of us, Augustin puts an arm around me and squeezes me tight. It gives me a funny feeling. I don't want him to let go.

"You handled that so well. And you didn't have a heart attack."

It takes me a few seconds to understand what he means.

"You're sturdier than you think. Let's get a move on. We've had enough emotion for one day, it's time to go home."

It starts snowing just as we get back to Dad's chalet. Tiny flakes that caress our cheeks and whiten our hair.

"Thanks for having walked me home."

Augustin looks down at me, his eyes sparkling with an inner light I don't dare analyze.

"Thank you for coming. You were really brave."

His voice is warm and gentle.

I feel a bit unsteady, and my keys slip out of my hand onto the snow. We both lean over at the same time to pick them up. Our fingers touch but neither of us makes a move to grab the keys. The seconds tick by.

"I've got to go," he says, almost regretfully, before standing up. "I have a class in half an hour."

"Yeah, of course."

He smiles at me.

"I'm happy."

"I'm happy too."

Augustin gives me a wink and adjusts my hat, which has slipped down a little. I had completely forgotten to give it back to him.

"See you soon, Mrs. Claus."

And he jogs off, leaving me standing in the snow with a goofy smile on my face.

When I get inside, I see I have a message from Eva.

I'm sick of studying! Hope you're having a better time than me!

Not too bad. Your brother took me along with him on one of his kids' cross-country ski classes.

Did you get back on the skis?

Not for long and they were only little kids. Not sure I want to do it again.

Ha ha! How did you get sucked into that?

Your brother asked me when we had dinner at your parents.

Typical! That's just like my brother! He could have just left you alone, but no, he takes you along as his minion! Did he not have a trainee with him?

Yes, but it was fine, I survived. I had a good time.

It was so cool being with him, but I'm not sure Eva would be happy to hear that.

Good for you! Next time it'll just be the two of us and we won't have a bunch of rug rats with us!

No point being a killjoy right now, but I'm not sure there will be another time.

I'd better go, I'm about to have a shower.

OK, no problem. And keep your distance from my brother otherwise he'll get you into trouble!

Keep my distance from Augustin?
Not sure I want to.
Should I tell Eva?
Not sure that's a good idea.
Am I staying clear of trouble? I don't think so, but I don't want to think about it.
Not now.

December

7

There's a farmers' market every Wednesday morning.

The Place de la Poste gets covered in awnings of every colour, and in the period running up to Christmas, it's even prettier. The stalls are decorated with string lights and fir branches. There are oranges and mandarins everywhere, roasted chestnuts, and mulled wine stands.

It smells so good!

It's *the* weekly catch-up for the people of Morzine: retirees, families, kids, dogs and, well, pigeons too, even though we don't like them much around here. Dad goes every Wednesday.

"I don't suppose we should buy a piece of raclette cheese?" says Dad as we walk past the cheese stand.

"No, but if you felt like getting some potchon, I wouldn't say no! Look, there's some in that food truck over there."

Potchon. There aren't many Savoyard dishes that I allow myself to eat, but this one…

Even the thought of it is making my mouth water!

When Mom used to come, she would make it for us, and I loved it. Potatoes, white wine, small pieces of goat's cheese and crushed tomatoes. You put all the ingredients in a dish and let it bubble away gently in the oven. It's absolutely delicious!

"And a bit of salad to go with it, I guess?"

"Of course, that goes without saying!"

We patiently wait our turn in front of the deli food truck. It's the same business we used to go to when I was younger.

"Is that your daughter?" asks the deli guy as we reach the front of the queue.

"Yes, this is April!"

"Oh, I wouldn't have recognized you! But, yes, I can see the resemblance. You have the same eyes as your Dad."

I frown. Dad's eyes are dark brown, almost black, and mine are... blue. I nod politely. He's obviously colour-blind.

"Oh, look! It's April!" interrupts his wife. "Gosh, you've changed! You've grown up. Are you on vacation at your father's?"

"Yes, I'm here until Christmas."

"I bet you planned that so you'd get spoiled," she says with a laugh. "You kids are all the same! And so you should be, too! I'm very happy to see you looking so well."

"Thank you!"

"You're welcome! So, Etienne, what can I get you?"

Dad puts in his order, and we wait for quarter of an hour. Just as we are leaving, he nudges me with his elbow.

"Hey, look who's here."

I look up and see Jeff heading toward us, a basket under his arm. When I said that the farmers' market in Morzine was the place to be…

His outfit is completely wacko – a pair of faded blue overalls, safety boots that should have been thrown out a long time ago, a red parka covered in stains and a bright yellow beanie that only barely covers his wild hair.

And that's not to mention the stink he gives off as he stops in front of us.

"Hi!" he says.

"Where have you come from?" asks Dad, who is just as surprised as I am.

"A dumpster!"

"I beg your pardon?"

"Like, literally! A client left his hearing aids on his breakfast tray. The waitress emptied it without looking, and the trash went out to the dumpster. They're worth about four grand, though, the guy was going nuts. We had to do everything we could to find them."

I can't hold my laughter in any longer.

"What a hero!"

"Yeah, Trashman! I should get a medal. I didn't even have time to change before going shopping. The market closes in thirty minutes, so I'd better hurry."

"OK, good luck," says Dad as he takes a step backward. Jeff smells so freaking bad!

"Oh, April, we're going to the Tibetan Café tonight, do you want to come? I can come and pick you up if you want?"

I have no desire whatsoever for a repeat of last time's fiasco. It's nothing to do with Jeff and the others, it's just that I'd rather avoid those types of evening. I know I wouldn't be any more relaxed than last time.

"I'm studying tonight, sorry."

"Oh… OK! Another time then!"

As Jeff strides off, Dad looks at him with a little smile at the corner of his mouth.

"Jimmy, Augustin, Jeff… you've become quite popular with the boys."

"Ha! And is this where you become the controlling father?"

"Not on your life! Jeff's a good guy."

I exhale deeply.

"Sure, but I'm just not interested."

"I see. One of the other two, perhaps?"

"Dad! I can't believe we're having this conversation!"

And he's actually laughing!

"Jimmy's a good guy too, but I have to say I have a soft spot for Augustin," he tells me, seriously this time.

"Well, you go out with him then!"

Dad raises his eyebrows.

"What fathers these days have to put up with! Come on, let's finish our shopping. I have lots to do this afternoon."

When we get back to the chalet, we're both surprised to see Mom's car pulled up just in front.

Dad and I look at each other.

"Did you know anything about this?"

I shake my head. As Mom sees us walk up, she gets out of the car.

"Hi, darling! I know, I didn't give you any warning, but I couldn't help making a little detour on the way back to Lyon to come and say hi!"

Thonon-Morzine, that's quite a detour.

Yep, that's Mom all right. She hates feeling like she's losing control, and she can't help doing whatever she can to get it back again.

Dad doesn't look too happy. I know what he's thinking.

It's not the fact that Mom is here that's bothering him, but rather why she's here – to make sure everything is OK. And by doing that, she's openly demonstrating her lack of trust in him.

And me.

She gives me a kiss and turns to look at Dad.

"Hello, Etienne. I hope I'm not bothering you?"

"No," he replies, doing his best to remain polite. "We've just come back from the market."

"Ah!" she says, taking a look in the basket. "You bought fresh vegetables, good for you!"

That's a bit underhanded. She's always thought that Dad doesn't look after himself well, and she probably imagined he was feeding me burgers. Well, she imagined wrong.

"I won't stay long," she goes on, "but I wouldn't say no to a big glass of water. I left without my water bottle, how silly!"

The little laugh she gives sounds completely fake. No one is fooled. Dad opens the door to the chalet and beckons her in. As soon as she's inside, she starts to inspect everything much more openly than last time.

It looks like she's trying to find something to comment on.

But there's nothing to comment on because Dad isn't at home much, and since I've been here, I've been doing a heap of housework. She can rest assured. I don't live in a completely sterile environment, but everything is clean and tidy nonetheless.

"So?" she asks, as she takes a seat at the living room table while Dad gets her a drink of water. "What are you getting up to during the day? It's been such good weather, you've been so lucky!"

I know my mother by heart, so I shouldn't be surprised by all this, but I'm just not able to calm my growing anger.

I've had it up to here with her questions!

"I told you yesterday. I've been studying, going out a bit, watching TV."

"Good! You'll be ready for your exams in January."

It's almost 12:30. Dad comes back in with a tray and lays out glasses, some water and some sugar-free soda on the table, as well as some peanuts, which no one touches.

"I see the roads have been cleared again," she says to Dad. "Has the snow let up a bit?"

He sits down across from her, not looking his most relaxed.

"It's been falling at night, but there haven't been any problems. The council has been making sure that no one gets blocked in. It's been an exceptional season so far."

"Yes, I know! Everyone will be raking it in," she replies with a laugh, implying Dad as well.

"Have you been able to get out in the snow a bit, too?" asks Mom. "You haven't been staying inside non-stop, I hope?"

It's best to say as little as possible here because she's just digging for information, so she can chime in and remind me of all the things I should and shouldn't be doing to keep well. I know all that, but Dad doesn't.

And he falls straight into the trap.

"Two days ago, we went for a trek not far from the Joux-Verte pass. I was lovely."

Mom carefully puts down her glass and her expression takes on a certain stiffness. She has the answer she was looking for, but now she has it, she's not happy.

"I see. How did you feel, April? Not too tired? Out-of-breath?"

"No, it was fine. We were going about the same speed as a wheelchair rolling through the snow."

"Don't get smart with me, my girl."

I don't answer.

"If you think you're going to be doing more of this kind of physical effort," she continues, "I wonder if it might be a good idea to do a little routine check-up at the hospital. What do you think? Dr. Tellier could write you a prescription for that, no problem."

"She doesn't need one. Everything is going just fine," interrupts Dad in a voice that should have set off warning bells for Mom.

This is going to end up in a fight, but isn't that what she wants?

I'm annoyed at her.

I am really, really annoyed at her.

I'm annoyed that she didn't realize how much I needed even a couple of weeks break between the two of us. I need to be on my own and prove to myself that I can be something more than a hermit crab that won't come out of its own shell.

After all this time keeping to myself, I feel like I'm finally making some progress. It feels like a win. But can Mom, with all her fears, ever understand that?

I doubt it.

So, I lose it.

"I also went out one night with friends, but don't worry, I didn't drink one drop of alcohol. I ate croziflette at the Favres' and it didn't kill me, and yesterday I went cross-country skiing with Augustin."

"April…"

"Mom, I'm nearly nineteen years old, and I have been through enough difficult moments to be able to decide on my own whether something is good for me or not."

"I understand you need to ease off a bit, but you mustn't let your guard down. You have to keep an eye out for any sign of weakness."

I can't let what she just said go by without biting back.

"I was running on a treadmill, monitored by sensors that were telling me everything was fine, and my heart failed. So how can anyone know? Am I going to have to shut myself away for the rest of my life? Live in bubble wrap? Make sure that everyone stays one metre away from me, and live on one square meal of pills so I don't ingurgitate something that might mean the end of me? That's not the kind of life I want, Mom. And you know what? I loved being back on skis, and if I wasn't so scared it would be bad for me, I could have eaten three plates of croziflette. I didn't but I should have! I'm going to go trekking with Dad again, further and higher, and I'll go out at night as often I want. You can't tell me what to do!"

"April," says Dad, trying to calm me down. "Don't get all worked up."

I leap to my feet.

"April this, April that! Don't do this, don't do that! I am so sick of people telling me what they think I should do. Sick of it! I only have one life, and it's up to me to decide how I want to live it!"

I grab my coat and slam the door behind me as I leave the chalet. I speed walk toward the village centre; far, far away from my mother.

I've had enough.

I just want a normal life and a normal family!

I want to be able to joke around, to make mistakes without fearing that death is just around the corner.

Damn it, is that too much to ask?

I head straight for the Blue Yeti, with tears in my eyes.

I wipe my face before going inside, then go and sit at the bar.

Jimmy stares at me.

"Are you all right?"

"No. My mother is pissing me off. I need a break."

He doesn't ask me any questions and serves me a strong coffee. Normally I wouldn't drink it – "it's too strong for me" – but I knock it back in one go. I don't care if it burns my tongue or sets off a tachycardia.

"Is that better?"

I take a deep breath and tell him everything.

"That is not cool," he says.

"No, it's not."

"Come with us to the Tibetan Café tonight, that'll take your mind off things.

"I'm not a huge fan of the place."

He nods in understanding.

"So, what are you going to do?"

"What everyone expects me to! Nothing."

"Don't say that. Come round to Margot's tomorrow, she's having a party. Her apartment isn't very big, but there won't be many of us. And Jeff'll be there," he adds with a teasing wink.

"Hmm… What time?"

"Ah, that's better! 8 pm!"

"I'll think about it. Anyway, I'd better go home. Thanks for listening. I hate fighting with my parents."

"You're right. Parents are so annoying, but we love them anyway."

I take my time on the way home. I think about my situation, about the fact that I've finally admitted that I can't go on wrapping myself in cotton wool forever. I want Mom to understand how I feel. But I don't think she'll be able to and that does my head in.

When I get back to the chalet, her car has gone, and Dad is waiting for me in the living room.

He has lit the fire and is sitting on the couch.

"Has Mom gone?"

"Yes. She thought it was best."

"I'm sorry I got so fired up."

"Come and sit over here with me."

I do as he says and sit next to him.

"I know how you feel, April. I understand because I always thought she was far too overprotective of you, but that's just how she is, and you can't change her."

"I know…"

"Your mother isn't perfect, but neither am I. I know how annoying and irrational she can be, and she shouldn't have reacted like that, but she has always been there for you."

He sighs.

"Dad, I know all this."

"No, listen to me. No one has given up as much as she has. I'm not saying this to make you feel guilty, but I want you to understand how hard it is for her to let go. I remember the day we were told you had a heart defect and that you needed an operation. You were barely two months old. She felt so powerless. I mean, goodness knows, we've had our differences. And yes, she can go too far and annoy the hell out of me, and yes, that probably won't change, but she loves you. Your mother loves you, April, more than anything. I'm so happy you're finally starting to enjoy life again, but you have to be patient with her. Listen to her point of view. Respect it and ensure she respects yours. Show her how much happier you are, and she will accept it, because she wants the best for you."

My cheeks are covered in tears. I know he's right.

"Come here, sweetheart."

He opens his arms and I snuggle up to him and cry. For a long time. When I go up to my bedroom a bit later, my phone is still in my bag. I get it out and find all the messages Mom has sent me.

> I'm sorry things went the way they did. I shouldn't have come.

> I'm always so worried about you, I can't help it.

> You're getting older, you're turning into a wonderful young woman, but you'll always be my baby.

> I'm going to let you spend the rest of your holiday with your father and not bother you. I love you.

My heart feels heavy, but my reply to her couldn't be any more sincere.

I love you, Mom.

I spent a long time on the phone with my mother. I know I'll never be able to change her, but I get the feeling she's starting to understand that she has to ease off.

But will she be able to? I doubt it.

I'm still afraid of dying, of making one mistake too many or of becoming even more trapped than I am now, but I need my freedom. The freedom to misjudge things, to mess up, to kick myself when I get something wrong, but also to be proud of myself.

I'm sick of being the perfect daughter, Mom has to understand that.

To try and make things right, I tell her everything that Dad said about her.

She's always thought he sees her as rigid and a pain in the neck, so she's surprised.

I have to admit that I am too.

Despite all their dramas and then the divorce that was the final nail in the coffin, I felt something in Dad that I'd never noticed before – the profound admiration he has for my mother. For a long time, I felt like I was the reason my parents got divorced.

I would say to myself, if I hadn't been sick, they would still be together.

And so, when they show the respect they have for one another, I see it as a sign that perhaps their feelings haven't completely disappeared.

Dad had told me he'd be away the whole day. In the morning, I bustled around the house, doing washing and even shovelling the snow away from the gate.

Things that normal girls my age probably wouldn't do, but hey, why be like everyone else?

At the end of the day, I flop onto the couch, and, still triggered by the message Benoit sent me three days earlier, I do something I haven't let myself do for the past year and a half. I unblock his TikTok profile and have a look at it.

I want to know what he's up to.

No, what I actually want is proof he's still a total loser.

I see video after video, each more ridiculous than the last. Reels showing off his naked torso in the bathroom, displaying the scar on his chest, and with the hashtags #superhero #fitandfrench #cute #gym.

His hair is longer than I remember, and he has a trim beard and more defined muscles.

I look at his almost perfect body and wonder what I found attractive about him apart from his looks.

He had serious health problems, maybe not quite as bad as mine, but he went through a difficult time. And yet he still doesn't get it.

I could almost pity him for how shallow his life is, but I remember how much I hate him for what he did to me.

I take a screenshot of one of his photos and send it to Eva.

> Look at this total jackass!

Did you go on his TikTok or am I dreaming?

> It's fine. I just wanted to remember how much I hate him.

Um... did you need to be reminded?

> No.

OK. So now you can block him again.

> Don't worry, I will. How're you?

OMG shame. I couldn't find an artifact that I photographed just yesterday. The director gave me hell for it. Can't wait to leave.

I can't wait to see you either. Tonight I'm going round to a friend of Jimmy's.

Jimmy ❤️
Give him a kiss for me if you see him!

I will!

I end our conversation and look at Benoit's account one last time.

Eva's right.

Just because he tried to get in touch with me doesn't mean that I should forget how hard I fought to get over him. I block him, for good this time, and throw my phone onto the couch.

Dad'll be home soon. I'm hungry so I get some dinner ready.

I can still feel the veggie lasagna sitting in my stomach when I get to Margot's place. I ate quickly so I wouldn't be late.

She opens the door with a big smile on her face.

"Hey! Nice to see you! Jimmy told me you were coming. He's over there with Jeff and Augustin. Make yourself at home. Can I get you a Coke Zero?"

I agree distractedly. Augustin is here, and I feel like nothing could make me happier. I look around but can't see him, even though Margot's studio isn't very big – one main room, a kitchenette and a mezzanine. There are about twenty people in here, but it feels like a hundred.

Everyone is standing with a glass in their hand.

Jeff is the first to notice I'm here and gives me a huge wave.

"Over here!"

I cross the room and find him next to a bay window that leads out onto the balcony. Nope, Augustin isn't here either.

"It's so cool you came. Look, I made an effort!" says Jeff, tugging on his unironed white shirt. "I hope you like it?"

I give an evasive reply.

"White's always a good choice."

"So, I hear you went cross-country skiing?"

"Yeah, on Tuesday, with a group of primary school kids."

Jeff leans toward me, his eyes shining.

"I'd be happy to help you get back on your feet. You can come skiing with me whenever you want. I'm always free from 4 pm onward, and that's when the ski lifts start to quieten down."

I narrow my eyes. I am sure he'll keep asking each time we see each other until I give in and say yes.

"Yeah, maybe. Augustin and Jimmy aren't with you?"

"Yeah, they are. They're upstairs in the mezzanine. Here, have a seat," he says, pointing to an armchair.

I barely have time to sit down before he joins me on the arm rest and pulls out his phone. Without saying a word, he leans next to me and takes a selfie.

"Hey!"

"Sorry, it's for my album of pretty girls!"

I see red.

"You're joking, I presume? You're not going to put that on Insta and make up some story?"

"No, who do you think I am? It's just a souvenir. Look, I have heaps, with everyone."

He scrolls through the photos on his phone, but I'm totally wound up and am struggling to keep my cool.

That was what Benoit did. Publish photos of me and then tell disgusting lies about me.

I try not get everything mixed up.

"Sorry. It's just that you should have asked."

"Why the sad face? Are you all right?" asks Margot as she returns with my glass.

Then she looks at Jeff suspiciously.

"What have you done now?"

He shrugs.

"Nothing. I just took a quick selfie, and April thought I was going to post it on social media."

Margot gets the same expression as the first time I met her.

"It's so annoying how you do that, Jeff. Have you ever heard of consent? You should ask permission before you take photos of people. Women aren't just there at your disposal as objects for you to post about. I mean, come on."

"Oh, calm down, you're not my mother. It was just a spur of the moment thing. April, do you want me to delete the photo?"

"No, that's fine. But don't post it."

Margot scowls at him and returns to the kitchen.

This is when I switch off.

Jeff starts some monologue about how he's always had good relationships with girls and how none have ever had any reason to complain about him. I think I even hear him say he's a good lay and wonder if I heard correctly.

I keep looking up toward the mezzanine. At this rate, it won't be long before I check out.

Then, after what seems like an eternity, Jimmy and Augustin come down, catch sight of us and come over. As soon as he sees me, Augustin gives me a wink. My heart starts to race.

It's completely ridiculous. What's happening to me? Jimmy, however, doesn't look so happy.

"So?" asks Jeff.

"She had a go at me."

"Sorry, dude. I'm going for a quick smoke on the balcony. You coming, April?"

I look at him in disbelief. Does he think I'd want to?

"No, thanks. Cigarettes and I don't get on."

"OK. I'll be back soon, honey," he says, devouring me with his eyes. "Don't go, all right?"

Honey? He's got to be kidding…

I'm mortified, and not just because Augustin is there to see it. What is going through Jeff's head? I mean, flirting is one thing, but he's so crass and unsubtle.

All of a sudden, I think of Eva. She would have handled this situation a thousand times better than me. She would have told him to get lost in front of everyone and not worried what people think.

But he's lucky. I'm not like that.

"He's hot for it!" mocks Jimmy once Jeff has gone. "He's not usually so sleazy, you must have caught his eye."

"Yeah, well, I'd rather I hadn't."

"Anyway, I'll be back in a minute. I'm just off to get a beer. Do you want one?" Jimmy asks Augustin.

"Not right now, thanks."

Augustin hasn't taken his eyes off me.

I feel like I'm getting lost in his eyes, and because I don't feel I can hold the gaze, I look for a distraction.

"Who was Jimmy talking about when he said someone had a go at him?"

"His girlfriend."

"The one who's complicated?"

He frowns.

"Did he tell you that?"

"No. Jeff."

"He blabbers too much."

I'd better not say that Jeff also told me a few stories about him. He wouldn't be happy.

"They've just broken up," he adds.

I nod, what else is there to say?

Jeff is back in no time, and he is relentless. He's barely joined our group again before he puts his arm around my shoulder.

"So, when are we going skiing, just the two of us?"

I stiffen.

I'm not going to be able to keep quiet, I've had enough. But because I don't want to make a scene at Margot's, I keep my cool and remove myself from under his arm as nicely as possible.

"Jeff, can you come with me onto the balcony?"

What an idiot. He can't read my mood and seems to think I'm interested. I'm going to have to tell him what I think and put things straight.

Once it's just the two of us, I look him in the eye.

"I think you're a nice guy, Jeff, but that's enough."

"Huh? You mean because of the selfie?"

I shake my head.

"The selfie, the touching, your over-familiarity, the way you keep going on about wanting to spend time with me. Let me be totally clear. I am not interested."

All the wind goes out of his sails.

Jeff scratches his beard and runs his hand through his hair.

"OK. I see."

"Good."

I cut off the conversation and go inside. Augustin isn't there anymore.

I grab my jacket from the armchair and slip it on. I don't want to stay here any longer. I feel uncomfortable, and now there's going to be a tense atmosphere.

I don't want to have to explain everything.

So I say goodbye to Margot, thank her and pretend that Dad needs me and that I've got to go. I've gone about five hundred metres through the snow when Augustin calls out to me.

"Hey! You snuck off quietly. Margot said you had to go home?"

I don't stop walking.

"Nothing serious. Go back to your friends."

"April, wait!"

He runs up and stops right in front of me, blocking my path.

"Was there a problem with Jeff?"

"I'm not sure it was really a problem, but it's fixed now anyway. Can I get past?"

I dodge around him and keep on walking.

I don't want to be having this conversation with him, because if I'm being totally honest, Jeff's attitude made me feel like a chunk of flesh at the meat market.

Augustin has never treated me like that, but once is enough.

"Do you like Jeff?"

I stop dead in my tracks. What the...!

"Is that the impression I gave? And even if I had? Is that any reason to behave like that? Or am I the only one who was shocked by his behaviour?"

"No, but..."

"Oh, come on! You've never been like that with me. He came charging round to my house to proposition me, he keeps trying to convince me to go on a private skiing lesson with him, he calls me 'honey,' touches me as if we've known each other forever. This isn't the 19th century, damn it! And even if it was, I'm sure most guys would have had more tact than he does."

"I'm sorry, I didn't realize it was that bad. I mean, I knew he liked you, but I didn't think he was being so insistent."

I shake my head and start walking again.

"Anyway. Now you know. And while we're at it, stop asking me all the time if I like a guy, just because I'm talking with him. Because at this rate, you'll start to think I like you!"

I can't believe I just said that. April, you're such a hypocrite!

"And do you?" he asks in all seriousness.

"You know you're my best friend's brother?"

"So?"

I give a nervous laugh.

"It's just wrong."

"Says who?"

My heart rate is starting to speed up.

"Hey, do I ever ask you questions?"

"You're the one who raised the subject," he replies calmly.

We walk in total silence for a few minutes, and when we're just twenty metres away from the chalet, Augustin says, "Have you ever asked yourself the same question?"

"What do you mean?"

"Whether I like you."

I miss a step. I can't speak.

"Umm…"

"I'm sure you have, so I'm going to answer it for you. Yes, I do."

A long silence ensues.

"But…"

I can literally feel the blood travelling through my veins.

I try and pull myself together.

"Um, look, I don't want to pretend to be all shy, but this is just too weird."

"Because Eva is my sister?"

"Yes! And you know what? We shouldn't even be having this conversation."

He smiles, and his smile is so disarming, so irresistible, so...

"Stop. That's enough. This is crazy. I'm going inside."

"Whatever you say. See you very soon, Mrs. Claus!" he says, as I open the gate.

I'm not going to turn around.

I'm not going to think about this conversation.

And I'm definitely not going to fall for him.

My head, my heart, everything is completely mixed up.

I can't think straight...

December
9

I'm not sure how on earth I managed to get to sleep. I was obsessed by what Augustin had said. It was much easier making him think that the two of us was a stupid idea than it was controlling the thoughts racing through my mind. He likes me, and despite me trying to convince him it's not true, it's totally mutual. How is it possible that, in the space of just three years, when the only thing that connected us was our shared lack of interest in the other, we are now imagining something happening between us? It's completely nuts! Even thinking about Eva makes me feel sick to my stomach. No one would ever want to find out that their best friend is going out with their brother. I don't feel good about this at all.

I mentally give myself a shake and get out of bed. It's 9 o'clock. Outside the fog is winding its way like a ribbon around the chalets, and it doesn't look as if it's going anywhere soon. It's a day for staying at home, which is going to work out just fine, as I'm behind on my studying. I pull on an oversized fleece sweater over my pyjamas and go downstairs. Dad already has his parka on, ready to leave.

"Hi. Are you going on a trek?"

"No," he replies, putting his beanie on his head, "not until this afternoon, and only then if the fog lifts. I've got to go and get my coffee machine in Annecy. It's been fixed."

"I bet you're pleased about that!" I say teasingly.

Since I got here, not one day has gone by without him saying that filter coffee is disgusting and he's going to throw the machine out the window.

"Do you want to come?"

I gesture toward my outfit and the woolly socks I have on my feet.

"I'm not sure the people of Annecy are ready for me! Will you be back for lunch?"

"Sure will!"

He gives me a kiss and heads off into the cold.

The fire is roaring, it's lovely and warm inside, and there's fresh bread that Dad went and got earlier in the morning. I make myself a cup of tea, swallow down my pills quickly and go into the living room, still lost in thought over what Augustin said last night.

Barely ten minutes go by before Dad comes back, slamming the door behind him.

"The warning light for the engine coolant has come on again, but I only filled it up yesterday. I just called my buddy who's a mechanic, and he's coming around in a few minutes. Damn car."

"Ah, what a pain. But you've had it for a while now."

My father has been driving a beat-up second-hand 4WD ever since I was six years old. He's already had it repaired about ten times. But I can see he's feeling grumpy, so I get up and give him a hug.

"Right, I'm off to have a shower!"

I get ready quickly and send a few messages back and forth to Mom. I can tell she's trying to back off and hardly asks me any questions. It feels strange. I'm not used to it. By the time I get back down, Dad is outside with his friend. I watch them through the window, and going by the expression on his face, it's not good news.

"So?" I ask when he comes in.

"It's the water pump, and he can't get one until Tuesday, or even Wednesday morning. But he did say there's one at his supplier in Annecy. I'll see if I can send someone to go get it."

I shrug my shoulders. There's nothing much I can say.

He takes out his telephone, and when I realize who he's calling, I freeze.

"Thanks, kid. The fog is starting to lift, so if all goes to plan, I'm meeting a client for a trek at 1 pm. But April will be here. She may as well go with you, then she can pick up my coffee machine. If you don't mind."

Augustin... He won't be aware of this, but if I was hooked up to an electrocardiogram, it would make a massive jump whenever I saw him or heard his name.

"Sounds good. See you later!" Dad says, and then puts the phone down.

"Um," I say, "when exactly is 'later'?"

"Early afternoon, I'll probably already be gone. You don't mind going with him?"

No. Yes. I don't know. Argh...

"It'd be good if you could, even if it was just to pick up the coffee machine."

I don't know what to say, so I just nod.

"Perfect! Shall we have pizza for lunch? I can't be bothered cooking."

"Dad…"

"Just the once?"

I smile at him.

"I'll get lunch for us. There's still some salad, eggs, cheese."

"That's not enough to keep me going. I need a steak!"

Well, since he asked so nicely!

Morzine and the fog are far behind us. I can see the sky over Annecy is greyer than the last time I was there, but to be honest, having Augustin next to me is enough to get rid of even the most persistent cloud.

He's driving his father's 4WD, a more recent model than Dad's. I can barely even feel the turns as we drive down the mountain. To my relief, during the trip he doesn't once mention yesterday's conversation. That's another plus for me – I love how Augustin isn't over-bearing like Jeff.

It takes us an hour and a half to get to Annecy and only thirty minutes to collect the coffee machine and the second-hand water pump.

"It's still early. Do you want to go for a walk in town?" asks Augustin.

There's something you should know about Annecy. In both summer and winter, it is probably the most romantic town in France. It has little canals running through it, a lake, half-timbered wooden houses, wrought-iron bridges and gorgeous cobbled streets. It's not called the Venice of the Alps for nothing. I have one really strong memory of Annecy. Whenever my parents walked through its streets, they always held hands, even if they had had a fight the day before. That's the power of this place, it makes you want to be in love.

Just thinking about it makes me gulp.

"Sure, if you want to."

"Are you hungry? I am. I didn't have time for lunch."

"I'm not that hungry right now, but we could go and get you a sandwich."

He bursts out laughing.

"Here we are in Annecy in the off-season, and all you can suggest is a snack? Do you have any other great ideas while you're at it?"

"Um…"

"Come on, Mrs. Claus, I'm sure you have a bit of room. I have an incredible place I want to show you!"

"OK, but stop calling me that!"

He gets a teasing look on his face.

"I don't think so… I can still picture you wearing that hat!"

"OK, fine, but at least not in public."

He raises an eyebrow.

"Because we're going to see each other in private?"

Taken by surprise, I open my mouth to say something, then close it. He starts laughing again.

"Got you!"

"Yeah, fair enough."

Augustin seems to know Annecy like the back of his hand. He parks right in the centre, next to the old town.

"It's just next door," he says, "right there."

He points to a restaurant with a red storefront.

"Chez Mamie Lise?"

"Yep. You'll see, it's great. It's always packed in the high season, you need to book way in advance."

As we walk inside, I can't help an awestruck smile coming over my face. It's just like a mountain chalet, with exposed beams, a ladder and a mezzanine with lots of objects on it – crates, milk churns, wooden sleds, teddy bears and heaps of cute Christmas elves. The walls are covered in old pine cladding, and there are red-and-white checked cloths on the tables. The backs of all the chairs have little hearts carved in them.

Woah…

"Do you like it?" asks Augustin, delighted.

"I love it."

"And you haven't even tasted Mamie Lise's fondue yet!"

I smile at him for two reasons. The first is because I'm happy to be here with him, and the second is because I feel so good I could eat almost anything! Normally I'm way more careful, but I know that Eva's arriving tomorrow, and there might not be another opportunity like this with Augustin. I've got to make the most of it.

Mamie Lise's fondue is amazing! It's made with fresh ginger and lemon zest – I've never had anything like it!

"Is it good?" he asks, his eyes sparkling.

"So good! But I won't be able to eat much."

He smiles. I eat the salad and a few pieces of bread dipped in the cheese. But that's all.

"It doesn't matter how much you eat, the main thing is that you're allowing yourself to eat!"

"Promise you won't tell Dad, otherwise he'll want to take me out to a restaurant every night!"

Augustin looks at me closely, as if he wants to ask me something.

"What?"

"How are things going to change for you when you go back to Lyon?"

It's so unexpected that it takes me a few seconds to think and give him an answer.

"You're making it sound like I've been here for ages and that everything is different. And I'm not sure that's the case."

"OK, let me re-phrase that. You've been here for a week and everything is different. Look," he says, as he points to my plate, "that's not just a small step, that's a giant leap!"

And, to better convince me, he stabs a bit of bread and a piece of dried meat that I hadn't dared eat, and stirs them through the cheese before offering it to me.

"Go on, eat that."

I do as he says, opening my mouth and chewing. It's the most delicious thing I've ever eaten.

"So? What do you think?"

"It'sh deliciou-sh…"

"I knew it. Life is beautiful, April, and it's waiting for you with open arms."

"Like you?" I ask without thinking. And regret it immediately. I should not have said that.

Augustin's eyes are shining. They seem even darker than usual. Instead of replying, he reaches out and wipes a corner of my mouth with his napkin.

"Can I give you a kiss?"

"What?"

He smiles.

"I want to give you a kiss, and I'm asking for your permission."

"Um… here? In front of everyone?"

He nods.

OK, I'm going to go into cardiac arrest again, that's for sure. My heart misses a beat.

"OK," I say in a squeaky voice.

Augustin gets up, leans over the table, and places a tiny kiss on my cheek. I can barely feel it. By the time he sits down, I still haven't taken a breath. I'm not sure if I'm frustrated or overjoyed.

"I didn't plan for that to happen," he says. "I mean, I didn't see it coming. I just felt a sudden urge come over me."

"I didn't see it coming either."

"I like you, April, I really like you. I'm not sure what's going on in my head, but I do know I want to spend more time with you."

Whoa…

"Me too."

He leaves it at that and just smiles at me, as if we didn't need to say anything else. I feel completely topsy-turvy.

"How about we skip dessert and go for a walk?" he says.

Which is exactly what I wanted to suggest.

"OK, but I have a request."

"What is it?"

"I'd like to pay, please."

"There is no way…"

"Up until now I've been amazed at all your qualities, but if you start getting all chauvinistic on me, you'll lose points, I'm warning you!"

He raises his hands in surrender. Sometimes a threat is the only thing that works.

"OK, I give in, but I just want… I mean, you can tell me if it's none of my business, but do you have a job?"

"So I can pay for the meal? No, but my grandparents on my Mom's side left me a bit of money. It's not much, but it means I can pay for this kind of thing."

"Oh, cool! Mine are so stingy. You have no idea!"

"So, make the most of it! Shall we go?"

In summer, Annecy's old town is full of bright flowers, but in winter, the Christmas market and all its decorations line the streets, bringing the façades and windows to life. There are little chalets everywhere, and reindeer all lit up. I had forgotten how pretty it is. Augustin and I walk up the Thiou River to Bacchus Bridge. We lean over its metal railing, adorned with fir branches, and look down into the water without saying a word. We stay like that for a long while, until the surface of the water becomes dimpled with fine droplets of water.

"Uh oh, it's starting to rain," says Augustin.

And then all of a sudden, it's pouring. I let out a cry in surprise, Augustin removes one arm from his parka and covers my head with one side of it while we run back toward the Passage de l'Évêché. We take shelter under the stone arch, soaked to the skin. Augustin's hair is plastered to his forehead; he looks like a Roman emperor.

I get a sudden fit of the giggles.

"If only you could see yourself! It's so funny – you totally suit your name! Octavius Augustus!"

But Augustin doesn't laugh. He stares calmly at me, with a slight furrow in his brow. He stretches out his arm and leans against the stone wall, just a few centimetres above me, his eyes unreadable. I stop laughing. Our faces are so close. Augustin doesn't make a move. He just watches me, as if he were searching my soul.

My breath catches. So does his. His gaze shifts from my eyes to my lips. I can tell he's going to kiss me. But he doesn't. I can feel the seconds ticking by, like an interminable countdown. A bomb that's about to explode. Neither of us care about the passers-by, the cold seeping into our bones, the time passing.

Augustin…

A whisper. A plea. A warning. Suddenly he closes his eyes, and I can see him regaining his composure.

"It's time to go."

"Now?"

He smiles at me.

"I don't want you to get sick because of me."

"Oh… don't worry about that."

I wish you'd kiss me. Why aren't you kissing me? Kiss me! I don't say a word, so he steps back.

He looks at me, and I can see something almost like pain in his eyes.

"When you want to, I'd rather you kiss me. Shall we go?"

I nod. I am in total disarray. I want to. But I don't dare.

"Yes, let's go."

It's almost 6 pm by the time I get home. It's dark. Dad has his Italian coffee pot back, his car will be fixed tomorrow, and it's sure to snow tonight – he's in seventh heaven. I retreat to my bedroom and lie down. I stare at the ceiling and relive every second of the afternoon I just spent with Augustin. Everything was perfect. The town, the rain, my beating heart. The kiss that didn't happen still haunts me. My stomach is full of butterflies, my mind is going in all directions. I was so ready and if I had been just a bit braver, I would have kissed him myself. Ahhhhh! I grab my pillow and stuff my face into it.

I should have done it!

On the way back we hardly said a word. It was weird, as if we were both lost in our own thoughts. Then at my front door, he smiled at me and said, "See you soon." That's all. It sounded like a promise, but Eva arrives tomorrow. Will that change everything? Maybe. Definitely. I don't know… I hope it doesn't. For crying out loud! Why does everything have to be so complicated?

I remove the pillow from my face, take a breath of fresh air and laugh nervously.

We haven't even swapped phone numbers. I mean, who even does that these days? I've known this guy since I was six and I don't have his cell phone number. That's not normal.

I close my eyes and try to empty my brain. Good luck with that! I pick up my phone and start stalking his Insta. There are photos of mountains, ski tricks, tracks in the snow, his instructor's certificate. He hasn't posted anything for weeks, and he doesn't have TikTok. So I DM him.

> Thanks for this afternoon. It was cool.

To my surprise, I see he's already read my message. And he's writing back!

> Thank you, Mrs. Claus. Can't wait to see you again.

Boom! There goes my heart!

> Me too... But I also wanted to say, don't mention this to Eva, OK?

And because great minds think alike, who should I get a message from, but Eva.

> Tomorrow

> Counting down the hours! When do you get here?

> As soon as I can. You'll be around?

> Nope, I've decided to go home early!

> Whatever!

> Where do you think I'll be, you idiot?

> Dunno, maybe you met some
> amazing guy and you didn't tell me?

Lucky Eva can't hear me gulp. It feels like I have something stuck in my throat. This is going to be so complicated.

> You still there?

> Hello? Don't tell me you've met someone?

> No way! What are you thinking! There's no one.

> Thought so! That would have been so cool!
> Anyway, I'd better go, have to pack! See you!

"That would have been so cool!" But it is, Eva, it is. It's never been so cool.

I hate lying to her, but how can I tell her what's going on without causing a total disaster? She sees Augustin as this guy who's just out to have fun and she feels sorry for the girls he's with. But I see something else in him. He is attentive and that makes me want to trust him. If I try and explain to her that in less than a week I've learned how to breathe again and that it's mostly thanks to her brother, she'll think I'm crazy.

I'm getting myself deeper and deeper into a difficult situation. I don't know how it will end, but I know one thing for sure: this *is* happening to me, and something is going to come of it. What? I'll find out sooner or later.

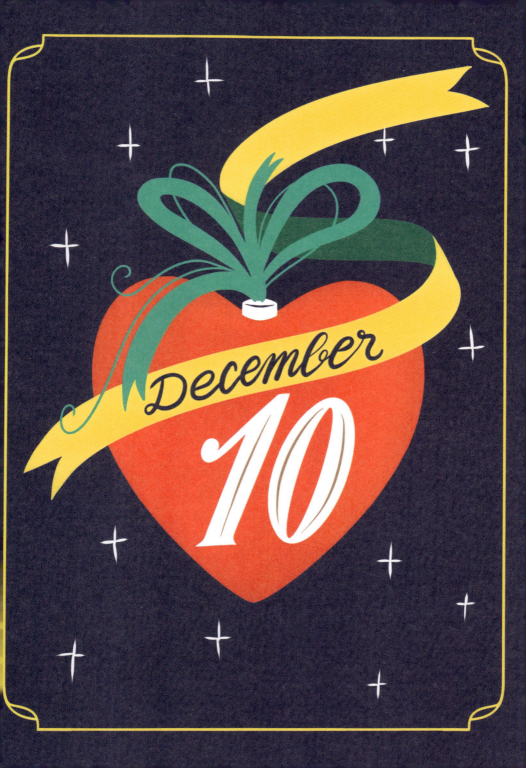

December
10

"Do you want to build a snowman? Come on, let's go play!"

What a wake-up call. I laugh as I hear Eva singing at the other end of the line.

"You're nuts!"

"I think some company is overdue, I've started talking to the pictures on the wall."

"Hang in there, Joan!"

"It gets a little lonely, all these empty rooms. Just watching the hours tick by!"

"OK, OK, I get it! Are you here yet?"

Eva laughs too.

"Yeah, I just arrived. I left at 6 am, can you believe it?! I'm beat."

I yawn and stretch. I've always said Eva has a screw loose.

"Wow, you must have been in a hurry to get here."

"You have no idea. I am so over my dissertation and being locked up in that museum! I started to think I'd shrivel up like the mummy on the first floor. And I haven't even finished the dissertation yet. I'm going to have to work on it during my vacation."

"We'll study together. I haven't gotten far either."

"Good idea! You didn't get too bored while I was away?"

I close my eyes for an instant. I hate lying to her.

"I went on a trek with Dad, and I've been out a couple of times. It hasn't been too bad."

"Good on you! You didn't get stuck in a rut! I am so happy to be here. Especially with all this snow! I haven't seen this much for years. I had Mom's old Mini, I thought I'd need chains to get up the mountain. Even the snow tires skidded a bit, crazy, eh?"

"It's been like this for over a week, not one night goes by without fresh powder. The ski resorts are loving it. So are the tourists."

"Speaking of skiing, have you been since you went with my brother?"

"Hello? I can't hear you? I'm just going through a tunnel, have bad reception. Hello?"

"Ha! If I don't see you on a pair of skis before I leave, you're going to hear about it! Anyway, are you coming over to my place or do you want me to keep singing?"

Eva knows *all* the songs from *Frozen* by heart so I'm definitely not choosing that option. But right now, I have another problem… A major one.

"Are you on your own?"

"Here at home? Yeah. Well, Dad's still here, but he'll be off to the store any minute. Why?"

Because if Augustin is there, Eva, I'll be hard pressed to keep my cool, if you see what I mean. I might even start kissing him and roll around in the snow with him, and completely forget you're there!

"Just wondering," I end up saying.

I look at my alarm clock on the bedside table. It's 9 on the dot.

"When should I come over?"

"In thirty minutes!"

"No way! I'm still in bed. Let me just get dressed, have a cup of tea, start to resemble a human being again, and I'll be there."

"OK! While I'm waiting, I'll get everything ready for our ritual."

My eyes widen in surprise.

"You really want us to make a snowman?"

"What do you think? Traditions are not to be meddled with!"

My mind is flooded with memories.

Up until three years ago, every year when I arrived, the first thing I would do was go to Eva's house and make a snowman.

When we started, we were quite competitive about it, but the results were never very convincing. Then we started to make them together. Inevitably, it always finished up with a snowball fight, where we fired them non-stop until one of us gave in. Then we'd go inside and have a hot chocolate and thick slices of fresh bread with butter and jam.

We wouldn't have missed it for anything. We've grown up a bit since then, so maybe it's kind of weird to still do it, except that when Eva gets an idea in her head, she doesn't ever let go!

Before I start to get ready, I take a quick look at Instagram.

Augustin hasn't written to me, but he has posted a new photo – a close-up of the tablecloth at Chez Mamie Lise. No one apart from me would understand.

I smile.

Unlike the last time I came, the Favres' house is now covered in Christmas decorations. There are fir branches laid out on all the windowsills, gold Christmas lights cascading down from the roof, stars attached to the railing around the deck, and in the garden there's a reindeer that must light up when night falls. The surrounding chalets all look sad and depressed in comparison.

"My parents really went to town," mutters Eva. "It gets worse every year."

"It's so pretty!"

"Not very environmentally friendly!"

"Party-pooper! They're LED lights!"

"If you like them so much, you should live here! The living room is in a complete state. It's like we're living in Santa's merry workshop! I'm overdosing on red! I hate it!"

"Well, I love it!"

Eva and I were destined to be friends. We are each other's exact opposite – both in our personalities and how we look. She's blond, I'm brunette, she's tall, I'm short, she has dark eyes and mine are blue, and as well, she's so bubbly, she makes friends in no time at all. My complete opposite.

Oh, and she's way more practical than I am too. For our traditional snowman, she put on her ski clothes, while I was stupid enough to wear jeans.

"OK, are you ready?" she says as she pulls her gloves on. "Here goes!"

It takes us about an hour to make a decent snowman, and we give it all we have. Ski goggles, scarf, hat... It's looking quite good, but it's come at a cost. My legs are soaked because I've been kneeling in the snow, and I'm freezing cold.

"The honour is all yours!" says Eva, handing me a carrot.

"Really?! Usually you have a tantrum when I say I want to do it."

"I must have matured!"

"Or turned into a granny!"

Just as I turn around and poke the carrot in, giving the snowman a nose, she takes the opportunity to throw a snowball at me.

"Hey! I had my back to you, you scheming minx!"

"Oh? Sorry."

And boom! She fires off another that hits me in the neck.

"Ah, just you wait!"

I bend over and grab a handful of snow that I aim right at her face.

"Yeah! Bull's eye!"

Eva spits out the powdery snow, wipes her face and bursts out laughing.

"You've always been a better shot than me. But you're not so good at anatomy!"

"Huh?"

"Your snowman and his carrot... Poor guy."

Eva walks up to it, pulls out the carrot and sticks it in just below its stomach.

"There! That's much better. Snowmanicus-phallus-giganticus!"

"Oh, come on, really?!"

"What? He doesn't care about having a big nose, what he really wants is a big..."

"Yeah, yeah, I get it!"

"At least he won't have any problems getting a girlfriend!"

She gets out her phone and hands it to me.

"Here, take a photo of me with this stud muffin!"

She stands next to it, and instead of putting an arm around its shoulders, she grabs the carrot and sticks out her tongue.

"Waaaaaaaa!"

"Oh man, you are such a fool!"

I take a few photos of her and then I join in for a selfie of the three of us, with Eva and I making crazy faces, shocked at Mr. Snowman's incredible protuberance.

We're so classy!

And we have no idea that Eva's father is looking out at us through the window, with a bemused look on his face.

"Um, would you like me to help you?" he asks as he opens the window.

Shame! Eva, however, doesn't miss a beat.

"Thanks, Dad! Hey, do you have any kiwis?"

Nicolas Favre rolls his eyes and closes the window, while the two of us snort with laughter.

"Come on," says Eva. "You'll get sick if you don't get those wet pants off. I'll lend you some and we can put yours in the dryer."

Once inside, she makes a quick stop in the kitchen to put the kettle on.

She gets a tray ready with two cups, tea and cookies, and heads straight for her room.

She throws herself on the bed, arms and legs out like a starfish, completely done in.

"I'm exhausted! Go and look in the closet, you'll find a pair of black leggings."

I get undressed. I'm so cold that my thighs are all red.

"You're still so fit."

"Huh?"

"You haven't gotten any exercise for ages, but you haven't lost your tone, and your legs are still muscly. My legs are as floppy as an old frog. And because I'm always scratching away in the dirt with bits of pottery, my fingers are disgusting," she adds, studying her hands with interest.

"What a load of crap!"

Eva is one of the prettiest girls I know. When I walk down the street next to her, I'm not usually the one people look at first. And she's not even aware of it. It's amazing.

I put the leggings on. The legs are so long that they wrinkle up around my ankles, making me feel like a little girl dressing up in her mother's clothes. But they do say that looking stupid never hurt anyone, and anyway, no one's going to see me.

"I can't be bothered going downstairs yet, we'll dry your pants later. Just put them on the heater in the meantime. Come over here," she says, tapping the bed with the flat of her hand.

Just like when we were kids and we used to lie on her bed next to each other, staring up at the ceiling. Then Eva turns onto her side, leaning on her elbow and looking straight at me.

"You didn't tell me whether you saw Jimmy again."

"Oh, yeah, I did. The day before yesterday."

"And you kept that info for yourself?"

I make a face. Eva and I haven't spoken much over the past few days. We just caught up quickly because I didn't have much to tell her.

Truth be told, I was mostly hiding things from her.

"He has been officially single for two days."

She sits up straight in one movement, folding her legs under her.

"You're kidding? I can't believe it! When did you turn into a locked box? Why didn't you tell me! Was it the girl from Paris?"

"Yes, but don't ask me for details, I don't know anything about it. I just know that they weren't getting along anymore."

Eva rubs her hands together.

"Ah, this is perfect!"

"You're here like two weeks max. You really want to try and hook up?"

And then I realize. I'm also going to be leaving in two weeks, and that hasn't stopped me from wanting to kiss her brother.

"Well, obviously!" replies Eva. "Just because you've been on the wagon for the last three years, doesn't mean that I'm the same! No offense, yeah? The guys in my year are so gross. They all have these overgrown beards, long dirty hair, a kind of a grubby, hippy look, you know what I mean?"

"Like Jeff, you mean. Yep, I know it."

"Jeff, the guy who works at the hostel?"

I nod and take the opportunity to tell her all about his horrible behaviour.

"I dunno why you're surprised. It's always like that during vacation. Everyone's trying to hook up. That reminds me, I'll have to ask my brother if he has another girl."

If I had antenna on my head, they would be shooting off sparks right now. Eva has no idea how tense I am.

"And if he has," she continues blithely, "I hope she's not like the previous nut case in Grenoble. I couldn't stand her."

"Why not?"

"She treated my brother like a little dog. Once she came around to my parents' house for dinner. I thought Mom was going to start bleeding, she had to bite her tongue the whole evening. This girl, she was at the dinner table, and she was like 'Darling, would you mind serving me again, please? Some water too, please. I'm sooooo thirsty,' 'Darling, I just hate peeling prawns, can you do it for me?' 'Darling, can you taste the dessert and let me know if it's too sweet?'"

In spite of myself, I snigger as I watch Eva act out the situation and put on a fake voice to imitate the girl.

"A punch in the face was what she needed!"

"I guess it wasn't the love of his life."

"No. So now he can pick up his old ways again."

"What do you mean?"

"My brother is a total player. Girls just fall into his lap, and all he has to do is help himself."

I hate hearing her say that and give a little shudder.

"Are you shivering? I told you you'd get sick."

What's making me sick is thinking that I too might be one of a long list of girls for him to have a good time with. I feel like I have a brick in my stomach.

"Are you OK?" asks Eva. "You've gone all pale."

"I'm just struggling to warm up."

To make sure I look the part, I grab my cup of tea off the bedside table and take a sip.

"Anyway, enough about my brother. What do you think of Jimmy?"

I answer without needing to think.

"He seems like a good guy."

"You think?"

"Yeah. He's nice and he has his head screwed on right."

"Not like my brother then, that's good."

I don't say a word. It's awful hearing her say those things about Augustin because I do not want to go through the same thing I did with Benoit. It's making me start to doubt myself.

"I want to have a real love story."

"Me too," I whisper, without even realizing.

"Oh, honeybun," she says, opening her arms wide to give me a hug. "Don't be sad! We're going to find our dream cupcakes, I promise!"

My shoulders start to shake as I feel a nervous giggle rise up.

I'm finding it hard to picture Augustin as a cupcake.

"You and your metaphors, honestly! You're one of a kind, Eva. I don't know what I'd do without you."

"You'd be bored senseless, that's what!"

Then she leans back, looks at me carefully, and starts up again.

"You want to know what I think? Just because I haven't ever truly fallen for a guy, that doesn't mean I'm never going have my own love story. And just because some bastard broke your heart, that doesn't mean you'll never find someone to mend it. You did that literally, and now you will figuratively too. And anyway, it's almost Christmas, anything is possible!"

Augustin wrapped up in Christmas paper, now there's an idea!

But Eva is right. The cracks in my heart go deep, and it's hard to learn to trust again. But is running away the best solution?

And justifying it by saying I don't want to take any risks? Is it right to be missing out on things like I have for the past three years?

Now I'm sure I want something else. I'm going to speak with Augustin the next time I see him.

I'll be totally honest and ask if he's just playing with me, then I'll be able to figure out whether he means anything to me or whether this is just a total fantasy.

I look at Eva and give her a smile. I feel myself opening up.

"You're right. We're the masters of our own destiny. Jimmy's going to fall for you, that's for sure. And I'm…"

Eva looks at me questioningly.

"And you're?"

I smile at her and then look at the plate of cookies and make a face.

"I'm hungry, shall we go and have a sandwich?"

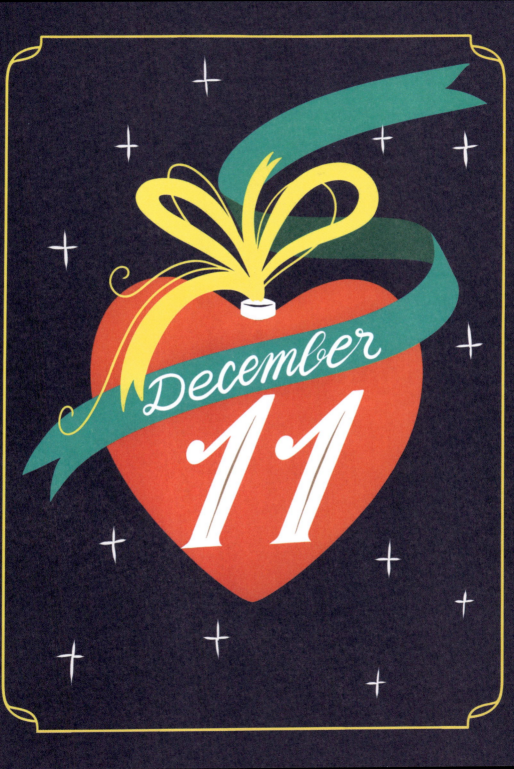

"Please come with me. I know it's not easy for you, but I can't go all on my own."

Eva is looking at me with puppy dog eyes, playing the role of the poor abandoned girl perfectly. She should have been an actor.

Barely twenty minutes ago she was describing her long and tiring evenings spent studying, her heart that is just waiting for the right person, and how timid and shy she is. What a pile of crap!

When I saw her turn up at my house earlier in the evening, I had a feeling there was something she wanted to ask me. And the fact that she didn't just pick up the phone to do it shows that she was banking on her incredible powers of persuasion.

And the worst thing is, those powers usually work.

"Please… It'll just be for an hour."

I let out a huge sigh.

"You are so annoying…"

"So you'll come?"

I shrug my shoulders.

"I know you won't give up until I say yes."

"Woohoo! I love you! You're the best friend ever!"

"But just to be perfectly clear, we'll only stay an hour, right?"

"Yes, I promise! I'll go home now and get changed, and then we can meet up in town."

Karaoke night at the Blue Yeti, 9:30 pm. All the things I hate most.

Sometimes I wish Eva and I had another close friend. If she had asked another friend to go with her, I would have been perfectly happy. I've already tried going out twice since I've been here, and both times I ended up going home earlier than expected.

It's just not my scene. I hope that nothing happens to remind Eva of that.

When I see her arrive at the agreed time, I wonder if she's playing a joke on me.

She is walking through the snow wearing heels, a red knee-length pencil dress and an open trench coat. Even her cleavage looks cold…

"You could have made an effort," she says, eyeing up my jeans, moon boots and puffer jacket, under which I'm wearing a turtleneck sweater. My outfit is simple and discreet, but most of all, weather appropriate.

"The theme tonight is 'Christmas Inside,'" she adds.

Ah ha, that explains the red dress…

"Hmm, I wanted to do a remake of *Lady and the Tramp*. No, seriously, did you come all the way from your house dressed like that? In the snow?"

She lets out a light, tinkling laugh that matches her look – lips in red lipstick and hair up in an artfully messy bun.

"I went by my parents' store to change. And I almost set the alarm off because I couldn't remember the code! But anyway, who cares about that, let's go in. It's freezing out here!"

Not surprising when you're dressed as if Morzine has suddenly developed a tropical climate...

Inside the Blue Yeti, almost everyone is wearing a Christmas hat. A couple of people are butchering the song *Someone Like You.*

I try not to show just how unbearable I find it and follow Eva to the bar.

The place is packed and there's barely even standing room. Eva's getting quite a bit of attention.

"I can't see him!" she yells in my ear as she removes her coat.

"Oh, don't worry, everyone in here has noticed you, so there's no reason Jimmy won't!"

She giggles and folds her trench coat over her arm before leaning over the counter.

"Is Jimmy here?"

"No, sorry," replies the waitress, "he's not working tonight!"

Eva looks at me, totally crestfallen.

"Oh, that sucks! Shall we stay and have a drink anyway?"

I shake my head. I'm eager to leave before my eardrums burst. I feel relieved as we walk out of the bar, but Eva on the other hand looks as if she's just had the worst news.

"Hey, there'll be other opportunities."

"Yeah, I know. It's just I feel a bit stupid. But maybe it's not such a bad thing – I may have gone a bit over the top," she says, pulling the lapels of her trench coat together.

"You want my opinion?"

She nods.

"Unless you dressed like that for your own pleasure, you really don't need to. At all."

"I hear you. I don't know what came over me."

I can't help laughing.

"Yeah, me neither! But at least if I need to dress up as Kim Kardashian one day, I know who to call!"

"Shut up! I'm going back to the store to get changed. Do you want to come?"

"How could I say no to an invitation like that?!"

The Favres' store is right nearby, in a two-storey, free-standing chalet, not far from the Pleney cable car. It's the biggest in town, and their store is the first you notice as you come into the street. It is completely covered in Christmas lights and flashing stars. But the most eye-catching thing is the window display, with a polar bear and three marmots skiing down a slope of artificial snow in a mountain setting. The Favres have always gotten right into the Christmas spirit. When I was young, I always looked forward to seeing what the display would be.

"I bet you love it," says Eva.

"Can't pull the wool over your eyes…"

"Oh man… You coming in?"

I nod and follow her to the service entrance, at the back of the chalet. She slips the key into the lock, and then I see her draw back a little.

"Um… I can't open it."

"Oh? Wait, let me try."

But no matter how I turn the key, nothing happens.

Until suddenly, the door opens abruptly, making us cry out.

"April? Eva?"

"Bloody hell!" Eva yells at Augustin. "What are you doing here? You gave us such a fright!"

He frowns and looks serious.

"It looks like someone waltzed into the store and then left but *didn't lock it behind her*. The alarm went off. Who could that've been?"

Even in the semi-darkness, I can see Eva grow pale.

"Oh, shit!"

"Shit, all right. Do you mind telling me what you were up to?"

"Um… I… I needed to get changed and…"

Augustin looks at me, then looks at Eva from head to toe, and realizes what happened.

"Right. I'll send a message to Mom and Dad to reassure them. I don't even want to know why you're dressed liked that."

"It's none of your business anyway. Let me past!"

Eva is so upset at having messed up that she almost shoves him out of the way.

"Are you OK?" asks Augustin.

I give a tense smile. I had wanted to see him again to talk with him properly, just not in such awkward circumstances.

"I'm a bit cold, would you mind if I came in too?"

"Oh, sorry. Of course not, come in."

The service entrance leads directly into the store room. It's a huge room filled with ski clothes, sleds, ski and trekking equipment... and right in the middle I see my best friend standing motionless, a pair of high heels in her hand and her trench coat over her arm.

It doesn't take me long to understand why.

Jimmy is standing stock still in front of the ski jackets, as stunned as she is.

It looks as if he's just discovered she's no longer sixteen years old.

I go up to Eva and whisper in her ear.

"Move. You look like a weirdo just standing there."

"Hey, hi, Jimmy! We stopped by the Blue Yeti. It was pretty wild."

"Mmm, yeah," he says, looking at Eva as she disappears behind a door. "I'm glad I'm not working tonight."

"Right, so it's all sorted. We'll wait for my sister and then we can go," says Augustin.

Jimmy frowns. "So why was the service entrance unlocked?"

"Because my sister mistook karaoke night for a night at the opera. She got changed in a hurry, and because she didn't want to miss the first act, she left without locking the door. Typical."

Luckily Eva doesn't see me smile, she would have been annoyed at me.

"I'm ready, sorry," she says, as she appears with her stuff in a backpack and wearing dark jeans, winter boots and a thick wool sweater. She fits in with the locals a lot better now.

"So, what are you two up to?" asks Jimmy.

Eva and I look at each other, but as I didn't want to go out in the first place, I'm not going to answer that!

"Do you want to come with us to Avoriaz? We're going bowling."

"Oh, yeah, great!" says Eva, all excited. "I haven't been bowling in ages!"

Well, imagine how long it's been for me then…

I glance over at Augustin, who seems willing. He zips up his parka and points to the door.

"The carriage is waiting for us outside, let's go."

There's no shuttle at this time of night, so we take Mr. Favre's 4WD.

I find myself in the front passenger seat and realize how wound up I am.

It feels just like when we went to Annecy two days ago. I can't help thinking of the passageway, of the kiss I was expecting but didn't come. *Get a grip!*

I close my eyes for a moment, sit up straight with my hands clasped between my thighs and do my best to make sure Eva doesn't suspect a thing.

Augustin looks at me for a few seconds. I look back at him, and he understands.

"Are you ready?" he asks, giving me a knowing wink.

"Let's go!"

Swept along by a northwesterly wind, fat snowflakes start to fall and crash against the windscreen.

Augustin keeps his hands on the steering wheel and is driving extra carefully. We can't even see the markings on the departmental road we're travelling along. Avoriaz is thirteen kilometres up the mountain from Morzine, with hair-pin bends most of the way. It usually takes twenty minutes to get there, but we've been driving for fifteen, and we haven't even gotten halfway.

Eva and Jimmy in the backseat don't seem to notice anything. They're chatting away non-step, laughing and sharing memories. They look like they're catching up on the two years they haven't seen each other. Eva is beside herself and doesn't stop smiling.

It's all going just as she hoped.

"Everything all right?" I ask Augustin, who is concentrating on the road, teeth clenched.

"I wonder if we shouldn't turn back."

His comment seems to wake Eva up.

"Wow, look how heavily it's snowing."

There's practically no visibility, and we can't even see a metre in front of us.

"I think you should stop," I say to Augustin, "it seems to be getting worse."

He nods, continues for a hundred metres or so and then pulls up safely into a driveway that leads to a mountain lodge.

"Sorry, but I don't think we'll make it to Avoriaz. We'll wait here a while until it calms down a bit and then go back down."

"Can't believe the winter we're having!" says Jimmy.

"I was born here, and I don't think I've ever seen so much snow," adds Eva. "We have enough gas, don't we? It's so cold, it'd be terrible if we ran out."

Augustin turns on the interior light.

"It's not the gas I'm worried about but how quickly the snow is covering the road. I'm going to call home and see what the story is."

He taps on his phone with a serious look on his face.

"Dad, we're blocked on the departmental road, just at the bottom of the drive up to the Syleno lodge. We were on our way to Avoriaz and the snow took us by surprise. Do you know what the forecast is?"

There's a few seconds' silence while Augustin listens to the phone.

"Yes, she's with me. Jimmy and April are too."

Another silence.

"OK, I'll wait." He hangs up.

"Apparently they've started to send out snowplows, but the snow isn't forecast to stop anytime soon."

"Are we going to be stuck here?" asks Eva, with a shiver.

While Augustin reassures his sister, I get out my phone and send a message to Dad. His reply is not encouraging.

"Dad says it's going to get worse. He doesn't think it's a good idea to go back down now – apparently there are cars stopped on the side of the road."

"Oh, fantastic," grumbles Eva. "So, we're going to have to spend the night in the car?"

It's not what she had imagined for her reunion with Jimmy. If the boys weren't able to hear me, I would have told her to make the most of it, we'll need to keep warm somehow. But instead I just give her a sorry smile.

We don't have a choice.

Augustin's phone rings ten minutes later. We listen in almost complete silence to him talking to his father. When he hangs up, his brows are furrowed even more.

"He says the same thing. He's trying to find a solution. If the worst comes to the worst, there are survival blankets in the trunk."

"Shit!" exclaims Eva.

"Dad knows the owner of the lodge," says Jimmy suddenly from the back. "I'll call him – maybe we could go there."

Their conversation lasts barely two minutes, plus another two minutes before his mom calls him back.

"We're in luck. The next clients arrive tomorrow so we can stay there tonight. There's a spare key hidden under a rock."

"Thank God!" says Eva. "Right, we should go, the last thing we want is to get stuck."

The road up to the lodge is no trouble with the 4WD, and we find the keys without a problem.

Inside, it's beautiful. The heating is on, ready for tomorrow's visitors.

"Wow! This is so nice!" says Eva excitedly.

"It used to be an old farming chalet," says Jimmy. "My parents wanted to buy it and renovate it. The owners have done an incredible job!"

With its wood interiors, huge bay windows that during the day look out over the most beautiful part of Morzine, four bedrooms, three bathrooms, an enormous living area and a fully equipped kitchen, it makes me want to stay for longer than just one night.

We find coffee and tea in a cupboard and make ourselves a cup, before settling into a comfortable red corner-sofa in the living area. We instinctively sit in the same pairs as we did in the car.

Eva is next to Jimmy, and I'm next to Augustin.

This is such a weird situation – Augustin likes his sister's best friend, and his sister likes his friend. It's almost funny – well, it would be if Eva thought so too. But my faint hopes disappear as I watch her and her brother sniping at each other.

"I can't believe you didn't check the forecast before you decided to go bowling. This isn't the Caribbean."

"Really?" he replies sarcastically. "So that's why you chose your prima donna outfit?"

"I don't know why you have such a problem with it, you don't usually mind high heels and short dresses. In fact, that's exactly the kind of look you go for."

He immediately tenses up.

He throws a quick glance in my direction, opens his mouth to say something but then decides to keep quiet.

The mood in the room changes.

Jimmy and I look at each other and without speaking, we come to the same conclusion.

We need to lighten the atmosphere.

"There's bound to be a pack of cards around here somewhere," he says. "Uno! I'm sure I'll find a pack of Uno in one of these drawers."

"I'll give you a hand!"

I get up and start rummaging through drawers with him. We find a pack. It looks like some cards are missing, but it'll do fine.

Eva is happy again, as if nothing has happened, and Augustin is far too reserved to show his annoyance at her comments.

He joins us around the coffee table and waits for the cards to get dealt.

We play round after round for a good hour, and then just before midnight, we stop. We're all tired.

It takes barely five minutes for us to choose our rooms. I send a message to Dad to tell him everything's fine and to reassure him that I always have at least one dose of my treatment with me. As I'm about to get into bed, I open the Instagram notification I just received. It's Augustin.

> Can we talk? I'm in the living room.

It's after midnight, and my legs feel a bit shaky as I go downstairs. Augustin is standing in front of the bay window watching the snow fall.

"Is the storm blowing over?"

"Yep, it's not snowing as heavily anymore. It's going to stop during the night," he says as he turns around. "Thanks for coming down."

I give him a smile.

"So, what did you want to talk about?"

I'm standing awkwardly in the middle of room, so he invites me to come and sit with him on the sofa.

"I'm not the kind of person you think I am," he begins.

I hold my breath. This is exactly the conversation I wanted to have with him.

"And what is it I think?"

He sighs.

"Eva and I have always struggled to communicate. You two have been friends for a long time, but I can imagine that she hasn't painted a nice portrait of me. Like the comment she made earlier."

He was offended, I could tell. When they were younger, Augustin and Eva fought like cats and dogs. He got annoyed that she was always following him around, and she said he was a pain in the ass because he was always complaining. I'm an only child, so I don't know what it's like to have a brother or sister, but I would have thought that things improve over the years.

But I don't want to beat around the bush, I need to say what I'm thinking.

"Are you just playing with me?"

He gets a dark look on his face.

"Is that what you think?"

We look at each other in silence for a few seconds, and as I don't reply, Augustin gives a deep sigh.

"Listen. I can imagine how it must sound when my sister talks about me, but I would hate it if you thought you were one of a long list of girls that I choose from depending on how I'm feeling. I'm not even twenty-two yet, and OK, I'm not looking to get married right away, but I'm not the person she says I am. I'm not some scumbag who has a girl in his bed every other night and who moves on to the next one right after. I've made mistakes, sure, but I've never used anyone. I admire you."

Well, that last comment takes me by surprise.

"You admire me?"

"You're a fighter."

I can't help but snort.

"It's not as if I had a choice. I just did the only thing I could – try and stay alive."

"I'm so glad you did."

"That's nice of you. I... what do you want from me?"

He takes his time before replying. Looking at me, lingering on my mouth, my eyes, my hair...

"I want you to give us a chance. I know it's crazy – you're my sister's best friend, we hadn't seen each other in three years, and all of a sudden, with just one look, something in me clicked. OK, I admit all that. But there *is* something between us, you can't deny it."

"No..."

"And I admit it's not the easiest situation. I'm not sure my sister will be happy, but I think it's worth the risk."

"Yeah... Did something really click for you with just one look?"

"Quicker than a look even, the blink of an eye."

He stretches out his hand toward my face and brushes away the hair that has fallen down onto my cheek.

"You are so pretty."

My eyes are wide open, and all I can see are his eyes, hungrily staring back at me.

There's a ball of fire in my stomach.

Our smiles have completely faded away. The tension between us is palpable. I want to touch him, and I know he feels the same, but when we hear the ceiling creak above, it reminds us that we're not alone, that the risk is too great here.

"I'd better go back to my room."

"Wait," he says, holding me by the hand as I get up, "you didn't answer me."

His fingers are warm. I look at his dishevelled hair, his burning dark eyes, and see something true in them, something unfiltered, a lack of guile.

I believe everything he said. One hundred per cent.

"I want to give us a chance, but I don't want Eva to know."

My hand is in his, and I can't bring myself to pull away.

"I don't work on Tuesday mornings. Come with me to Les Lindarets."

"Les Lindarets? Why?"

"So we can get to know each other better. Just the two of us."

I smile at him, and without knowing what excuse I could possibly give Eva if she wants to hang out, I say yes.

"OK!"

Without warning, he lifts my hand to his lips and kisses the back of it. No one has ever done that to me before. A shiver goes through my whole body, from head to toe.

And I gently pull away.

"See you tomorrow."

When we get up, the sky is blue, and the road is clear. Like other things here, the weather is surprising too. The sun and the snowplows have done their job, and we're able to leave practically straight away. It's just after 8 o'clock.

There's a strange atmosphere, no one's really saying anything. I put it down to the short night we all had, but nothing usually stops Eva from talking. She is unusually quiet, even in the car. She gets in the back seat with me, but barely looks at me and instead stares out at the snowy landscape. I hope she didn't overhear the conversation I had with Augustin.

Thinking about that possibility gives me a terrible sensation in my gut, and I can't even pluck up the courage to send her a discreet message to ask her what's going on. Augustin drops Jimmy off in town, then brings his sister home. All she does is give me a wave. Then he drives me back to the chalet.

"Eva seemed weird," I say, as soon as we're on our own.

"I noticed."

His answer was a bit curt. Which makes me worry even more.

"Is there a problem between the two of us?"

Augustin forces a smile.

"No, not at all. Are you still on for tomorrow?"

"Yes, of course."

He rummages through his pocket and pulls out a piece of paper.

"Here. We haven't even swapped numbers. I'll send you a message to let you know where and when, OK? But make sure you bring waterproof clothes. There's lots of snow up there. And bring your snowshoes. You think you'll be OK with this?"

"I survived cross-country skiing, a Savoyard fondue and a snowstorm, I should be all right."

I smile at him and put my hand on the door handle, ready to get out of the car.

"Hey… wait," he says, putting a hand on my shoulder. "You're even prettier first thing in the morning."

"That's because you're not seeing straight!" I reply with a laugh. "See you tomorrow!"

When I go inside the chalet, Dad is already gone. He has left a note on the table, which makes me smile.

The ice rink in the main square has just been installed. If you want to make the most of it before it gets busy, now's your chance. Ask at the information centre! I'll be back at 5 pm! XXX

My father, who hasn't seemed to notice I'm not a kid anymore…

I go up to my bedroom and get my stuff ready before having a shower. Afterward I'll need to study. I feel so anxious about Eva, and when I get back from the bathroom, there's a message from her on WhatsApp.

> I did something stupid…

>> What happened? You want me to call you?

> No, I'd rather not… I slept with Jimmy.

>> What?

I'm this close to adding "already?" but I don't. No point in making her feel worse. If she's reacting like this, then she really feels bad about it.

> I don't know what to say.
> I couldn't stop myself.

>> You wanted to, right?

Yes, of course, he was lovely, it's just that... What's he going to think of me?

Um, the same thing you think of him? That he wanted to? That you both wanted to? What else would he think?

That I'm an easy lay?

Hey, wait. You think he was lovely, but you're easy? No way!! If you're easy, then so is he! You both wanted to so where's the problem?

I just feel like shit... He barely spoke to me this morning.

You want my advice? Call and tell him how you're feeling. If he thinks you're easy, he's not worth it.

Yeah, maybe. Thanks for being there...

That's what friends are for. And it'll be fine. You're amazing. XXX

But when I put the phone down, I feel so wound up. I hate it that she thinks of herself like that. I hate it that society has conditioned us to believe such stupid things! Why should it be fine for a guy and not a girl? Jimmy had better be OK with all this, otherwise he's dead.

I get dressed and try to focus on my study. But I can't even do an hour's work, I keep thinking about Eva.

What are you still doing here? She needs you!

I jump off my bed and race down the stairs. In under five minutes, I'm wearing my boots, jacket, gloves and hat, and I'm outside. It takes me twenty minutes to walk to Eva's house.

She's at home alone. She's been crying and her eyes are all red. She's wearing a hideous flannel bathrobe.

"Hey... you shouldn't be getting in such a state for something that's just in your mind. Have you called Jimmy?"

She sniffs.

"He's at work and won't answer. Oh, I just feel so awful!"

The waterworks start again, so I give her a big hug.

"Stop beating yourself up. You haven't done anything wrong."

"You think?"

"I'm sure. Go and get dressed, we're going for a walk."

"Where are we going?"

"To town!"

"There is no way we're going to town, we're bound to see Jimmy!"

Argh! She's going round in circles.

"So what? You'll be able to ask him what he thinks of you."

She shakes her head like a child. Then I have another idea, one that's much more fun.

"Eva, get dressed, we're going ice skating."

She's always loved skating. Even though the rink in the town centre will probably be too small for us and even though it's not officially open, I know she'll love it. When we were small, we used to go to the covered rink, which is ten times bigger. Eva skated like a pro, while I would spend half my time sitting on the ice on my butt. Each to their own.

But she's not convinced.

"Do you really want to go ice skating?"

"If it makes you smile again, then yes. But only on the rink in the square!"

She furrows her brow as if she's trying to understand.

"Whoever you are, begone from the body of my friend."

I burst into laughter.

"Come on. Just tell yourself it's the mountain air. But I'm warning you, this offer is only going to come up once, and it expires in… um… twenty seconds! One…"

"Wait, are you serious?"

"Two…"

"What the…"

"Three…"

"OK, OK! I'll go and get dressed! April Hamon, imprisoned in her own body for the last three years, who has always hated ice skating, wants to take me to the outdoor rink? I can't believe it."

"Only so you get your smile back, don't think this is going to become a habit."

The things we do for our friends.

I almost didn't survive. There are some people who have no sense of balance, and I am most definitely one of them. Although Morzine is not yet at the height of the winter tourist season, those that are here had a field day watching me fall over. Fifteen times at least. Peak humiliation. I wouldn't be surprised if I ended up on an embarrassing social media video.

"Wow! That was amazing," says Eva, as she sits down on a bench to put her boots back on. "That did me a world of good. Thanks for having insisted!"

The skating rink is so small that she must have done at least fifty laps. It almost made me feel dizzy watching her go round and round, but she has her smile back and that's the main thing.

"Do you know what I feel like now?" she asks.

"Let me guess… A hot chocolate with marshmallows."

"Yes!"

I smile. I saw that one coming.

We walk through the village on snowy sidewalks, while carefully avoiding the Blue Yeti. We end up in front of a place I've never seen before. It's out of this world. Simon's Coffee Bar. It's in a chalet all decorated with twinkling lights, pine branches and a string of silvery stars. Outside there are gondola cabins covered in snow, and inside each one there's a wooden table for two and benches with cushions and sheepskins on them. It's like it appeared out of nowhere.

"OK, please tell me we're going to stop here," says Eva, who can barely contain herself.

How could I possibly say no? This place is incredible.

We climb into a gondola and place our order. A huge hot chocolate for her and an orange peel tea for me.

"I'm loving hanging out with you," Eva tells me. "I don't know what's sparked it, but I love the vibe you're giving off at the moment. The last time we saw each other, you didn't even want to go and have a coffee just round the corner from your house."

What sparked it? It's this place and everything that goes with it. I so want to tell Eva about what I'm going through, I want to tell her all about Augustin and how he makes me feel, but I know I might ruin it all.

Eva leans back in her chair and smiles at me. I decide to try something.

"It was actually your brother who first helped me get over some of my fears."

"Oh?"

"Yeah, when we went skiing with the kids."

She looks surprised.

"Really?"

"Yeah, it was so nice of him."

She gives a strange laugh.

"Luckily you're not his type, otherwise I would have lost it."

"Umm..."

"Don't worry, it's not you, it's just that he prefers girls who are up for a good time."

I nearly choke on my tea, then try my best to make it seem less awkward.

"You still don't get on with Augustin. Why not?"

She sighs.

"It's not that. I think I'm still holding something against him."

"What?"

"You haven't been here for three years. I haven't told you everything that happened."

I frown.

"What do you mean?"

"Do you remember Melodie, the girl who was in my year at high school? She repeated a year."

I nod.

"Three years ago, Augustin had a thing with her, and it ended badly. She was so into him and went around telling everyone that he was the one. She was totally obsessed."

"Oh yeah, I remember now, you told me about her."

"Yeah. Well, one night they were at the same party, and they slept together."

I can feel myself becoming tense.

"And?"

"And my brother had drunk too much. The next day, he told Melodie that he didn't want to go out with her, that it was a mistake. He had just started his sports studies, and he wasn't looking for a serious relationship."

Eva's expression became grim.

"She tried to kill herself a few weeks later."

I can't hide my distress. Augustin had told me he had made mistakes, but I never imagined this.

"Shit…"

"Yeah, it really was. Augustin was nineteen. Melodie's parents wanted to press charges for statutory rape, but she was seventeen, so it probably wouldn't have been admissible. She wouldn't let them take it any further. There was a terrible atmosphere at school for quite a few months. Until Melodie's parents decided to move to the south of France."

I am in shock.

"You never told me about this."

"You'd just been hospitalized after your heart failure, it wasn't really the right time."

"No… I wasn't interested in anything apart from what I was going through. And so you're still angry with Augustin?"

Eva leans back in her seat.

"It ruined part of my time at high school – I was the sister of a complete bastard."

"I'm sure he's changed since then…" I murmur.

She laughs cynically.

"Dream on! Then there was that girl I couldn't stand, then he calmed down a bit, and now he goes for anything that moves. It's just the way he is."

If I could, I would block my ears. Eva is wrong about her brother. Augustin could have gone for me, in fact I wouldn't have stopped him, but he didn't. And last night he was genuine.

Every single part of me is crying out to believe that.

"Hmm," she says, looking at me. "You don't look as if you agree with me, but believe me, I know him better than anyone else."

I give a tight smile.

How can I contradict her without giving away the fact that Augustin and I have gotten closer? She would never be able to accept it. Ever since the beginning I thought this might be the case, but now I'm sure.

The situation is so screwed up. Totally screwed up.

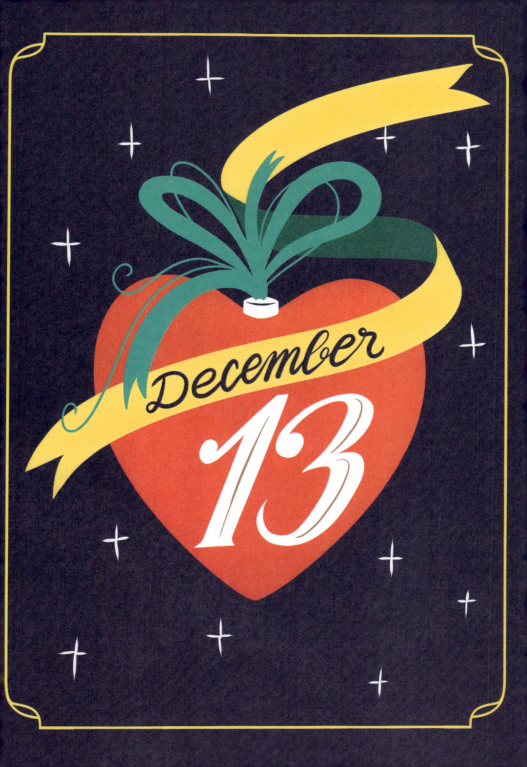

In the end, Augustin decides to pick me up with his father's car.

Dad is tidying up some paperwork and catches sight of me as I walk past his office. It's not quite 9 o'clock.

"You're up and about early this morning," he says, seeing I'm already dressed. "Oh, are you going up the mountain?"

The fact that I'm wearing my cross-country skiing outfit doesn't escape his notice.

"Um, yes… Augustin offered to… We're going snow-shoeing at Les Lindarets."

"Oh? Is Eva going too?"

"Um… probably, yeah."

I hesitate for a fraction of second, so he raises an eyebrow.

"You're not sure?"

"What I mean is… Dad, why are you even so interested?"

He lifts his hands in surrender.

"OK, OK, do what you want."

My foot is just on the top stair when Dad adds, "Actually April, I haven't seen you study for a few days, you don't think…?"

Now it's my turn to make a face.

"When I got here you were disappointed that I hadn't made plans to do any activities, and just as I'm about to go outside, you want me to stay in and study?"

"That's not what I said. I'm very glad you've finally decided to socialize and go out. I just want to be sure you're able to keep up with everything."

Dad never really worried about my schoolwork. He could see that everything was fine and didn't interfere, so I'm surprised by his comment. But still, I don't want him to think that it's not his business, so I go into the office and give him a kiss on the cheek.

"Don't worry, everything is fine."

In theory, anyway. Because in practice, even though I fall asleep surrounded by my papers, I'm not achieving much.

Do I need to start taking it up a notch? No. Before I came to Morzine, I worked so hard.

Everything is fine.

"Have you heard from your mother?" Dad asks.

"We chat a bit by message every night. She's busy with her translations."

"There haven't been any more clashes between the two of you?"

I give him a wink of shared understanding.

"She doesn't ask me any questions, so I don't tell her what I'm up to!"

Bizarrely, instead of playing along as he always has, he gets a look of concern on his face.

"What is it?"

"No… no, nothing. Have fun. I'm not working today, but I've got to go into the information centre for a bit of a catch-up meeting. Don't wait for me for lunch."

As I leave his office, I struggle to hide my irritation.

What exactly is he worried about?

That I've decided to have a real vacation after being locked up for so long at home? He's been wanting me to come and get some fresh air for months, and now that I'm here, it's as if he's reproaching me for not studying enough and not telling Mom what I'm up to?

My parents are going to drive me crazy, they really are.

I go into the garage and dig out my old snowshoes and poles. They're all still in perfect condition. I gulp down a cup of hot tea and a banana, and then send a message to Augustin before he gets here. I don't want him to knock at the door and bump into Dad.

There has been enough interrogation for one morning.

When I come out of the chalet, he's waiting for me in the 4WD. I throw my snowshoes and poles in the back and sit in the front passenger seat, making sure he can't see my annoyance.

"Hi, Mrs. Claus! Sleep well?"

"Really well! Um… just because I don't want to keep worrying about it, is Eva going out this morning?"

"Nope! She said she's going to be studying. Are you ready?"

I nod, then Augustin looks me up and down.

I'm wearing my red beanie with two pompoms.

"What?"

"Nothing, I love it!" And he starts the car.

I'm looking forward to going to Les Lindarets.

Everyone here knows about it, it's a truly special little village. In summer there are more goats than inhabitants! They wander freely through the streets, and visitors can even pet them. It's such a fun place to visit. And then in autumn, the goats go back down to the valley until spring, the village gradually covers over with snow, and it's no longer possible to get there by car.

For our excursion today, Augustin drives to Montriond and then along the lake, which is nestled between steep cliffs. It's magical to see it completely frozen over.

When I was younger, we'd often come cross-country skiing here as a family. We'd even see divers under the ice. Those guys are completely bonkers. Imagine staying thirty minutes underwater at a temperature of not even 4° C! But in summer it's fantastic. Eva and I used to go kayaking or stand up paddling, not to mention sunbathing!

Augustin drives past the lake and parks in the hamlet of Ardent, full of wooden chalets all decorated with Christmas lights, not far from the cable car.

"What a perfect day!" he exclaims as he gets out of the 4WD. "We'd better make the most of it. The weather's meant to change just before Christmas."

He gets a backpack out of the trunk, puts it on and then gives me a smile.

"Ready?"

"I haven't been snowshoeing in ages, so take it easy with me, OK?"

His little smile is so cute, I can feel myself falling for him.

"Maybe I will, maybe I won't! Come on, let's do this."

With our snowshoes under one arm, poles in the other hand, hat and gloves on, and sunglasses pushed back on our heads, we walk through the hamlet and head up to the cable car.

The cable car operator helps us into one of the cars, where it's just the two of us for the five-minute journey.

Augustin leans against the window and doesn't say a word. He's looking at me intently with brightly shining eyes.

It feels like the cabin is getting smaller and that time is coming to a stop. My legs have turned to jelly and all I can do is return his gaze.

He attracts me like a magnet.

I try to snap out of it and dig around in my pocket for my lip balm, which I apply distractedly. Augustin follows each of my movements with a fascination that unsettles me even more. It's only once the cabin comes to a stop that he seems to gain control of himself again.

He gets out first and gives me his hand.

"This is us. Here, let me help you."

On the flat plateau at Les Lindarets, the snow is even deeper. This is where lots of ski lifts leave from and head in every direction. It's like a hub.

It's the week before Christmas, there are more and more people; skiers everywhere, both downhill and cross-country, people trekking and snowshoeing. I didn't feel like this when

I went to the Joux-Verte pass with Dad or when I met up with Augustin at Super Morzine, but I can feel a prickling sensation on the soles of my feet, and I almost feel like crying. I used to love skiing.

"Is something wrong?" asks Augustin.

I put my sunglasses on properly; I don't want him to see that I'm upset.

"No, no, not at all!"

He frowns. I don't think my little act fooled him.

Augustin draws closer, pulling my sunglasses down and looking into my eyes.

"Are you crying?"

I sniff and quickly wipe my cheeks. I feel so stupid!

"No, it's nothing. I just feel a bit emotional."

"Why? Are you scared?"

"No, I… Three years ago, I would come here with Eva or even on my own, and nothing scared me. I spent entire days on my skis. It felt like nothing could happen to me, that the operations I had when I was little would be enough to keep me safe, to make me normal like everyone else and…"

I start crying again, this time properly.

"I'm so sorry, I'm so stupid." Augustin sticks his poles into the snow and gathers me into his arms. He is so tall. Held tightly against his chest, I can feel myself letting go. I am so lame! I really didn't mean for this to happen.

"I'm ruining everything…"

"No, don't say that. It's totally the opposite. This is good, because every time you hit a wall, you get up again and are able to push your limits out a bit further."

I give another sniff.

"You have a funny way of looking at things."

"I'm not you, and you have every right to tell me I don't know what I'm talking about, but I reckon it's not just nostalgia for the past that's making you upset. You *want* to be doing things again."

I pull away from him slightly and look up at him.

He's right. He is totally right. I want to be normal again, to ski and… to kiss him. Without thinking, I stand on the tips of my toes, slide my hand behind his neck and give him a long kiss on the lips.

Augustin is speechless.

"I did not see that coming!"

"Me neither!"

And for no reason, in the middle of a whole bunch of people who couldn't care less, we burst out laughing like two idiots.

Just what I needed!

I think that's what I like most about him – the bond he creates between us and the calm sense of strength he gives off. Both of these things make me want to trust him, no matter what I've heard about him. I don't have much experience in terms of relationships. The only one I've had was a total disaster.

With Benoit I was also the first to instigate a real kiss, and until then I had never dared touch a boy's mouth. We were sitting on a bench in the day room of the cardio department, and thirty seconds later his tongue was in my mouth. Benoit took without asking.

Whereas Augustin receives without forcing himself on me. He doesn't jump down my throat and that's what makes all the difference. He is a good person. I can feel it deep within me and I want him to know it.

"It's so good being with you."

"I feel the same!" he says as he gently brushes away a lock of hair that has come out from under my hat, "April Hamon, I think it's time for you to start again. Skiing that is, but if you started kissing me again, I wouldn't say no!"

I give him a cheeky look.

"Right here, right now, one seems more likely than the other."

He smiles and puts his sunglasses on again.

"Anything is possible, you'll see. One step after another. Are you with me?"

"Yes!"

I also love how he doesn't make a big deal out of a situation he knows I find difficult. I'm not sure if one day I'll be able to ski like I used to, but when I'm around him, it feels like there are fewer barriers.

He puts on his snowshoes, helps me tighten my straps and we're away. The goat village – with no goats in winter – is down the mountain a bit, maybe a hundred metres below us.

It's a small hamlet with real Savoyard chalets hugging the mountain side. At this time of year, the roofs are covered in a thick layer of snow. There must be at least fifty centimetres. There are no cars, you can only get here by snowmobile, on foot or by ski. The place gives off a feeling of timelessness I've always loved.

To get to the hamlet, we walk on the edge of the trail; skiers shoot past us at top speed.

I don't have the most recent showshoes, but they're comfortable enough, and it doesn't feel like I have anything attached to my boots. I'm surprised I don't find the walk difficult. Even on the slopes we make good progress, and we reach the village in just ten minutes.

At this time of day, people are mostly going straight through, but there are still some outside sitting at tables in sheepskin-lined chairs and enjoying a hot drink in the sun.

"This is not the only reason I brought you here, but almost," says Augustin with a smile. "I hope you didn't have a huge breakfast!"

I shake my head. I'm dying of hunger, the banana I ate wasn't enough to fill me up.

We sit down outside at La Ferme des Lindarets, a wood and stone chalet covered in snow. The entrance porch is decorated with flashing multicoloured lights. There is a Christmas wreath hanging against the façade, and angels and stars dangle from the windows. It's a shame we can't see it at night.

"Their waffles are delicious, and the hot chocolate too. Does that sound good?"

I nod because I don't want to be a spoilsport, but when Augustin orders and asks for the sugar on the side, it tugs at my heartstrings.

"You're always so attentive," I murmur.

"It's not hard. I can see what you're thinking, and I want you to feel at ease."

"I do."

Augustin smiles at me, but for a brief instant I sense he's preoccupied.

"Are you all right?"

He takes off his hat and runs his fingers through his hair to straighten out the kinks.

"I'm not trying to win points, you know. This is just how I am."

"I... I don't feel like you're trying to manipulate me."

"Despite what my sister told you?"

I feel my face grow pale.

"Um... what are you talking about?"

"I had to go home and collect something yesterday morning, I heard you talking. She says I'm a player."

I don't know what to say.

"I messed up," he says. "Once. And I'm only too aware of it. I'm not trying to make excuses by saying I drank too much, even though that's what happened. I slept with a girl who a few weeks later wanted to commit suicide because I didn't want to be in a relationship with her."

"I know..." I say softly.

He doesn't ask me how I know. I'm sure he can guess.

"I regret what I did, but I shouldn't have to pay for it for the rest of my life."

"I understand. I'm sorry that Eva can't get past this."

"I tried to go and see Melodie in the hospital, to talk with her, but her parents didn't let me. They had confiscated her phone, blocked her social media. I was never able to apologize or even tell her how sorry I was. April, I'm not that kind of guy."

The waiter arrives with our order, and we stop talking. When he leaves again, I reach out and place my hand on his.

"You don't have to justify yourself. I believe you. I believe in you because I can see the type of person you are. I wouldn't be here otherwise."

His eyes shine with an emotion that makes him even more endearing.

And endearing he is. He affects me in a way no one else ever has. Not even Benoit.

"This is going to be complicated," he says. "Eva might not accept our relationship."

"I know..."

"Do you still want to try?"

"Yes."

I am absolutely certain of it.

"There's another thing..."

"Yes?"

"When we were in the lodge, my room was just below Jimmy's. I heard them. I guess Eva told you?"

I swallow. I can't remain impassive. Nor can I lie.

"Yes. How do you feel about it?"

"Fine. It's her life and her choices, not mine."

"I wish she thought the way you do."

He smiles at me.

"We'll see. But for now, it's just you and me."

His waffle is covered in whipped cream. He dips his finger in, and before I have time to react, he puts some on the tip of my nose.

"Hey!"

I respond in kind and get him with a good dollop. The ensuing laughter is enough to make everyone turn around, but who cares, it feels like we're the only people on Earth.

Augustin gets his phone out and suggests we take a selfie to immortalize one of our most attractive looks.

When I go back to Lyon, this will be a moment to cherish.

But I don't want to think about that now, about what will happen afterward, about the distance, about how Eva will react once she eventually discovers my relationship with her brother.

Maybe she'll understand that Augustin and I aren't that different from her and Jimmy. And if she refuses to understand, then I'll continue to fight, because the only thing I know for sure is that choosing between them is the same as giving up.

And I refuse to choose between Eva and Augustin.

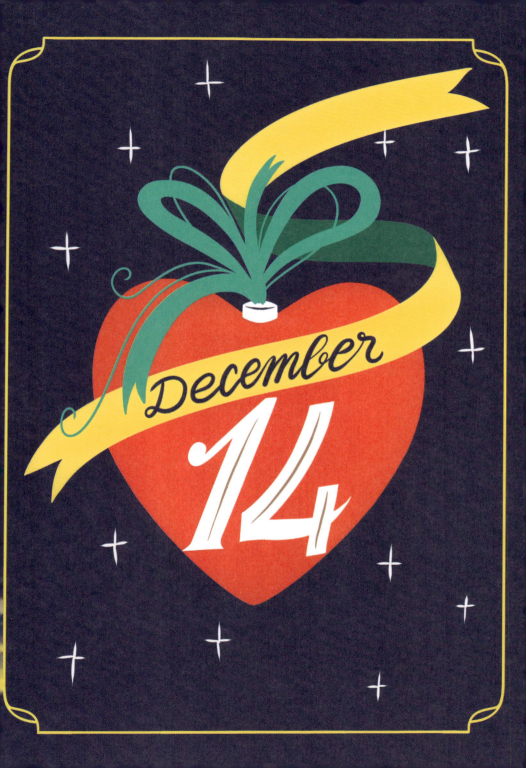

I got up from my chair feeling like I could move mountains. I haven't had that much energy for such a long time. When I got home, I turned the house upside-down, cleaning and tidying from top to bottom. I organized all my study papers, sorted through the old clothes that have been in my closet for three years and made chocolate cookies. When Dad gets back at midday with a bag of groceries from the market, the table is set, the meal is ready and the music is on full-bore, with me singing my lungs out.

I even dance up to him – I've never seen him so surprised.

"Are you celebrating something?"

"Life!"

He raises an eyebrow.

"Has life done something special to you in the last twenty-four hours?"

There's no way I can tell him I'm falling for the most awesome guy on Earth.

Nor can I tell him that the something special is Augustin. Dad would try and bring me back down to reality, and I don't want that. It's not often I've ever been this happy.

"Hmm… it's just that I'm getting better and better," I say instead. "Are you hungry? I made pasta with pesto."

What I actually did was open a jar of pesto before its use by date became a thing of the past.

"It's good to see you so happy. What's brought all this about?" he asks as he empties his basket.

"The mountain air! All this oxygen, the cold, it's… invigorating."

I can see that Dad only half believes me.

"Is there a boy under here?" he asks, as he sits at the table.

I make an effort not to give anything away.

"You're always jumping to conclusions!"

"All right, all right! But this kind of thing happens at your age."

I manage to cleverly change the subject.

"What about you? Have you ever wanted to start a new relationship?"

He puts down his glass of water, clearly disconcerted by my question.

"No."

His answer is so terse that I almost swear it contains a note of bitterness. When I once asked my mother the same question, she said that she didn't have the headspace for it, that she would rather focus on my future and that she couldn't imagine becoming involved with another man. I remember that the way she talked about this "other man" felt to me like a confession, as if my mother had given her heart to one man only and she would never be able to love another.

"Do you still have feelings for Mom?" I can see his eyes narrow.

"What kind of a question is that?"

"Did you still love each other when you broke up?"

"April, what has come over you? Your mother and I have been separated for three years and divorced for eighteen months. That's all behind us now, there's no point going back over it."

I shrug my shoulders.

"I always thought you two made a good couple."

"We fought all the time."

"Because you didn't agree or didn't have the same fears about me. But before I was born, I'm sure you were really close."

Dad sighs.

"April, I hope you don't feel responsible for anything that happened. It wasn't you, it was just life that separated us. Our differences of opinion."

"OK. But I'm a big girl now, and sometimes I can't help thinking that if you or Mom are not able to move on, maybe it's because things aren't completely over between you."

Dad looks at me as if I were an alien. I hadn't planned on this conversation, but now that we're having it, I realize that my parents' divorce never seemed logical to me. It seemed instead as if it were an easy way out of all the problems they hadn't been able to manage.

When Mom behaves in a reserved way with Dad, I get the feeling it's to protect her from herself and from what she might still feel toward him. And when he tries to be kind and remind her that they used to have a bond, he is always hurt when she shuts him down.

"April, I don't know what's going on in your head, but I would advise you to move on to something else. It's totally over between your mother and me."

"So that's why you still have a photo of her on your bedside table?"

I saw it this morning while vacuuming his room. It's an old shot from when they were still young. They're holding my hands. I must have been about five.

It takes him a few seconds to process what I've said.

"You're in the photo too."

Like a family.

I smile at him. I don't want to intrude into his personal life anymore.

"Whatever you say! Do you want more pasta?"

After lunch I head to Eva's with my backpack, ready to study while she works on her dissertation. We've both fallen behind, so we've decided to spend the afternoon trying to catch up.

Dad can feel totally reassured.

When I get to hers at about 2 pm, the house is empty. Her parents are working at the store the whole day, and Augustin is busy with lessons until 5 pm.

I don't want any complicated situations, so I'll make sure I leave before he gets back.

"Shall we work in my room?" asks Eva.

I nod. Her window looks out over the valley and is nice and bright, even though today the clouds are so low, they're practically hanging off the mountain.

As I go in, I see a little Christmas tree on her dresser, and next to it an advent calendar. Each day until December 24 she gets a little Christmas decoration to hang on the tree.

Eva has always loved that sort of stuff.

"I have so much to tell you!" she says straight away, sitting cross-legged on her bed. "I listened to your advice, and I spoke to Jimmy last night."

"And?"

She sighs.

"I didn't say anything for two days, and neither did he. I was sure he regretted it, and he thought the same about me. It wasn't that he was trying to avoid me when we left the lodge, it's just that he felt embarrassed."

"Why?"

"My brother heard us."

This obviously comes as no surprise to me. I hate having to pretend and play a double game, but I don't have a choice.

"Oh... Awkward..."

"Yeah, his room was just below, and well... it didn't take him long to figure out we weren't doing jumping jacks."

I can't help smiling. Eva and her descriptions.

"So, how do you feel about that?"

"I dunno. It's weird, but my brother hasn't even spoken to me about it. He hasn't taken it badly at all. But then I guess that's totally his style!"

I frown in irritation.

"You show him no mercy, do you. Would you rather he got annoyed?"

"Of course not! But his approach has always been 'each to their own.' He doesn't care about other people. And for once, that suits me just perfectly."

"And Jimmy?"

"He was worried that Augustin would get upset or that it might ruin their friendship, but that's not the case, so he's fine."

The weight I can feel growing in my stomach is starting to bear me down.

My heart is racing, as if I were in an exam. Surely now Eva might understand what I'm going through. I wonder if it might be the right time to talk to her about it.

I try to give a little laugh and approach the subject delicately.

"Can you imagine me in the same situation?"

Her face literally crumples in horror.

"What, you mean, you and my brother? Ugh, I can't imagine anything worse. I don't even want to think about it!"

OK. So that makes me feel a bit annoyed.

"But what would be so different?"

"Like, everything! He's known you since you were a kid, it'd be like he was going out with... I dunno, his half-sister or something! It would be so gross."

I'm sure I've gone completely white. I'd never thought about it like that.

"And if in some parallel universe you did go out with my brother, our friendship would definitely be over because we'd no longer spend any time together."

She sighs and pushes a hand through her hair.

"And also... I would hate that to happen because he wouldn't take it seriously. It'd last, what... a few weeks during the vacation? And then what? You'd be in Lyon, and he'd be here? You don't want to be with a guy like him, believe me! Sure, he's nice enough, but being in a relationship with him would not be fun."

Eva suddenly lies down and stretches out her arms and legs. It's like she has completely moved on from what she just said.

"I think I'm in love..."

And I can't say a word. I feel like I have a ball of pins in my throat. Eva is my best friend, one of the people I love most in the world, but she's not being fair. She has this black-and-white vision of her brother that is so demeaning. And as well, she and Jimmy are doing exactly what she wouldn't accept from Augustin.

I can't believe she just spoke like that. She's never been so vindictive. Augustin can't keep paying eternally for something he did three years ago. And as for thinking that Eva and I would grow apart, it would be exactly the opposite, I'd feel even closer to her.

More than I do at the moment, that's for sure.

"Are you OK?" she asks as she turns and looks at me. "You don't look like your usual self."

I can't tell her the truth. Then we really would have a fight, and that's not what I want. I suppress my feeling of discomfort and try to give her a smile.

"I'm fine. How about we do some studying?"

We work hard all afternoon and barely say a word to each other. Eva is focusing on her bachelor's dissertation, and I'm studying my legal clauses, and even though I can't stop thinking about the situation, I still achieve more than I have in the past fortnight.

It's almost 6 pm when I say I should be thinking about getting home. Time has just flown by.

It's dark and the fog is thick on the ground. Eva gives a huge yawn.

"Why don't you stay the night here? Then tomorrow we could go do some Christmas shopping?"

What, and be under the same roof as Augustin and have to pretend there's nothing between us? It brings me out in a cold sweat just thinking about it.

"I can't, I've got to do some more work otherwise I'm not going to be able to keep up. But we could go shopping the day after?"

I feel ashamed.

Eva sighs. "OK, good idea. I haven't bought any presents yet. And anyway, I still have another ten or so pages to write. I'd like to get it all done before Christmas so I can make the most of my vacation. What are you and your father doing for Christmas?"

I smile.

"A romantic meal just the two of us!"

"Wooo! That'll be fun!"

"It's been such a long time that I'm actually looking forward to spending it with him."

I get off the bed, gather up all my stuff and pull on my parka.

I really have to go.

Eva's phone rings at exactly the same time.

"Damn, it's Jimmy! Do you mind if I don't walk you home?"

I shake my head, blow her a kiss and go downstairs… just as Augustin is opening the door.

We both come to a stop in surprise, then he closes the door behind him and walks over to me.

"Eva is upstairs," I mumble hastily.

"OK. Were you on your way out?"

"Yeah, we spent all afternoon studying, and it's getting late."

"Do you want me to take you home?"

I glance outside. Aside from the fact that I want to be with him, the weather outside is awful, and I'd feel safer.

"I would like you to. But wouldn't Eva find that weird?"

"She probably didn't hear me come in. I'll just say that I'm heading back into town and that I'll drop you off on the way. Give me a minute, I'm starving. I'll grab something to eat, and we can go."

I nod a bit miserably. All this lying and scheming is not like me at all.

I don't know how long this is going to last, but I'm not the kind of person that can keep a secret like this for very long.

I go into the kitchen.

"Augustin? I think I'll go home on my own."

"What? Why?"

"I don't feel comfortable about lying to Eva."

He frowns.

"Do you want us to talk to her?"

"No! No…"

Not now, not after everything she just said.

"It's just that…"

"You feel like you're betraying her?"

I lower my head. Augustin comes closer.

"Hey… look at me. I don't want to create any problems for you or interfere in your relationship with my sister. If, for whatever reason you might have, you'd rather we didn't take this any further, then tell me."

It's enough to make me want to cry.

"That's not what I want."

"Me neither."

In the most natural way possible, he leans forward, and I turn my mouth up to him. Our kiss should have been brief. We're in his kitchen, at his house, with Eva just above our heads, but we can't stop ourselves. As soon as he touches me, I feel warmth course through me. I wrap my arms around his neck, give myself up to the feeling and kiss him deeply. Without realizing it, we move backward until I'm up against the wall.

It's our first real kiss, and it's even more magical than I thought it would be.

Then all of a sudden, he releases me and leans back against the island unit.

"Oh, you're here?" says Eva as she comes into the kitchen. Then she sees me.

It is so hard to act natural, with my lips and my heart still feeling his touch.

"And you haven't left yet?"

She looks questioningly between us.

"She was just on her way out as I came in. The fog is still thick, so I offered her a ride, but she didn't want to bother me."

Eva looks out the window and puts on a serious look.

"Are you scared of my brother?" she teases, making a veiled reference to everything she'd said before.

My smile is more forced than ever.

"No, not at all."

"The weather's terrible, it's dark, and with all these cars around, I'd feel much better if you didn't walk home. Is it still OK if you take her, Gus?"

"No problem."

"You want me to come with you?" she asks me.

"No, no!"

I answer with such haste that she looks at me oddly.

I pull myself together.

"You said you wanted to keep working on your dissertation, I don't want to interrupt you when you're on a roll. But you can come over after you're done and sleep at mine if you want?"

I glance over at Augustin, who is hiding a laugh, I can tell.

"Aww, thanks. But not tonight, I'll probably end up going to bed late, but I promise, I'll come on a weeknight!"

I smile at her.

"OK. All right, then, I'm ready to go."

I say goodbye to Eva and get into the 4WD with Augustin.

"Did you do acting classes as a kid?" he asks jokingly.

"Oh, stop it. I hate having to do this."

He starts the car and sets off. It's only a five-minute drive.

"What are you doing tomorrow morning, Mrs. Claus?"

"Nothing, why?"

"I want to try something out with you."

"Huh? What kind of thing?"

He gives me a wide grin.

"The kind of thing you're going to love! Here's a hint, wear your old skiing gear if you still have it."

"I do! But…"

"Shh. I'm not saying anything else."

He turns into Route des Nants, clearly pleased with himself.

"I'll meet you tomorrow at 8:30 in front of the ski school."

"That's super early!"

"Well, at least we can be sure we won't come across Eva by surprise," he says with a wink. He leans over me to open the door and sneaks in a kiss on the way past.

"See you tomorrow, Mrs. Claus."

I stay standing on the porch, grinning like a fool, until his car disappears up the road.

Eva's not the only one who thinks she's in love…

December
15

It's 8:30 on the dot when I get to our meeting point. Augustin is wearing his ski instructor outfit and is already there waiting for me.

I keep my distance. There are lots of people around, and I don't feel brave enough to kiss him. He doesn't kiss me either.

My old white ski outfit hasn't let me down. It's still in perfect condition, apart from a hole in the middle of the thigh that Mom repaired by sewing on a Minnie Mouse patch.

It's probably the first thing that Augustin notices, and it makes him smile.

"Is Mrs. Claus a Disney fan?

I poke my tongue out at him.

"So, what's the plan for today? A snowball fight?"

"Way better than that," he answers with a smile.

He digs into his pocket and pulls out a smartwatch. "Here."

I look at the watch without moving.

Mom had given me one for my fourteenth birthday so that I could better track my heartbeat when I went skiing or trekking in the mountains. Dad got angry, he hated the idea of an object that would control me and make me slow down and live in fear. They had a terrible fight about it, and the watch ended up in the trash. Since then, I've often been tempted to buy one, but haven't for fear that I'd end up addicted to it.

I already impose so many limits on myself.

"What should I do with this?" I ask Augustin.

"When you came round for dinner at my parents' place with your dad, you said you only did exercise when you were being monitored, right?"

I frown.

"Um, yes."

"So, here's what I suggest. You come skiing with me, you wear the watch, and I connect the data to my phone. You don't need to look at it, so you won't get stressed, but I can check your heart rate as we go."

"Are you serious?"

It's like he's asking me to jump from a plane without a parachute but has promised he'll catch me. I'm not sure he realizes how full on this is.

"Couldn't be more serious," he says, full of enthusiasm. "Just for half an hour, or more if you want. We'll start with the beginner's slope over there."

He points to the white expanse at the foot of the Pleney runs.

"I... I'm not sure this is a good idea."

"I might be wrong, but I get the feeling you want to. I could tell when we were at Les Lindarets. You want to ski. You miss skiing. It's the fear that's holding you back."

"It's not easy to get over, you know…"

He uncurls my clenched fingers and places the watch in my hand.

"I'm not asking you to trust only me, but also to trust yourself. You can do this."

"Augustin, the hardest thing is trusting myself."

"I know, but I saw you run after that little girl who was heading straight for the cliff. You did that without a second thought, because it was instinctive."

"Yes, but…"

"Listen to me before you start arguing. Anything could have happened to you that day. No one was checking your heart rate. And today we will be."

He takes me by the hands.

"April, I tried to find out as much as I could about this before I suggested it to you. You can do this if you follow the rules. It won't be any more active than the cross-country skiing or trekking we've already done together. You'll warm up first and you won't go over 170 beats per minute."

My head is spinning.

"It's a bit more complicated than that…"

"Well, then explain it to me."

I think it over before speaking.

"Someone who has had a transplant can exercise, but their heart doesn't behave like it does for other people. It needs time to adjust. Making a sudden effort is impossible. That's why I found it so difficult to breathe after running to catch that kid. After I had the operation and started rehabilitation, I learnt that in a normal person, the sympathetic nervous system regulates the heart rate and allows sudden movement. But when I had the operation, parasympathetic nerves were severed, and so I've got to rely on adrenaline to give me that momentum because my body can't prepare itself for sudden effort. Do you see what I mean? I know, I'm not supposed to be able to control this kind of thing, but I'm scared that my body won't know how to manage on its own, that it'll get carried away and won't be able to stop."

"Do you think you'll be able to master that fear?"

I take a deep breath.

"I don't know."

"Do you want to try?"

I look down at my boots without answering.

"If you're worried I'll make a mistake, check the watch. Then both of us will be able to keep an eye on it."

"Promise we'll go slowly?"

"Yes. One thing at a time. And you decide when you want to stop."

"OK..."

His face lights up, while mine, I'm sure, is totally pale.

He helps me put the watch on, checks that it's connected to his phone and smiles at me.

"Eighty, that's nothing! Come on, let's go get you some skis!"

To be honest, I'm not sure if it's fear or excitement that's making my heart beat so fast. Probably both. The adrenaline is already racing through my veins. I follow Augustin into the ski school chalet. It's the first time I've been inside it.

There are Christmas decorations everywhere, but the tired-looking lights and plastic tree must be at least a thousand years old. It's too early for classes to have started yet, so the instructors are still sitting around the table having a coffee.

No one looks up as we come in.

Augustin goes to a store room with skis and boots in it.

"We always have extra material in case we need it. What size shoe are you?"

"Thirty-eight."

"And your height?"

"One metre sixty."

"You're a little pipsqueak!" he laughs. "Here, try these."

I sit on a bench and pull the boots onto my feet. They're much more comfortable than the ones I have at home. Plenty of technological advances have happened in three years.

Augustin comes back with some skis, checks them against my height, pops a helmet on my head and smiles.

"Are you warm enough or do you need another thermal layer?"

It's so darn cute how he looks out for me. It makes me want him even more.

"I'm OK, thanks. I get sick quite easily now that I've had the operation, so I put lots of layers on."

"Good. Let's go then! The beginner's slope will be the perfect warm-up. We'll go nice and easy."

With my skis over my shoulder and poles in hand, I walk like a robot through a gaggle of children.

Augustin makes us walk up a bit of a slope to reach the beginners rope tow. If he had brought me here three years ago, I would have laughed at him, but I am not as confident anymore. I'm even feeling a bit apprehensive.

"I don't need to explain how this works, do I?"

I shake my head, click my boots into the skis and grab the bar before I think too much and change my mind.

I let myself be gently pulled up the slope. I haven't forgotten how to do it.

"Darn, I was half-hoping you might fall off," says Augustin teasingly.

"Phew! I haven't lost my touch!"

He looks delighted.

"Great. Because we're not going to stay on this slope forever! Are you ready to follow me? Let's go!"

It's like I never stopped skiing. The slope is so short and flat, it's frustratingly easy.

We're down in not even four minutes, and it's as if my body has just woken up from a deep sleep. It's starving. It wants more.

One day, my father told me that skiing is like visiting a chocolate factory. You eat one and you can't stop.

And that's exactly what is happening.

I haven't forgotten any of the sensations of skiing, and I want to start again right away.

"One hundred beats per minute," says Augustin, checking his phone. "Another go?"

I nod in agreement.

After the third time down, my heart rate is still just as steady, so I agree to go on the cable car that will take us to the plateau at Le Pléney. The blue trails are easy, but they're longer.

"Is everything OK?" asks Augustin, as he takes a look at his phone. "Are you a bit scared?"

"Yeah, a bit."

In the cable car he takes my hand and squeezes it gently.

"You're doing a great job. I don't even need to remind you what to do. This is going to be fine. We'll take the Grizzli trail and make our way gently down to the Nants trail. We can stop whenever you want, OK?"

I nod. If there's one person I can trust, it's him.

By the time we get out of the cable car at Le Pléney, there are a few more people around. We're at 1,500m altitude and the air is cold and invigorating. The forest is below us, the snow conditions are perfect and the sky is a stunning blue, but that's not enough to calm my feelings of anxiety.

"One ten," says Augustin. "Everything is going to be fine."

I adjust my neck warmer, put my skis on, lower my sunglasses and take a deep breath.

"OK. Let's go before I change my mind."

"OK. Just follow me! We'll go slowly at first so you can warm up, and as soon as you feel ready, pick up the speed a little and go down in big zigzags."

I have skiing in my DNA. I know what I've got to do. I relax my arms as much as I can, I bend my knees slightly and soften my ankles. I keep my back straight and lean slightly forward. We're off!

Augustin glides past me effortlessly, and I follow him without thinking, going down the slope from left to right to control my speed.

I realize that I'm super nervous. I keep touching the exact spot on my chest where I was operated. My arms are out too straight, and my knees aren't bent enough. After barely five minutes, I lose my balance and fall over.

"Are you OK?" Augustin calls out.

"Yes," I reply and get back up.

He looks at his phone and waits for me to catch up to him.

"You're feeling stressed, but your heart rate is doing really well."

I breathe out and nod.

"Shall we go again?"

"Yes! You go first this time!"

Now it's my turn.

"You're doing so well. Trust yourself!" cries Augustin.

I used to be an excellent skier, and the three-year break shouldn't have changed anything. I have the skills, I just need to let go of my fear.

At one point it feels like my heart is speeding up more than it should, and I fall over again.

I take off my helmet and sunglasses and throw them onto the snow. I'm on the verge of crying.

"I can't do it..."

"Yes, you can. It's all in your head. You're feeding your own fear and it's slowing you down."

I picture myself as a sulky kid with my arms crossed over my chest, and I can tell I'm not far from turning that mental image into reality.

"It's not intentional, you know."

"I know. And you're already doing so well."

"How far are we from the closest ski lift?"

"The Plateau de Nyon is less than a kilometre away, we can take the lift down from there."

"OK. Thank you."

Augustin smiles at me and helps me up.

"We've done half the slope. Now you know we're getting the ski lift back down, try and make the most of the rest of it, OK?"

I nod. I try to trust in myself and start the hill down with a bit more suppleness and less fear. The snow isn't out to get me. The other skiers are a good distance away. There are no obstacles in front of me.

I try to let go of the fear and stop thinking about my movements and breathing. I try to let my body take control.

I try to live.

We go through a stand of trees, and when we come out the other side, we've already reached the ski lifts. I didn't fall over one single time. I didn't fall over, and I liked it.

It's not only a victory, it's proof that life, myself and everything I've given up has been worth it for what I'm in the process of recreating.

"One hundred and forty! That's perfect!"

"Is that all?"

"Sure is! You were just getting into it. Next time it'll be even better. But now you need some energy. Here, have this."

He gets out a muesli bar from inside his jacket and hands it to me. It's all these caring gestures that make him special to me.

I smile at him and realize I'm starving. I wolf the bar down in two seconds flat.

"It's not quite 9.30. Before we go back down, would you like to go up to the Pas de l'Aigle?" he asks. "We take the Nyon cable car then the ski lift up to the peak, and then we can go back down to Morzine the same way, nice and easy."

I can't hide my excitement.

I've never been there before; the lookout was installed the year I had my operation. Everyone has told me that it's the most beautiful viewpoint in the whole Portes de Soleil resort. It's at 2,000 metres altitude, and you walk out onto a glass footbridge with 350 metres of nothingness beneath you. Apparently, it's both magical and terrifying.

Augustin doesn't waste a second. He asks the cable car operator to look after our skis and helmets, and the two of us go up. But unfortunately when we get there, the access ramp is closed for the day. I'm so disappointed. The other skiers who also wanted to go to the lookout make do by taking photos from a distance.

"Oh no…"

"Let's just do it anyway!"

"But the guy in the hut over there will see us."

Augustin doesn't listen and walks over to the footbridge. He lifts the chain that blocks our entry and slips underneath it, before holding it up for me.

"Your turn!"

"But we can't!"

"We're not allowed to, but we're still going to! See, I just did!"

"You're crazy!"

I cast aside my principles, take a quick look around and duck under the chain.

"Come on, let's go or we're going to get caught," he says as he gives me his hand.

We hurry along the fifteen or so metres until we get to the end, where I come to a complete standstill.

Affixed to the mountainside, the metal footbridge extends outward, giving us an incredible view. Even covered by a thin layer of snow, the glass plates beneath our feet don't seem thick enough to protect us from the vast emptiness below. It's an indescribable feeling, like we're standing on nothing. And a breathtaking landscape opens up before us.

We can see everything: Morzine, Lake Geneva, Mont Blanc... As we turn full circle, the great expanse of the Alps unfolds before us.

"It makes me feel so tiny. I could never have imagined it would be so beautiful."

I realize that I've never felt so alive, and it brings tears to my eyes.

I almost missed out on experiencing this. Inhabiting a wounded body, tethered to my scars as if they were a lifebuoy, I denied myself everything.

I never want to be like that again.

I look at Augustin with misty eyes.

"Thank you. This is magnificent."

"You're magnificent."

He's looking at me hungrily, and I'm pulled into his gaze.

Even surrounded by this exceptional landscape, with the sky so blue, all I can see is him. A tremor passes through my body. Augustin leans forward as I stretch toward him, both of us drawn to the other. Our foreheads touch, our eyes close, our breathing rises and falls in time. Nothing exists outside the two of us.

"Hey, what are you doing?" a voice suddenly yells. "You're not allowed on there! Come back here right now!"

We come out of our semi-trance and turn to look at the man on the other side of the footbridge, waving his arms about above a paunchy belly.

"We've been spotted!" says Augustin with a laugh. "We'd better hurry, he looks as if he's going to have a fit."

"And you're a ski instructor as well! Oh, that's a great example you're setting!" roars the lift operator in anger. "That was so thoughtless. What if the footbridge was closed for repairs because it was dangerous? Did you think of that?"

"Sorry, sir," apologizes Augustin in a slightly mocking voice as he takes me by the shoulder and pulls me close. "We won't do it again. We promise, sir."

"Oh, you can be sure about that, I never forget a face!" he says, pointing his finger at Augustin.

I'm so close to cracking up at how serious the guy is.

But I don't, as all of a sudden, I notice two skiers, barely ten metres away.

A boy and a girl.

The girl looks absolutely furious. I stop breathing.

It's Jimmy and Eva.

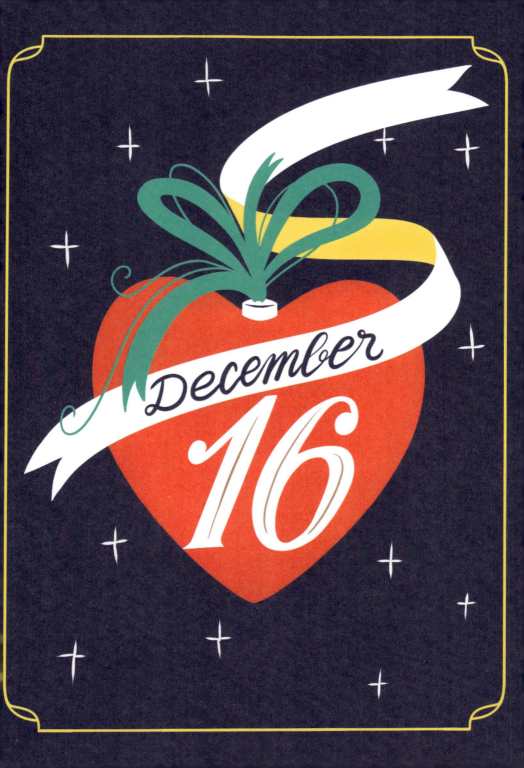

December
16

The sun is shining through the curtains in my bedroom, and before I even open my eyes, the scene from yesterday morning flashes through my mind. I can remember everything, each word, each movement.

It's awful.

The ground feels like it's giving way beneath my feet. Augustin hasn't yet seen his sister and Jimmy, he's still holding me tight. It's too late to try and wriggle free; I'm rooted to the spot. I know exactly what we must look like. There's no possible doubt.

"What's up?" he asks me.

"Eva and Jimmy are just over there…"

He looks up toward the cable car and finally sees them. They're on their skis with their sunglasses on their heads.

"Shit…"

"Augustin, I… she is going to react so badly."

"I know. You mind if I try and talk to her?"

I nod, feeling sick to the stomach. I have no idea how I should react or what I should say to Eva.

We go through the open gate without a second glance at the lift operator, who's waiting impatiently for us, and walk toward Eva and Jimmy.

"Hi," says Jimmy, who doesn't seem bothered. Eva is looking straight at me, her eyes dark with anger and her jaw clenched.

"You've been making a complete fool out of me," she snaps immediately.

"Eva..." Augustin starts to say.

"You, shut the hell up. I should have guessed. I should have picked up on this. God, I've been stupid. How long has this been going on, eh? How long have you two been making a fool of me?"

"No one has been making a fool of you."

In a fury, she turns to her brother.

"Oh, yeah? And what do you call this? A grey zone? A parallel dimension? The multiverse? What I just saw there, the two of you cosying up at the end of the footbridge, that didn't happen? Who's going to believe that? You've just got to have them all, don't you? You disgust me."

I try and talk.

"Eva..."

"And I don't want to hear your excuses. If you've been stupid enough to fall for his charm, then too bad. I gave you enough warning."

"You're not being fair."

"What? You betrayed me! You lied! I asked if you wanted to catch up today and you said, 'I can't, I've got to work, I'm getting so far behind...' When did you become so underhanded, April? Was it when they changed your heart?" she says maliciously.

I turn pale.

"That's going too far," Augustin warns.

"Oh, yeah? I've never made anyone go to the hospital and then abandoned them like a piece of shit, so don't come lecturing me! Do what you want. It's your problem. You can go screw each other senseless if you want, but just do it far, far away from me!"

Now it's Augustin who looks like he's been slapped.

Eva puts her sunglasses on again and heads off toward the slopes in a rage.

Augustin and I don't move. Jimmy is looking at us in turn and doesn't know what to say. I don't think he's judging us. I think he's just as shocked as we are.

"Sorry, I'm the one who asked her to come up here this morning. I wasn't working and she said she wanted to go skiing. If I had known, I wouldn't have come."

"It's not your fault," says Augustin.

Jimmy looks at me questioningly.

"Are you really together?"

I nod in assent.

"Well, it doesn't worry me. It's no weirder than me and your sister," he says to Augustin.

"Yeah… She doesn't look as if she shares your opinion, though."

"I'll try and talk to her."

"That's nice, but don't let it create any problems for the two of you. I'll see her tonight once she's calmed down."

"OK," answers Jimmy. "I'd better go. It's a steep trail. It's not great that she's tackling it when she's so worked up."

Augustin agrees. Jimmy gives me an awkward smile and follows after Eva. I want to cry so badly that I can't even say a *word. It feels like I've been struck by lightning. I'm completely empty. This is the first time that Eva has spoken to me with such malice. I feel shaken and miserable.*

"Hey..."

Augustin turns me around so I'm facing him.

"It's going to be OK."

"No, I don't think it is."

"Yes, it will. You'll see. My sister can get worked up in no time, and then she calms down again."

I don't think it will be the same this time. Augustin hasn't heard her talking the way I have. But I don't want to say anything; I don't have the heart to make things sound any worse than they are. Truth be told, Eva does have a sharp tongue. She's fallen out with lots of people because of it. She's totally uncompromising and can't abide the slightest error. For her, friendship is sacred, and I betrayed her because I wasn't brave enough.

"I hope you're right..."

I haven't heard from her since. She has read but ignored all my messages and calls. It's making me feel sick. I just want to be able to talk to her and explain things, but what could I even say? That yes, I deliberately lied to her?

That was wrong of me, but does she realize that refusing to talk to me is only going to deepen the divide between us? Yes, I'm guilty of not having said anything because I was scared I'd have to end a relationship that was important to me, but I refuse to feel guilty for finally being happy. She should understand me better than anyone else.

She waited a long time for Jimmy, she knows what it's like. If only she would talk to me. I've only just gotten up and already I can't stop thinking about it. It's going to be a long day.

After lunch, while Dad is off on a trek until at least 3 pm, I decide to go to the Blue Yeti, hoping that Jimmy might have more news. Augustin certainly hasn't had any luck. Last night, she shut herself up her room and refused to talk to him.

The weather is as beautiful as it was yesterday, but the temperatures have dropped sharply. It's cold but dry. I dress warmly and walk through town. Tomorrow's going to be a big day. Friday's the day when one lot of people leaves and another arrives. But today the streets are almost empty, as if everyone was making the most of the snow. The Blue Yeti is no different. I go in, but there's not a soul to be seen. Jimmy is drying glasses behind the bar.

"Hi!"

"Hey, April! Are things any better?"

I shake my head and sit on one of the bar stools.

"No news from Eva, she's completely ignoring me."

"Yeah, she's really pissed off."

"Mmm… Have you tried talking to her?"

He sighs and puts his dish towel on the edge of the sink.

"She refuses to talk about it."

"Yeah, that's just like her."

"I'm sorry. It'll all blow over eventually. Can I get you anything?"

Leaning with my elbows on the bar, I remind myself of an alcoholic who desperately needs vodka. If I did drink, I would already have downed three glasses. I shake my head.

"No, thanks. I'd be better off studying than running this over and over in my head. Can you give her a message for me?"

Instead of answering, Jimmy gets a funny expression on his face, and I see him looking through the window.

"I think you'll be able to give it to her yourself..."

Just then, Eva comes in and stops in the doorway as she sees me.

"I'll come back later," she finally says and turns around.

"Eva, wait!"

I dash out and catch up with her on the sidewalk.

"Please, wait, I just want us to talk."

"What could we possibly have to say to each other?"

Her voice is so curt. I've never heard her talk to me like that.

"I... I'm sorry."

"Not as sorry as I am."

"Can we go somewhere and talk about this?"

"Not interested."

"Eva, look, I'm not proud that I lied to you, but I want to explain why."

She gives a cynical laugh.

"Oh, don't worry about that, I think I've figured it out all on my own. My brother turned on the charm, it made you feel special, and you fell for it. Well, you're out of luck, because you're going to end up getting hurt. What you went through with Benoit will be nothing compared to this, believe me."

"Why are you so hard on him?"

"Why? Because he's a predator, he's almost twenty-two and that's all he thinks about!"

"That's not fair. Jimmy's also twenty-two, and you don't say those things about him."

"As far as I know, no one has tried to commit suicide because of him."

She keeps on bringing this up. The situation must really have made her suffer.

"Your brother's not like that with me."

Her face becomes expressionless.

"Not yet, you mean. Wait until you sleep with him, and then we'll talk about it! Because you haven't yet, have you?"

"That's unfair. You're not giving him a chance. You and I have known each other since we were six. You did everything before me – had a boyfriend, kissed someone, had sex, and it was always you who ended things. Remember that guy Hugo, over the summer vacation? You were eighteen, he was seventeen, and you broke his heart because you just wanted a summer fling, and when he went back home, you didn't want to keep in touch with him."

"Hey, stop right there. He and I had an arrangement, that's what we agreed on. Augustin never made any agreements with anyone, he just took what he wanted and then cut and run."

"It wasn't like that and you know it."

"Were you there?"

"No, but you told me about it, and so has he. Eva, I just can't believe this is actually the problem. Can you please tell me what this is really about?"

Her nostrils are flared, her jaw is clenched and her lips are trembling a little. A passer-by would think she's about to go for my throat. I've never seen her like this.

"Are you in love with my brother?"

My breath catches and it takes a few seconds before I can answer.

"Yes…"

"Oh my god, I can't believe it. This is crazy. Just like that? Overnight?"

"Eva, he… has changed everything for me. He's pushing me to do things I thought I'd never be able to do again. He's caring, he's attentive, he… he makes me happy."

She gives me a black look.

"You can't be with my brother."

"Why?"

"Because he's my brother, damn it!"

Now it's my turn to clench my fists.

"Do you realize what you're saying? You're going out with your brother's best friend, and that's completely fine, but the opposite isn't? Can't you see that?"

"He's my brother! I've shared all my secrets, all my fears, all my dreams with you, and now you hook up with him?"

"I don't understand. Are you worried I'll tell him everything you've said?"

She clicks her tongue in annoyance, as if I'm purposely not understanding.

"It's just wrong! It's as if… damn it, April, you're like my sister. How can you expect me to accept this? Jimmy and Augustin don't have the same relationship that we do. They haven't known each other for as long, they're not as close as we are. And also, what's this about him magically changing things for you? He's never been there for you but somehow he miraculously solves all your problems with a wave of his magic wand? That's totally crazy!"

"Are you comparing yourself to him?"

"Yes! Can I just remind you who was there when you needed it? Who comforted you, reassured you, held your hand and spent hours on the phone with you when you were at rock bottom? Was it him? No. It was me."

"And I'd do exactly the same for you, but what does that have to do with Augustin? Are you scared I'll love him more than you?"

"That's total bull! I know my brother. You two won't last. You'll end up in tears, and there's no way I'll be there for you because I've already told you what's going to happen. But I'm still going to give you one last piece of advice: stop before it does. And if you don't, well, then, don't bother coming to talk to me about it."

This time, I can't hold it in anymore.

"You can think whatever you like about your brother, but don't tell me what I should be doing. I have the right to live my own life without asking your opinion or getting your permission. And if you're not happy? Well, you know what? Too bad, I'll do without you!"

Eva gives me the death stare, shoves past me and goes inside the Blue Yeti. I feel unsteady. My legs are trembling. We've never fought like that. Ever. I lean against the wall of a chalet and hold back my tears. It feels like I'm in a bad dream. I want to snap out of it, this can't be true!

I walk home on autopilot. Apparently, Dad has just gotten back.

"You all right, sweetie? You look a bit off-colour. Have you been crying?"

I don't say anything, and he comes up to me.

"April?"

And that's when I break into tears. Huge noisy sobs.

"Hey... darling girl, what happened?"

I give a sniff.

"I just lost my best friend."

"But..."

He takes me by the shoulder and leads me into the living room. We both sit on the couch. I'm finding it hard to stop crying.

"Come on, it'll be OK," he whispers, holding me tight. "Try and tell me what's going on."

"I'm so ashamed, Dad, you have no idea... but I'm in love."

Dad listens without interrupting me. I don't want to leave anything out. I tell him everything, my feelings, the lies I told, the way I feel I've been coming back to life and how my world has now suddenly collapsed.

"So, that's it. Now you know everything."

He frowns.

"If you were a friend, I'd ask if I could give you some advice. But because you're my daughter, I'm just going to give it to you anyway."

What he says next does not fill me with confidence.

"I'm so happy you're finally coming out of your shell and that you're ready to tackle new challenges. Love is always a good driver for that, as long as you're not blinded by it."

"What do you mean?"

"I don't agree with how Eva has reacted, she's not being fair. But I do think you might be going a bit fast, and it would be a shame to lose such an important friendship for something that might not work out."

It's like a cold shower.

"So you don't think Augustin's a responsible person either?"

"No, that's not it. But he's not even twenty-two. You're nineteen and you don't know what life is going to bring. You should take some time and think about what I've said."

I stiffen.

"So now I'm the one you think isn't responsible."

"Oh, come on, April, that's not what I said!"

"Yes, you did. You don't think my feelings for Augustin are worth risking my friendship with Eva. That's obvious. But so far, it's not Augustin who's giving me a hard time, it's Eva!"

"You're getting defensive."

"Of course I'm getting defensive! I've just explained to you that I've never been so happy in my entire life, and that

I want this to continue, and all you can say is just think about it first? Think about what, Dad? About whether I have the right to be happy just because my best friend might not like it?"

"Sweetie, you're generalizing. I didn't say Eva was right, I just said you should weigh up the pros and cons."

I get up in one movement, supercharged with emotions.

"I love him. It's as simple as that. And if you and Eva can't accept that, then you both care less about me than you claim! I'm going to my room."

"April!"

But I don't look back. I don't want to talk anymore.

I am so over today. I just want it to be finished.

I throw myself onto my bed and close my eyes for a long moment before opening them and looking up at the ceiling.

Dad is way off base. And Eva is the most irrational I've ever seen her. She is totally over-reacting and basing her reactions on something that happened such a long time ago. She should have moved on by now.

She is my best friend, and she is so important to me. And my father is probably the man I love most in the world. This situation is totally unbearable, but they're the ones being difficult here.

I pick up my phone, about to send a message to Augustin, but then I change my mind. What is there to say? That my father doesn't trust him?

I drop my phone back on the bed, pick up my pillow and stuff my face into it to stop myself from screaming. Then I do the only thing I can right now, I pick up a folder from under my bed and spread out all my worksheets.

Study and forget everything else.

At the very end of the day, I get a message from Augustin.

Jimmy told me about Eva.
I'm sorry.

You're not the only one…

I didn't sleep well, and when I awake to the sound of my phone beeping with a notification, I'm in a terrible mood. It's my mother.

Are you already awake?

Hi Mom, yes, I just woke up.

Are you feeling better?

How do you mean?

I do not like where this is going.

I spoke with Dad last night, he told me about Eva.

And there we go. Why do they both always feel the need to share every little detail about me? It's insufferable. Now I wish I hadn't even spoken to him about it. What was I thinking?

> I'd rather not talk about it, Mom…

She ignores what I just said. Typical.

I agree with him that Eva is overreacting and she shouldn't be threatening to end your friendship, but you also need to take a step back and think about things. Augustin is young and so are you. It might not end up being serious.

> Mom, sorry if this sounds rude, but I don't want your and Dad's opinion.

I'm sure you don't, but that's not going to stop us from telling you what we think. Our role is to protect and guide you.

> I don't need you to protect me, but to trust me and allow me to make my own decisions.
> I'm going now Mom, because I don't want to talk about it and you can't stop me from having my own opinion.

You're your father's daughter... OK, I'll let you be. But if you want to talk about it, I'm here. Love you. 😙

As I switch off my phone screen, I feel on edge. I would much rather have gotten a cutting message from Eva saying she's mad at me than have to talk things through with my mother.

I get up and go straight to the shower. The hot water might wash away my grumpy mood.

By the time I get down to the kitchen, it's 9 o'clock, and Dad has already gone. He's left me a note on the table.

Hi, sweetheart,
I hope you're feeling a bit better. I'm away all morning, I have a meeting with the information centre. I don't think I'll be back for lunch. And this afternoon I'm taking some clients to Lake Montriond. I should be back around 4pm, then I have tomorrow off! Do you want to go out for dinner? I'm a terrible cook, but I know where we can get some excellent potchons.
XXX Dad

My parents' attitude annoys me, but I don't want to fight with Dad. I get out my phone and send a message wishing him a nice day and that going to a restaurant is a great idea.

Then I quickly swallow down my breakfast and force myself to study for a few hours. At 12 o'clock I've had enough. Eva still isn't talking to me, and Augustin is working all day, so I decide to go for a walk into town.

Except I forgot that today is the first day of the school vacation and that the Christmas celebrations start tonight in Morzine. I soon start to wish I had gone for a walk in the forest. The sidewalks are packed, there's not one free seat outside the cafés, there are huge queues for the cable car and the shops are heaving. The sun is shining, but all the chalets, buildings and street lamps are festooned with fairy lights and stars in preparation for the evening, and Christmas music is playing from speakers around the central part of town. The whole place is buzzing. There are overexcited children running about, people are wearing red hats, the atmosphere is brilliant, almost magical. It's exactly what I've always loved about Morzine, but when I left the house, I wasn't looking for crowds.

I'm about to head down a side street when I bump into Jeff just as he's coming out of a store. He freezes and so do I. We haven't seen each other since I gave him a piece of my mind at Margot's. There is an initial moment of awkwardness between us, and then I smile at him.

"Hi, Jeff!"

"Hey, how're you doing?"

"Good, good. You're not working today?"

"No, I took a day off, I had some shopping to do." He scratches his head. "Um, look. I'm sorry about last time. Sometimes I can be a bit heavy-handed."

That's the least you can say!

"Oh, don't worry about it."

"Cool. I hear you and Gus are together?"

"News travels fast!"

"Yeah, Jimmy told Margot and me. I wouldn't have imagined the two of you together."

I raise my eyebrows.

"I mean, you're both really cool, it's just that Gus isn't someone who's looking for a serious relationship, and you're, well…"

OK. I don't know why everyone feels they have to tell me these things and give me their opinion about the two of us, but it's really starting to annoy me.

"You know what? I'm not some kind of delicate flower, so you can all stop imagining that I'm going to get caught in his evil trap and that it's just a one-off thing."

"That's not what I said. It's just…"

I put my hand up to stop him.

"Of course that's what you said, and that's what you think. Everyone clearly has their own opinion on the matter, but I just want people to stop going on to me about it."

"Sorry, I didn't mean to offend. I like you, and I just don't want anything bad to happen to you, I mean… what with your heart and everything."

Oh, come on!

"My heart is doing just fine, thank you very much, and it would be even better if everyone just minded their own business. Anyway, I've got to go. Say hi to Margot for me."

I don't wait for him to say bye, but jostle past him crossly and walk quickly away.

Going by what everyone says, Augustin's not quite the devil, but he does give him a run for his money. In terms of girls, that is, so therefore with me. I'm so fed up of hearing this kind of garbage. Because even though I'm sure of myself, I hate that it's starting to touch a nerve – it's making me doubt. Augustin and I haven't gone very far yet, but if we did, I do not want to come to grief.

It's 1 pm. Augustin must be having his lunch break now or about to. I decide to go to the ski school and see if he's there. I want to talk to him about this, otherwise it's going to drive me nuts. I'm leaving in a week, I need to find out whether the two of us are serious, or whether I just should make the most of it before I go home.

When I get there, he's walking toward the chalet with a snowboard under his arm and his glasses pushed back on his head. With the sun we've been having the past few days, his face is even more tanned, and to me he looks amazing.

"Hey! Hi there, Mrs. Claus! This is a nice surprise!"

He leans over and kisses me on my lips. Now that the secret is out, no need to hide things anymore.

"Hey, I was wondering if you had a bit of free time before your next class, I'd like to talk to you."

"Nothing serious, I hope?"

"No, not at all! It's just… it's a bit tricky talking about it like this."

"OK. My 2 o'clock class was cancelled, and it was my last. Do you want us to go to yours?"

"No!"

I reply with such force that he frowns. How can I tell him that I'd rather my father didn't see the two of us together?

"Actually, I'd prefer it if we were alone."

"You're being very mysterious."

"Yeah, I… Sorry. We could grab a sandwich and go and eat it on a bench somewhere?"

I smile at him to lighten the mood. Augustin looks like he's thinking.

"With all these people out and about, it might not be very private. How about this for an idea. I have a friend who's away for a fortnight at his parents, and he left me the keys to his apartment so I can feed his goldfish."

I wonder whether he's joking with me.

"No, I'm serious! I'll just grab my bag, we'll get something to eat and then we can go?"

I agree and follow him to a food truck selling paninis and fries, which I haven't eaten in ages.

We order our food then walk to a three-storey chalet in the centre of town, similar to the one Margot lives in. Augustin's friend lives in an attic studio on the top floor. It doesn't have any windows but light comes in through the skylights. It's a no-frills kind of place – a sofabed, a chest of drawers with an aquarium on it, a television, a kitchenette, a table and two chairs – but it's a total mess.

Augustin puts our bags on the table, gets a couple of glasses out of the cupboard, along with a jug of water, and points to a chair.

"Take a seat, I'll be ready in two minutes."

When he gets back, he has swapped his ski clothes for a pair of blue jeans and a thick, wool roll-neck sweater. My breath catches. He is so good-looking.

"How's Eva?" I ask as soon as he sits down next to me.

"Dunno," he says without looking at me.

"She still won't talk to you?"

"Mmm," he says in assent.

"What's it like in front of your parents?"

"We pretend. She refuses to listen to me, and I'm sick of trying to talk to her."

"I'm so sorry."

As I lower my gaze, Augustin lifts my chin up with his finger to make me look at him.

"This is not your fault. It's no one's fault. Falling in love isn't a crime, is it?"

My heart misses a beat.

"Does that mean you're in love with me?"

He smiles.

"Only a girl would ask that question when the answer is right in front of her. Of course I am."

All of a sudden, I feel so stupid for having doubted him. Because of other people and what they say, what they think.

"I'm in love with you too…"

"I know. And that's why you and I are going to make it out of this mess. Eva will come round eventually."

"Gus, everyone seems to think that you and I are a bad idea, that you're a player and that I'm just too naive to realize it."

His face clouds over.

"I don't know who 'everyone' is, and to be honest, I don't care. I've had one serious relationship. All the others were short-lived, sure, but what do all these 'people' expect? That I'm going to get married at twenty and have kids at twenty-two? Well, you know what? I'm a guy like any other, like plenty of other guys, and like plenty of girls, actually. And who could blame me for falling in love with you? No one..."

He gets up, takes my hand and leads me to the sofabed.

"This is the second time we've had this conversation. I don't want this to keep coming between us, I want you to trust me."

"But we don't know what's going to happen after Christmas, when I go back home."

"Lyon is only two and a half hours from here, you think that bothers me?"

I smile at him.

"I don't have my driver's license..."

"I'll do the driving for the both of us, at the weekend, during vacation."

"April," he says, taking both my hands and looking deep into my eyes. "I'm going to ask you this question again. Do you want to give our relationship a chance, despite my sister, despite all the others and despite your fears?"

I don't need to think twice.

"I do."

Then, as I realize what I just said, I burst out laughing.

"It sounds like I just accepted a marriage proposal!"

He pushes his hand through his hair.

"Yeah, well, not straight away, OK! Shall we have something to eat? I'm ravenous!" We make light work of the paninis, but I don't want to leave straight away, so when Augustin suggests we watch some Netflix, I agree happily.

We blob out on the open sofabed, my head against his chest and his arm around my shoulders. We're watching absolute trash, a crummy show about zombies that just makes me drowsy. I fall asleep, and Augustin doesn't wake me. When I open my eyes, the sun has already gone down, the television is off, and he is caressing my hair. I sit up and stretch, I feel a bit sluggish.

"Ohh... I think I fell asleep."

"No? Really?"

"Did you finish watching the show?"

"Yep."

"And how did it end?"

"In tragedy. All the zombies were killed, and the humans finally won. But the future is grim, they're going to have to keep fighting it out until the end."

"LOL!"

"It's 5 o'clock, do you want me to take you home?"

I start to lose myself in his gaze. His eyes are almost black, but they still shine so brightly.

"Not really... not yet. Unless you have something else you should be doing?"

"No."

Then he leans over me and kisses me. It feels as if my whole body has been set alight, as if I'm burning alive. This kiss is different from the others; it's more urgent, less hesitant, more daring, more powerful. And this time, I keep nothing back.

I'm soon lying down again on the sofabed, with Augustin half on top of me. His body is heavy, but I don't care. His hands run down my shoulders, my waist and my hips, while mine hold onto him tightly. Then I feel his fingers slip under my wool sweater, under my cotton t-shirt. They touch my skin and move up my stomach. I tense. Augustin freezes.

"Do you want me to stop?"

"No… it's just that you're going to touch it."

His face clouds over.

"Touch what?"

"My scar."

His fingers clench, just above my belly button.

"Oh. Does it… hurt?"

"No, not anymore, but it feels weird. It's a sensation I can't explain, and apart from me and my doctor, no one has ever touched it."

He removes his hand.

"Well, let's just leave it for a bit, then. I don't want you to feel uncomfortable."

I smile at him. Augustin is not only patient and intelligent, but gentle too.

"This scar is a part of me now. I forget I even have it when it's hidden under my clothes, but when I catch sight of it, it reminds me that it wasn't always there. And I get a bit anxious. It's hard to look at. It's still quite new and not very nice."

"I'm sure it is."

No, it isn't. It's a thin line that's about twenty centimetres long. It runs down between my breasts and ends just below in a knot of pink flesh. I remember when I showed it to Eva the first time, she started crying. That still happens to me sometimes. I know it will never completely disappear, but it'll fade over time.

Augustin leans on an elbow and locks eyes with me.

"You are a warrior, and this scar is proof that you won the battle. You can be proud of it."

"One day, maybe, but right now I still can't."

With his free hand, he caresses my cheek, from my temple down to my jaw.

"I want to find out everything about you. Everything I don't know."

"Why?"

"Because I've never met anyone as amazing as you. And also, if you don't talk to me and distract me, I'm going to want to jump on you again, and that's not allowed!"

"Yes, it is," I say in a tiny voice, "I give you my permission."

He becomes perfectly still. He looks as if he's holding his breath.

"I need to know... I'm sorry if this is embarrassing, you don't need to answer if you don't want to."

"Yes?"

"Have you ever been with anyone? I mean sexually?"

Now it's my turn to stop breathing.

"Yes... once."

Augustin senses the distress in my eyes, the lump in my throat.

"It didn't go well?"

I close my eyes and gather up my courage so that I can tell him the truth. I want him to know that in my heart there was a terrible storm, that it's about to break out again, but that I want to calm it once and for all, with him.

I'm going to tell him everything.

I don't want there to be any grey areas between us.

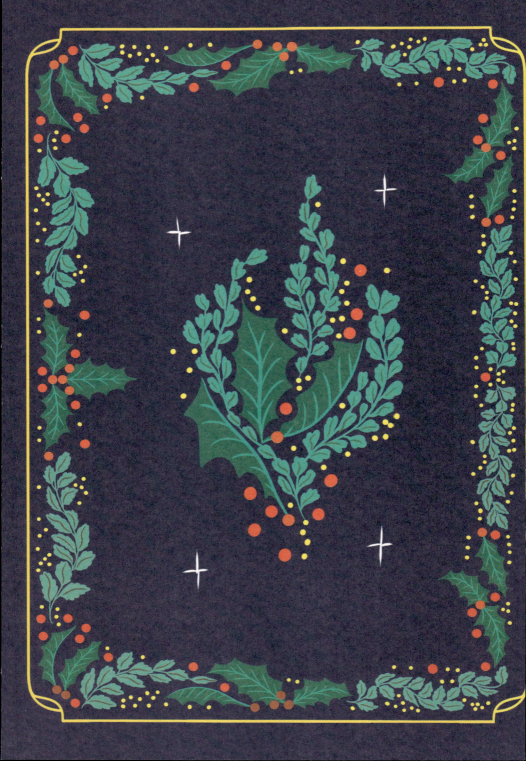

"His name was Benoit, and he was in the same hospital department as me, paediatric cardiology. He's part of the reason I wasn't able to fit back into my world when I got out of the hospital."

Augustin is sitting across from me, quiet and tense, like someone who doesn't know what to expect. I don't want to be overdramatic, so I try and wear a more neutral expression and relax a little.

"He was there for three weeks. We saw each other every day and ate in each other's rooms. We both had our own computer, so we watched TV shows, played on Roblox and sent messages to each other when we weren't in the same room. Basically, we were always together in some way. He was nice and funny, and he made me forget that I could die at any moment."

"Then he stopped being just a friend?" says Augustin, in a voice that is more sombre than usual.

"Yeah. It happened when I was told there might be a heart for me. The boy who saved my life was brain dead. He had

had a terrible motorbike accident, but his parents were still holding out hope, they didn't want to give up. It was such a hard time. I felt like this would be my only opportunity, and that if his parents refused to give me the transplant, I might not live."

"That must have been awful," says Augustin, as he sees my eyes growing damp.

"I was so scared that it wouldn't work, that I wouldn't be able to do all the things that a girl my age should. I had never been in love before, I didn't think too much about it. That night, I went to see Benoit in his room. I wanted to find out what it was like because maybe I would never have another chance. He didn't say no."

Augustin closes his eyes for a moment and smiles at me sadly. Not because I gave myself to a boy, but because I did it for the wrong reasons. I know he understands.

"The next day, I was told that the boy's parents had agreed to switch off the machine and donate his heart. I was operated on the same afternoon, and when I got back to the cardiology department a few days later, Benoit was no longer in the hospital."

"Did you know he'd be gone?"

"No, he hadn't said anything. I tried to contact him a few times, but he never replied."

"And did you find out what happened to him?"

"Yeah… I found his TikTok account. And that was the worst part. He had posted these gifs of him showing off his chest, with comments like 'When you get laid on your last day in the hospital.' And his friends were congratulating him. He didn't care about me at all."

Augustin is so stunned he doesn't even touch me. The silence between us stretches out, until finally he says, "I get why you find it hard to trust me."

"But you're not like him. You and Benoit have nothing in common."

"That's not what my sister thinks."

I take his hands and look deep into his eyes, hoping to convey my sincerity.

"But she's wrong! Augustin, I trust you."

"I don't want to hurry you. In fact, I want you to trust me one hundred per cent before we go any further."

"I do trust you one hundred per cent."

He touches my cheek with such delicacy that I barely feel it. Then, out of the blue, my stomach starts to make the most incredible noise. The timing! Augustin laughs.

"Do you want to go out and get something or should we just see what we find in the cupboards?"

"Too many people outside."

"OK."

We find a tin of ravioli, a packet of crackers and a jar of applesauce. Then we choose a film and eat in front of the television, sitting cross-legged on the open sofabed.

Time has no hold on us; I feel completely disconnected from the real world. When I'm with Augustin, hours pass like minutes, and once the film ends and we're lying side by side, snuggled up under a duvet, I say to myself I'll just spend another hour or two with him before I go home. We're holding each other close. I listen to him telling me about his life, his dreams and all the things we could do together.

It's completely dark, we can barely hear the people partying outside, so I end up falling asleep, more at peace than I've ever been before.

I wake up with a start at 10 o'clock in the morning, still fully dressed. I look at Augustin next to me. He's sound asleep.

Shit, shit, shit!

Dad will be beside himself with worry. I get off the sofabed in a hurry, grab my phone and see the ton of messages and missed calls. The last time he had tried to call me was at 2 am, but my phone was on silent.

Even Mom apparently left me a message, but it might not have anything to do with the situation.

"Gus… Augustin!" I give him a shake.

"Hmm…"

"We fell asleep, and I didn't let anyone at home know!"

He opens his eyes and sits bolt upright.

"Shit!"

"You can say that again. Dad is going to kill me…"

He gets off the sofabed and rubs his hair.

"My car isn't far away, I'll drive you home right now."

"I didn't even tell him where I was last night."

Augustin looks at his phone and grows pale.

"Your father tried to call me…"

He listens to the voice message, makes a face, then puts on the speaker phone.

"Augustin, it's Etienne. Eva says that April might be with you. Can you please let me know if she is? Call me back as soon as you can."

"Come on, grab your coat, let's go. It'll be fine, don't worry."

But I am worrying. I've never done anything like this to my parents, never, and I hate the idea of Dad being scared for me.

When we get to the chalet, there's a light on in the kitchen.

"It'd be better if I went in on my own."

He nods and leans over to give me a quick kiss.

"Call and tell me how it goes, OK? I'm not working today, so I can answer."

"I promise."

I smile at him, take my courage in both hands and, with my heart beating wildly, walk up to the front door. When I open it, Dad comes out of the kitchen, totally worked up.

"For crying out loud, April, have you seen the time? Where in the hell were you?"

"I'm sorry, Dad. I didn't plan this. I went into town yesterday and spent the afternoon with Augustin. We were at a friend's apartment, and I lost track of time."

"You lost track of time? You've got to be kidding me. I called you so many times! I thought something had happened! Damn it, April, we didn't bring you up to behave like this!"

"I'm sorry."

"You're going to have to explain yourself to your mother. She called several times last night to find out if you were home."

My face drains of colour.

"Were you the one who called her?"

"No, she rang to find out if you had patched things up with Eva. She wanted to speak with you, and I had to tell her I didn't know where you were. For Pete's sake! You're out of control here, April, you need to pull yourself together!"

"Dad, I said I was sorry."

"Well, that's not enough! I hardly see you study, you get into a fight with your best friend because you've suddenly decided to go out with her brother and you spend the night away from home without even letting me know."

"I have been studying, I spent hours at it yesterday. If you were here more often, you'd realize that."

"Are you blaming me for going out and working?"

"No, you're the one blaming me. I'm not ten years old anymore, Dad. I know how to manage my own time."

He gives me a challenging look.

"I like Augustin, but I'm disappointed in him. I think he's having a bad influence on you."

Oh, whatever!

"He doesn't have any influence over me at all, and I want all of you to stop judging him as if he were some kind of dangerous criminal."

"Now, don't exaggerate; that's not what I said!"

"I know exactly what you said, and you're wrong!"

My phone starts to ring.

"Oh, so now you've decided to take your phone off silent mode?" asks Dad cynically.

I don't respond and concentrate on answering the phone. It's Mom. She's hysterical.

"Mom, calm down, I'm home. Everything's fine."

"Do you realize what you put us through? Your father and I were worried sick. I almost got in the car and drove up there in the middle of the night! Were you with Augustin?"

"Yes. I'm sorry, I should have let you know."

"Yes, you should have. But what you will do now is stop seeing that boy!"

What the…!

"Mom, I'm too old for this! I'm not going to start asking for your permission."

"April!" thunders Dad, without knowing what my comment was about.

I'm going to explode. I'm totally wired, so I hang up on my mother and head for the front door.

"Where are you going?" barks Dad.

"I'm going out, and this time I'm letting you know!"

He doesn't try and stop me. I have tears in my eyes. I hate what they're doing.

OK, sure, I didn't let them know where I was, but they've turned it into such a drama. I'm not a little girl anymore or some fragile little creature. I'm allowed to live my own life! And if they think I'm going to stop seeing Augustin, then they're dreaming!

I practically run toward town, while trying to call Augustin. He doesn't answer, so I leave a message asking if he can meet me at the Blue Yeti.

"I'm so sick of them, I'm so sick of them, I'm so sick of them!"

I'm bellowing like an ox in the middle of the street, but who cares if I look crazy.

When I get there, Jimmy's not behind the counter, his father is. I order a latte and just as I start drinking it, Augustin arrives. He has swapped his instructor's ski suit for one of his own. He sits down at my table, and I tell him what happened, but doing so doesn't calm me down. It makes things worse.

"Are you about to go skiing?" I finally ask him.

"Yes."

"I'll come with you."

"What?"

"I want to go skiing. Now. I need to let off steam."

His frowns.

"You're quite hyped up, I'm not sure it's a good idea. And there are lots of people out today."

"We'll go backcountry. I'm sure you know a safe place that's not too hard and where there's no one around? I really need to do something."

Augustin looks like he's weighing up the pros and the cons.

"Have you had anything to eat?"

"No, not yet."

"OK. Let's start with that." He orders me some bread, butter and strawberry jam. I think of my mother and laugh as I take a big mouthful.

"What is it?" he asks.

"If my mother saw what you had given me for breakfast, she'd hate you even more!"

He furrows his brow.

"Does she really hate me?"

"No… I mean, I think she'd hate anyone who makes me deviate from the path she's put me on. She gets carried away far too easily."

"I can understand why."

"That's because you don't know her! She could turn a doctor into a hypochondriac!"

"I guess she's worried about you." He looks so serious.

"For sure. But that doesn't change the fact that sometimes she can be impossible. And even though last night I should have let them know where I was, that doesn't give them the right to try and dictate my life. I'm almost nineteen. I should be able to make mistakes and then improve without them laying into me."

"Well, that's what I'm going to do if you play up when we're skiing!"

"That's not going to happen! Right, I'm done. Let's go!"

We cautiously drop in at home for me to change, but Dad's 4WD isn't there.

There are only two of us, so Augustin can't take the snow-mobile. We go on the cable car. The deal is that I've got to warm up on a blue trail to see if things go better than last time. I have no problem whatsoever. Roused by the fight I had with my parents, it even seems easy. My heart rate is good, and I don't fall over once.

"We'll go off-piste at Chamossière," says Augustin. "We don't have to trek anywhere from the top of the chairlift, and up there the snow cover is perfect and really stable."

"Cool!"

"But there's an open section without any trees, and it's easy to pick up speed on the downhill if you're not careful."

I hear him, but today I'm not afraid. I know I'm in safe hands – Augustin would never take me to a place he's not sure of.

"I'll be careful."

"OK, then. Let's go."

It's 1 pm by the time we get up to an altitude of 2,000 metres. Even though the sky is more overcast than the day before, the air is dry and invigorating. It almost catches in our throats. It's windier than down in the village, which is normal, but the landscape below us is incredible, studded with jagged rocks and intensely green spruce trees. For just one moment, the pristine vast expanse makes me forget what happened this morning. Nothing can compare to the mountains. It's hard to believe I did without them for so long.

"Are you going to be OK?" asks Augustin, as he looks at his phone to check my heart rate.

"I think so."

"You're not scared?"

"Um… a bit, but I don't want to think about it too much or I'll change my mind. Shall we go?"

"Yeah, but nice and easy, don't go too fast, OK? Make sure you control your speed, your movements, your posture.

Let yourself go but do the snowplow whenever you need to. Are you ready?"

"Ready!"

I take a deep breath and set off first. My body isn't able to do too much effort straight off, so I take my time. I zigzag down the hill, savouring each of my movements, which have never seemed so fluid. The undulations in the terrain are easy to manage, the snow is excellent, and it almost doesn't seem like we're skiing off-piste. At such an altitude, it's amazing.

We ski like that for a while, then Augustin passes in front of me, perfectly in control.

"I'll go ahead for a bit! Just keep to my tracks!"

I control my speed, and two hundred metres farther on we start a steeper downhill section.

Of course, I follow his instructions, he knows exactly what he's doing, and it's perfect – he establishes the rhythm for me. I trust him one hundred per cent. There is no one around, just the two of us. No noise apart from the sound of our skis on the powder. I feel a kind of euphoria, and when I see him stop a few metres below, I decide to keep going. To challenge myself to manage on my own, gently, carefully.

"Hey," cries out Augustin, as I ski past him. "Be careful, stay right in the centre!"

"Yes, boss!"

I do as he says, I go by the book, but I'm having the time of my life. I would never have thought I'd be able to ski again so easily. It feels so good! All around us, the sharp mountain ridges almost make me dizzy. Everything seems bigger and more beautiful here. I feel intoxicated, I'm in my element. This is my place.

At one point, the slope seems to flatten out for a few metres. As I'm not going very fast, I open my arms out wide, spread my legs out a little and close my eyes for a few seconds. The feeling of freedom is exceptional, undefinable and heady. But when I open my eyes again, I start to feel dizzy. I do the snowplow to slow down, and my body stiffens. My breathing accelerates. I try to gain control of myself, but I lose my balance and fall, rolling through the snow for several metres. One of my skis comes off, my poles fly away, I can hear Augustin calling my name, and then I come to a stop on my back. I'm breathing jerkily and automatically put my hand onto my heart.

"April!"

Augustin throws himself down at my side.

"Can't... breathe..."

I see his panicked face, his lips moving.

And then nothing.

My hospital room at Thonon-les-Bains looks like all the others I've ever been in. White, cold, austere and soulless. An electrocardiogram – or ECG for short – beeps at regular intervals. I have sensors all over my chest.

I got here yesterday after my fainting attack at high altitude and went through the emergency room, with all the associated tests and stress.

I hate being here, but what happened was serious. I had tachycardia, where my heart started beating much faster than normal, and I fainted. Now they're checking it to make sure the situation isn't serious.

"Good morning! Breakfast time! Did you sleep well?" cries the assistant nurse, as if I was deaf.

The fact that every two hours a nurse came to check my ECG prevented me from sleeping well, but I choose to lie.

"Yes, thank you. I'm not very hungry though."

"I'll leave you the tray anyway, shall I? You can eat it whenever you want! Coffee, tea, hot chocolate?"

"Tea, please."

She fills a paper cup, dumps a teabag in it and smiles at me.

While all this is going on, a nurse comes in.

"Hello, Miss Hamon! How do you feel this morning?"

"I'm OK, thanks."

"Your ECG is excellent. The doctor apologizes for not having been able to stop by last night before you were transferred here, but he'll be here early in the afternoon to talk things over with you."

"Do you think I'll be able to leave today?"

She shines an infrared thermometer on my forehead and looks at the result.

"Perfect! You'll have to check with him, sorry. And until then, you'll be keeping the sensors too, I'm afraid."

"OK. Can I have a shower? I bet I stink."

"Of course. I'll take all this off for you and then you can go. Will you need a hand?"

"No, thanks. Just a towel if there is one."

"The assistant nurse will get one for you. Oh, and your father called. He's going to come in before midday with some of your belongings."

"How... how is he?"

Yesterday I was in the emergency room, and they hadn't let him come and see me.

I let know him by message that my phone battery was going to run out, but I can imagine the state he must be in. I feel so guilty. Not to mention Augustin, who after having seen me fly off in the helicopter had to stay at his place for the same reason, and I wasn't able to contact him.

"We let him know you were doing well, and your Mom too, don't worry," she says, as she removes the electrodes.

Mom… I can't say I'm looking forward to seeing her come through the door.

"OK, that's all done! I'll leave you now, Miss Hamon. The assistant nurse will bring you everything you need for the shower."

"Thank you."

With no television or phone, time crawls by at the most depressing pace. And all I seem to do is keep going over what happened again and again – seeing stars, gradually losing my breath, the helicopter coming to get me.

I'm going to go crazy if I keep thinking like this. I need to take my mind off things. I press the button and call the nurse.

"Excuse me, is there an iPhone charger I can borrow?"

The nurse smiles.

"No, sorry. Time must be dragging."

"Yes, a little."

"It's not quite visiting hours, but I can make an exception. Your boyfriend has just arrived in the waiting room, would you like to see him?"

Augustin…

My heart starts to beat a bit faster. The nurse smiles as she sees the electrocardiogram speed up.

"Apparently you like the sound of that!"

"Yes... Please bring him in."

She leaves the room, and Augustin comes in almost straight away.

"Hey..."

He stops in the doorway, looking tired and worried.

I pull the sheets up around me and beckon him in.

He comes toward me as if he were walking on eggs, as if he's scared to break something, then he leans over and gives me a gentle kiss on the forehead.

"How do you feel?"

"I didn't sleep much last night, I'm exhausted."

"You're in good hands."

I nod. I can't bring myself to say anything else. For now.

"I'm sorry I got you into this situation. Really."

"Don't say sorry. I'm the one who should apologize. I wasn't careful enough. I should have been looking at your heart rate more often."

"You were looking, but you wouldn't have been able to stop it anyway, it happened all at once."

"At least you've been on your first helicopter flight," he says, trying to make a joke. "And next time we'll be more careful!"

I find it difficult to swallow. I want to cry. He's wrong.

There can't be another time... I was so scared.

I was unconscious for only a few minutes, and Augustin had already called the emergency services, but when the helicopter came to get me and I found myself swinging on a stretcher being pulled up through the air, it was like being confronted with my own death for the second time.

I remember the day I had my cardiac arrest. I was conscious while people were busy all around me. My mother was there, she was holding my hand.

But not this time.

I was alone and terrified by the idea that I had thrown everything away for just a few hours of skiing.

Augustin has no idea what I am thinking. He smiles at me.

When he's there, it's like I'm seeing him at the end of a tunnel, like he's holding out his hand and telling me not to be afraid. It's like he's surrounded in light.

I want to be able to envisage the future with certainty, to imagine fulfilling my dreams and not missing out on anything. He can act freely in all the magnificent things he does, but that is not how my life will unfold for me. I've got to accept that.

"Hey, Mrs. Claus, are you all right? Would you rather I left?"

We are interrupted by a couple of gentle knocks on the door.

"Yes?"

"Hi, darling, it's me," says Dad as he walks in. "Are you feeling better?"

When Dad takes me in his arms, I feel like crying, but I don't want to make things worse.

"It's OK, Dad, it's not serious."

Dad stands up again and turns toward Augustin, who has stepped back a little.

"Would you mind leaving us, please?"

I immediately notice his curt tone of voice, but Augustin replies quietly, "I'm sorry, Etienne, I should have been more careful."

"Yes, you should have. But we'll talk about that later."

He nods and tries to smile as he looks at me.

"Try to rest. I'll come and visit later, OK?"

I don't dare reply and just nod in answer.

"What came over you?" asks my father in a gentle voice as he sits on the bed.

"I was so angry. I just had to let off steam. Please don't blame Augustin, it's not his fault. He didn't want to, but I insisted. It was thoughtless, I know."

Dad sighs. I get the feeling he doesn't want to continue the conversation, and I'm grateful for it.

"I let your mother know yesterday, she's on her way."

"How did you manage to hold her back for so long?"

"I didn't. It was the doctors who managed to convince her to wait overnight before getting in her car. But I can assure you the nurses won't forget her for a while, she harassed them non-stop over the phone."

I smile at him.

"Dad… please don't hold it against Augustin, it's not his fault."

"I'll talk to him in good time. But meanwhile, there's someone here to see you."

I frown, but he goes out the door and signals to someone in the corridor. I wait for a few seconds and see Eva, whose eyes are all red. In five seconds, I start bawling my eyes out, and she runs toward me.

"You're not allowed to give us such a fright!"

"Oh, Eva…"

She gives me a huge hug, sobs and cries with me, then stands up.

"I'm even more angry with you now, but at the same time I'm so happy to see you're doing OK. I must have been worried to have set out in my car with so much snow. Don't ever do that again."

I dry my tears and close my eyes for a moment.

"It's not going to happen again."

What with all the different examinations I had, x-rays, blood tests, I feel like I've been here forever, and I know I don't ever want to go through this again.

"I went and got a few bits and pieces for you at home before I came," says Dad. "As well as your phone charger. They're in the car, I'll just go and get them."

When he leaves, Eva gives me a stern look.

"Everyone sends their love, Jimmy, Jeff, Margot. But you and my brother, you really messed up."

"I don't want to talk about it."

"Yeah, I can imagine."

No, she can't imagine just how much.

"Thank you for coming…"

Eva smiles at me.

"That's what friends are for."

Mom gets here just as I'm finishing my meal. She's looking tired and drawn, and can't have slept much. But there's something else in her look that I will never forget – disappointment.

It's as if someone is squeezing my stomach into a ball.

Dad comes in with her and goes and sits in an armchair next to the window. Mom comes over and looks at me, her eyes filled with emotion.

"I'm fine, Mom."

She leans over me and hugs me tightly, without saying a word. Then she sits on my bed and looks at me for a long time before starting to speak.

"As soon as I brought you into the world, I knew that you mattered more than anything. I even knew that I wouldn't have any other children, because I wouldn't be able to love them as much as I love you. When I first saw you – this little being that was so fragile, but braver than a Viking warrior – I knew I would be capable of giving up my life for you, that I would fight to the death so that you could live. You were born sick, but nothing and nobody was ever going to stop me from believing that everything would turn out all right. I have scaled mountains of fear, conquered uncertainties and dismantled the prejudices that said you weren't going to pull through. I didn't give up, not even for a second. I carried you, I believed in you with the power of two, but never, ever did I imagine I'd have to fight you."

Tears flood my eyes.

"Your body is your temple. It's the most precious thing you have, and no one is worth you putting it in danger. No one. You understand?"

"I'm sorry."

Mom remains impassive.

"You are not to see this boy again."

I look at my father through the veil of my tears, but he doesn't react. All of a sudden, I feel so alone.

"It's not Augustin's fault, Mom. He didn't want to, but I insisted."

"That just confirms what I said, you're not ready. Neither of you realized how serious the situation was."

"I'm upset with him," says my father. "It's not because I hold him responsible, but because he wasn't brave enough to stand up to you. He didn't act like a man."

"What does that even mean 'act like a man'? What kind of stock phrase is that? Men are allowed to hesitate, to cry, and anyway, damn it, that's not his role! Everything is *my* fault. If he hadn't come with me, I probably would have gone on my own, and then there wouldn't have been anyone to call for help. You should be thanking him, not blaming him. I'm the only guilty one here."

My voice breaks, and I start sobbing.

"April…" Mom says gently, putting her hand on my shoulder. "You have to think about yourself, about your health, your…"

"You think I don't know that? What I am supposed to do? Deprive myself of everything in the meantime? Stop living when I'm going to die anyway? Mom, in fifteen years this heart will be fit for the trash, maybe even before that, so I want to be able to make some good of it!"

"Yes, I understand, darling, but not like this. If you're careful, if you take care of your body, when the time comes you'll receive another transplant and you'll live for many years. You'll have children if you want to, and you will live a happy life."

"And who with? Some perfect guy you choose for me?"

Mom ignores my words.

"Your father and I have discussed it already; you and I are going back to Lyon tonight. You need to rest and think about the situation."

I'm finding it hard to breathe. I'm suffocating.

The doctor comes in at exactly that moment. My parents get up.

"Hello, Miss Hamon. Your ECGs are perfect and so are the results from your blood tests. The biomarkers for heart failure present no particular anomalies. The altitude, sudden physical activity and adrenaline in all likelihood caused the arrhythmia and hyperventilation. But your heart is doing extremely well."

"Can she leave?" asks my mother.

"Yes, absolutely. I'll take care of the paperwork, Miss Hamon, the nurse will come and remove the electrodes, and then you can get dressed. However, I do ask that you remain vigilant and, this is very important, do not forget to take your immunosuppressor treatment. The occasional omission doesn't have a serious effect, but should this become more frequent, it would…"

"Did you forget to take your medication?" interrupts my mother, looking at me.

"Madam, everything is fine. She is fully up to date, we gave her a capsule."

I can see that Mom is making a huge effort not to blow up in front of the doctor. Once he leaves the room, she pinches the bridge of her nose.

"It really is time for you to pull yourself together. Really."

She's breathing as if she can't get enough air.

"I've got to leave, or I'm going to say something I'll regret. I am disappointed in you, April, so disappointed."

I can feel the tears pricking my eyes as she turns on her heels and disappears into the corridor. Dad looks at me with his lips tightly closed.

"I'm going to let you get dressed. Give us a call when you're ready."

As my ECG speeds up, I feel like everything is crumbling around me.

I just spent three extraordinary weeks, a taste of the carefree life I had been giving up for the past three years, but I hadn't allowed myself to truly think about things, and Mom is right, I went too far. I was deep in denial, and I forgot that this new heart doesn't really belong to me.

And, maybe even worse than that, I took risks. I put myself in danger and I laid too much responsibility on Augustin.

That's the reality.

But the other reality is that my heart is breaking, because for both his good and mine, I've got to put a stop to this.

I've got to tell him.

I've got to find the courage to tell him.

I can't see him again.

It's over.

December

20

A snowstorm has just started up, the roads are blocked, did you make it to the chalet?

Hi Mrs. Claus. The hospital told me you were going home this afternoon. Can I call in and see you?

You must be exhausted, you haven't even read my messages.

"888" voicemail: 12/19, 16:35. The caller did not leave a message.

It's 6 pm, you're still not answering, it's still snowing. I tried calling, got your voicemail. Are you OK?

OK, just spoke to your dad, he said you're tired and not to disturb you. Reply when you can. Thinking of you.

The messages are all from yesterday. I still haven't replied to Augustin, and I make sure he can't see that I've read them. I'm not able to answer him, I can't bring myself to tell him. I know I owe him an explanation, I know that if I don't do it, he'll end up getting upset and thinking that I'm mad at him or that I hold him responsible for what happened, but I just don't have the courage to talk to him.

The weather turned yesterday when we got back from the hospital. Mom and I are stuck here because the roads are blocked. Last night she slept on the couch in the office. As I get up, my heart and my stomach are in pieces. My thoughts are going round in circles, so I decide to write to Augustin.

I'm sorry I wasn't brave enough to reply before. I've been living in a dream, but reality has caught up with me. I've got to look after myself, and not take any risks. I can't be with you in a situation like this, it's too dangerous, I refuse to make you bear the responsibility for my mistakes. I'm going back to Lyon as soon as I can.
I loved being with you, it felt like I was truly alive again, and I'm so grateful for that, but we can't see each other anymore.

His reply comes through almost immediately.

> Are your parents forcing you to do this?

> This is what I want...

> So you're breaking up with me by text?

> I'm sorry, but it's better for both of us. Please respect my wishes.

> And what about mine?

Suddenly my phone rings. It's him. My heart starts to beat faster, I can't answer, I don't have the strength. I'm going to break down if I hear his voice. Augustin tries once, twice, three times. Then he stops.

> Please don't try and call me anymore. I'm sorry. For everything.

That's all I manage to say.

I wait a few seconds more, motionless, but I don't hear from him again. I'm doing my best to hold back my sobs – I'm the one who has created this mess, I've got to accept that — but I can't hold back the single tear that drops onto my telephone screen. I've never hated my life so much.

I go to the window and look out at the snowflakes swirling in all directions. It reminds me of the night we spent in the mountain lodge. I frown. Mom will never be able to drive in these conditions.

When I go downstairs, I find her in the kitchen. It doesn't look as if Dad is there.

"So, I don't think we're going to be leaving anytime soon," she says. "How do you feel this morning?"

"Better, thanks."

"Have you been crying?"

And I start up again. I sniff and rub my hand across my cheeks to wipe away the tears.

"April…" she says gently, sitting down next to me and taking my hands. "It's not with a light heart that I'm asking you to go home with me."

I have no desire whatsoever to talk about this.

"Mom. I know what I've got to do. I know what's at stake, and I've told Augustin it's over between us. It's hard enough as it is, so let's not talk about it, please."

My voice is harder than I would have wanted, but if I let it soften, I really will crumble.

Mom nods in understanding, gives me a lopsided smile and leaves the room.

I busy myself in tidying the kitchen, then I go and have a shower, before trying to lose myself in my studying. But it doesn't work. I was so convincing that Augustin didn't even try and change my mind. My heart feels like it has smashed into thousands of pieces. I want it to stop snowing so we can leave as quickly as possible. Leave Morzine behind me, put it out of my mind, and maybe never come back.

There's a strange atmosphere in the house when I go down just before lunch. A feeling of déjà-vu that reminds me of happier times. I stop halfway down the stairs and watch them. My parents are both sitting on the couch, facing each other, with a glass of wine in hand.

"After all that, it's not so bad that the two of you have to stay here," my father is saying. "Even if the situation isn't ideal."

Mom throws her head back and laughs.

"Sometimes life takes us down strange paths, but yes, you're right. We've got to stay strong for April."

Dad makes a sign of agreement.

"If you have to stay tonight as well, you can have my bed. The office is so uncomfortable."

They exchange a silent look that conveys much more. I can sense their shared memories of intimacy. My mother slept in that bed for so many years. With my father.

There are candles flickering on the coffee table, flames are crackling in the fireplace, the Christmas lights on the tree are gently blinking on and off, and my parents are smiling at one another. Something is happening between them. Something tender.

Around 3 pm, just as the snowstorm is quietening down a little, there's a ring at the door. Mom is still locked away in the office, and Dad is outside chopping wood – the height of the illusion of the perfect family. I open the door and see Eva. She smiles at me, wrapped up in her ski gear.

"With all this snow, I thought I'd never make it here. Are your parents around?"

"They're busy."

"I want to talk to you. Shall we go for a walk?"

If I stay here I'll just keep brooding on things. I leave a note for my parents, dress warmly and shut the door noisily behind me.

The roads are all blocked. The snowplows haven't gone by yet, and no vehicles are even attempting to venture out. With last night's icy wind, the thick layer of snow is almost frozen.

Eva and I walk for a few minutes in silence. I can't speak. I keep thinking of Augustin, of our situation, of us, of what a waste it all is.

Out of the blue, just before we arrive near the centre of town, Eva stops at a wooden bus shelter covered in Christmas decorations.

"OK! Come and sit down with me."

She takes a place on the bench and taps the seat next to her. I sit down. I recognize her determined look, I know I won't be able to get out of this.

"Augustin refuses to talk to anyone. He's stuck at home because there's an avalanche risk, so he's locked himself away in his room. If anyone tries to talk to him, he just tells them to buzz off."

I look down.

"I'm not saying this to make you feel guilty, I just want to know what's going on. You're not just going home, you've broken up?"

"Yeah… I told him it was over, that I wasn't the right person for him, that it was a mistake and that I need to look after myself more."

Eva is watching me closely. I get the feeling she's studying me and reading my innermost thoughts.

"Do you really like him?"

"Yes…"

"And have you for a long time?"

"No. I didn't see it coming… neither did he."

Eva gives me a sad smile and a sombre look comes over her face.

"He loves you too, that's for sure."

"I'm not ready for this. I took risks I shouldn't have, I forgot to take my medication, I behaved as if I don't need to be careful, and I also put him in a situation that could have been much more serious. And all that for some brief moments of pleasure…"

"For the feeling of being alive…" she finishes for me. "And you deserve it."

She's right, but I got carried away.

"I was too hard on my brother. I was nasty," she murmurs.

Despite the situation, I'm happy to hear her admit it.

"Your brother is not who you seem to think he is. He's a good person."

"I know. I overreacted because I was so angry at him."

"Because of Melodie, the girl who was at school with you?"

"Yeah, but also because of what happened after."

She can see I don't understand, so she takes a deep breath, gathering herself to explain.

"I didn't tell you everything… Once Melodie had left school, I became a target. Some people had decided I should go through the same thing she had."

"The same thing?"

"There was this guy I had a crush on. He invited me to a party at his, there were lots of us. I had had a bit to drink, and I ended up in a room with him, I totally wanted to. We slept together – it was my first time – and the next day he dumped me saying it was because of my brother, that was all I deserved. If you knew how much I hated Augustin for that…" she adds with emotion.

My hand flies to my throat. I feel like I've suffered a blow, I'm speechless. Eva's eyes are glistening.

"Was that Kevin, your first time?"

She nods, lowering her eyes.

"Oh, Eva, you never explained it to me like that! You told me you had done it because you were curious, and it wasn't anything serious."

"You had just had your heart failure, you didn't know about my brother, and I felt so ashamed."

Her story with Kevin makes me realize why she felt so strongly when Benoit broke my heart. She always knew exactly the right thing to say. I could never have guessed why. Now, three years late, I try and give her a hug, but she stops me and looks deep into my eyes.

"That's all in the past now, even though my first thought with Jimmy was that he'd do the same, and even though I was so angry at my brother. April, this is hard to explain, but everything got all mixed up in my head because… I was scared

I'd lose you. I was scared you wouldn't need me anymore and that my brother would replace me in your heart."

"That would never happen. You're like a sister to me."

She smiles.

"I know. And that doesn't mean that my brother is also your brother. I'm sorry I said those awful things."

I close my eyes. I feel like crying again.

"I know you didn't truly think that."

She looks at me and gives an unhappy smile. I try to find something else to say. I don't want to rub salt into the wound.

"How are you and Jimmy?"

"Good, he's so cool. We see each other just about every day."

"You waited such a long time for him. I'm happy for you."

I take a deep breath to try and dislodge the lump in my throat. My breath judders noisily. Eva puts her hand on my arm.

"Hey… If you and Augustin love each other, then it can't end like this."

Just then, a group of children speeds past on sleds. Their bright laughter echoes in the street. They're all wearing red Christmas hats, which reminds me of the cross-country ski outing I did with Augustin and the laughs we shared. I start to feel all choked up, and stupidly, a tear trails down my cheek.

"Oh, no…" says Eva, taking me in her arms. "Come on, my little stinkbum."

With my head against her shoulder, I hear myself give a nervous giggle.

No one has ever compared me to a skunk before!

Eva starts to laugh too.

"Stinkbum is a term of endearment!"

I look my best friend in the eye.

"I am so sorry I lied to you and didn't trust you."

"Let's put that behind us. You did what you had to because I wasn't ready. I was being stupid. Now, listen to me very carefully, April Hamon," she says, grabbing me by the shoulders. "Don't leave things like this if it doesn't feel right. I can totally see where you're coming from, your parents, pressure from your mom who's worried for you, your own fears, but they're all just technicalities."

"Technicalities?"

"Exactly. What matters is the present moment, the things you've yet to experience, what you want to do with this heart of yours. What matters is you. Not your parents, not me, not what the doctors say, just you. Do you love my brother? Well, tell him. Are you scared? Well, tell him. Do you still want to try again? Well, tell him. Tell him and let him show you he can give you the support you need. He's always liked looking after people and animals, he can do this."

One of the things I have always loved about Eva is the incredible aura of freedom that radiates from her. Liberty above all things. For the first time since I got back from the hospital, a ray of light is starting to pierce the darkness in which I had become lost. Thanks to Eva.

I can't help smiling. What a turnaround!

The flaky side of me coming out!

We look at each for a moment, face to face. We've found each other again, together, united, the world's two best friends.

"Thank you."

"You are welcome! Do you want me to talk to him?"

"No, I… I've got to think about all this."

"OK, OK! Let it stew for a while, you're right! But, while we're waiting for it to marinate for a bit, do you want to go and get a waffle in town? I'm starving!"

Stinkbum and the Greedy Pig, I'm sure there's a story in there somewhere!

When I get home at about half past five, it's snowing again, and the wind is blowing harder than ever. Our house looks like a solitary chalet in a Siberian blizzard. I can't see more than one metre ahead of me, and it's even hard to walk.

"We were starting to get worried," says Mom.

I give a sigh.

"Mom, this isn't going to be easy if you get worried every time I go out."

"I'm sorry, it's because of the snow. There's a severe weather warning, and it's not supposed to let up until tomorrow morning. I think we're stuck here."

"You know that you both can stay here for as long as you need," says Dad.

"That's a lovely offer, but I have things I need to do in Lyon. Do you know how long this weather is going to last?"

"No idea. The warning is in place until tomorrow at least. You can use my office to work in, if you want."

Mom sighs and looks at me.

"OK. Lucky all my files are on the cloud. Right, I'm going to grin and bear it. The fire is going, that's one good thing!"

Dad smiles at her. I think he's happy. Around 7 pm, while I'm studying before dinner, I can hear music from downstairs. It's coming from the living room. I'm intrigued and go down, just barely managing to hold back an "oh!" of surprise. My parents are dancing arm in arm. They're dancing in the living room!

"Hey! Come and dance with us!" cries Dad, as if this were perfectly normal. "Your mother and I haven't lost it! Come on, I'll show you some dance steps! One, two, three! One, two, three!"

I'm disgusted, and without thinking, I go straight to the TV and turn it off.

"What the hell are you up to?"

I stare at them in turn. My parents are taken aback.

"We're stuck here because of the snow, I've been working all day, and your father was chopping wood. A bit of down-time never hurt anyone."

I look at Dad. He nods in support of Mom.

Oh, come on!

"Um, you do remember you're divorced?"

"That's not appropriate, April," replies my father.

Not appropriate? This time I do explode.

"I'll tell you what's not appropriate. I've just had to dump the person who helped me out of a situation I had been bogged down in for years, who gave me back my smile, some-thing my own parents hadn't been able to do. Breaking up with him hurt like hell, and here you are, the two of you, dancing the salsa as if it was the best news you'd ever heard? Look at you! For the past three years you've fought over the slightest thing – about me, about the weather, about whatever it is that sets the two of you off, and all of a sudden, you're in total agreement, but at my expense? How do you think that makes me feel?"

"April…" Mom starts to speak.

"No, I don't want to hear it. If you want to get in each other's pants, then go for it. Just not in front of me. All I'm asking for is a bit of decency, given what I've had to sacrifice. I'm going upstairs. Don't bother coming and getting me for dinner, I'm not hungry. Good night."

If there had been a door, I would have slammed it, but my words are so strong they convey the same effect.

I throw myself on my bed, consumed by an unexpected rage. It was the fact of seeing them together that caused it, that made me explode. I don't care what the two of them intend to do, and perhaps if I were a little less selfish, I'd even be happy for them. But I can't. Not like this. Not after I feel like I've been torn into a thousand pieces. I hate that they're benefitting from my awful situation.

Tonight I need time to vent my anger, and I know my parents will leave me alone. Tomorrow they'll tell me all about it, and maybe I'll have enough courage to listen to them without judging. Maybe I'll be able to feel happy for them.

Tomorrow. Maybe.

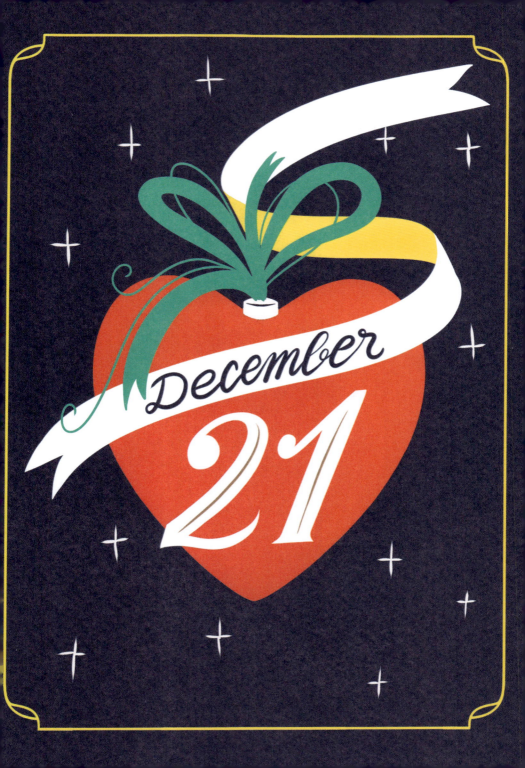

No surprises here, but I spent all evening and all night thinking. I thought about what Eva said to me, about my parents and about the strange state of mind they're in. I thought about myself too, my choices and what my life could be if I made different decisions. I also thought about Augustin, that ray of light that has shone into my life, about his smile that sparks my own, about his sense of joy that has lifted me out of my deep anxiety. So I picked up my phone to tell him something obvious.

> Thinking of you.

The message was sent but not delivered. He can't have been connected. I looked at those three words on my phone, several times, breaking them down without fully understanding them. What if I just said what I was feeling or that

I wanted to go back on my decision and instead overcome the fear that has been a part of me for years.

I'm not sure of myself. I feel completely lost.

It's after 8 by the time I head down to the kitchen, and I don't think Dad's around. Mom is sitting with a cup of coffee, reading a magazine.

"Hi, Mom."

She lifts her head.

"Good morning! Did a night's sleep do you good?"

"Yes, thank you."

"Your father is doing some shopping in town. With all the snow last night, he still can't go trekking. And the two of us are still stuck here too."

I look out the window and am greeted by an incredible sight. There must be twice as much snow as there was yesterday, all crystallized into tiny frozen stars. I've often come to Morzine, and I can't remember ever having experienced such weather. It's as if the snow had rested during the day so it could blow in a tempest at night.

I sit at the table. There's some toast on a plate and the kettle is still warm. I pour myself a cup of hot water and put a teabag in.

Mom returns to her reading as if nothing has happened. But I know her so well. She's waiting for me to mention last night's outburst. And she knows me just as well because I'm not going to be able to let this fester away for long. In fact, I'm going to have to say something right now.

"Mom?"

"Yes?" she replies distractedly.

"I need to know what's going on between you and Dad."

She takes a sip of coffee and turns a page of her magazine, as calm as can be.

"Just life, April, for better or for worse."

Well, that's an answer that gives nothing away. I hate that.

"OK, so would you say this is... for better?"

Now I have her attention. She folds her arms across her chest and looks me steadfastly.

"I'm still in love with your father."

Just like that, without warning, no holds barred. Boom!

I close my eyes for an instant. After my parents separated, I dreamed of hearing that sentence. I had even asked Mom if she still loved him, but my words fell into a pit of nothingness. And now, three years later, here they are, having swung back toward me like a boomerang. I'm older now. Mom doesn't mince words.

Fine, then. Neither will I.

"Is it because you finally both agree about my state of health and on the kind of life I should lead that all of a sudden you see him as your ideal man?"

She pales. That was a low blow, but I couldn't help it.

"That's not fair."

"You're not being fair with me either."

She closes her magazine and looks at me.

"Yesterday you thought we were happy about your situation, but you're wrong. You thought we were celebrating our victory. That wasn't it. There's nothing positive about all this, just things that could have been avoided. I'm not blind.

I could see you were unhappy and that you had to make a huge sacrifice, but I also know you by heart, and I want to ask you a question. Had you made a decision about what to do before I got to the hospital?"

I decide to speak frankly.

"I saw it coming. Because I knew that those 'things that could have been avoided' were a result of how tightly I kept myself reined in for all those years, but I think it's more complicated than that."

"What do you mean?"

"I was right to push the boundaries of the space I was trapped in. But I shouldn't have leaped into the unknown without a safety net. And I shouldn't have told Augustin it was over between us."

And just like that, as the words come out of my mouth, I know it's true. I should never have told him that! I was so wrong!

Mom frowns.

"That's a bit extreme."

"You think? Well, I don't. Do you love Dad? I love this man."

"I don't think it's quite the same."

"Actually, I think that in this case, you and I are quite similar."

"Go on."

"My situation made you realize that you regret breaking up with Dad. My situation made me realize that I regret having told Augustin it would be better if we went our separate ways."

"Oh, come on, April, you can't compare living together for several years, marriage and bringing a child into the world with a relationship that's only lasted a couple of weeks!"

"I'm not making that comparison, Mom, I'm just saying that I really do love him, for all the good he's done for me, for all the bad stuff he's made me forget, for all the love in each of his actions and thoughts. If you can't understand that then maybe you've never truly been in love?"

"What? Oh, that's a good one!"

"Well, you see, Mom, when you say that Augustin is just a short-lived crush, I feel like saying the same thing to you."

Mom shrugs her shoulders scornfully. But I think she knows I'm right.

"Mom," I go on. "Yesterday I got angry with you and Dad, and that was wrong. I feel bad about that."

Seeing her questioning look, I continue.

"After that night in the hospital, I told Augustin that it was over because I didn't want him to end up in the same situation one day because of me. But I was holding him responsible for everything. I was unconsciously accusing him of not having been good enough, but I was the problem, not him, and it was so cowardly of me to have turned my back on him."

"You have been doing some soul-searching, haven't you!"

"And I suppose you think I'm wrong?"

Mom thinks for a few seconds before replying.

"No, I think you're right. OK, hell is freezing over as we speak!"

"And maybe you also think I shouldn't have told him it was over between us?"

Mom gives a little smile.

"Now you're going a bit far, aren't you?"

"You think? You know, Mom, I've grown up. Enough to know that I love him, and to tell you, face to face, that I'm not going to pretend it's not true and that he's not important to me."

My mother looks as if she has just had a bucket of ice-cold water tipped over her head. As if she has realized that I'm not five years old anymore. She takes a deep breath, lowers her eyes a moment and then looks at me again, woman to woman.

"Cutting the umbilical cord is harder than I thought, especially in our situation. I guess I owe you an apology, because in some ways it's my fault you weren't careful enough."

"Your fault?"

"Too much pressure, too much anxiety coming from me."

"Do you really think that?"

Mom's voice cracks.

"I'm just so scared I'll lose you. That's my only excuse. I can see that you have become a wonderful and courageous young woman. Seeing you change so much scares me because... I can't control everything anymore, and I don't seem to be able to let go of your hand."

And she bursts into tears. I get up and take her into my arms.

"Oh, Mom. I don't want you to let go of my hand, I just want you to stop squashing my fingers."

Her little giggle, mixed with sobs, is muffled by my pyjama top.

"You need to trust me more, Mom. The trust you place in me is what will carry me forward. I don't want to have to fight you every time I decide to do something that doesn't fit with your program."

"Neither do I."

She's holding my hand, so I pull up a chair and sit opposite her.

"I need you, Mom, you're my guardian angel."

"And you're my angel, plain and simple."

We hug each other tight for a few seconds, as if to mark a new beginning, and then I pull away a little.

"You know what I'd like?"

"No?"

"Given that it looks as if our family has decided to come together again, I'd like us to spend Christmas here, all three of us, snowstorm or no."

"Hmm… OK, but your dad's not allowed to cook!"

"Suits me fine!"

I watch her thumb caressing the back of my hand.

"Are you both ready to get back together? After just forty-eight hours?"

She smiles at me.

"No… I mean, not straight away. We need to get to know one another again and build up our relationship. You know, for a long time I thought your father was too casual, and I was the one who was determined. But maybe I was wrong."

"What made you change your mind? What brought you together so suddenly?"

Her eyes are damp as she replies, "The fear of losing you…"

As I realize that they separated because of me but now, again because of me, they're finding their way back to each other, this phrase makes so much sense. I find it difficult to hide my emotion.

"I love you both so very much."

"And we love you too."

We smile at each other for a few seconds, then I pick up my phone to see if Augustin has replied to my message. It's still undelivered. Mom gets a resigned look on her face.

"I suppose you want to contact Augustin now?"

"If he ever gets back online, yes. I'm going to leave him a voice message."

"April… Your father is not going to be as accommodating as I am, you know. He is still upset at Augustin."

"But that's not fair! All he did was follow me."

"I'll speak with him."

I nod my head, grab my cup and a slice of toast without butter and walk toward the stairs. I turn back before leaving the kitchen.

"Mom, not right away. Do you mind if we wait until after Christmas? It's stormy enough around here as it is!"

"OK. That's sensible."

"See, I can be… under torture!"

I shut myself in my bedroom and dial Augustin's number. It rings without stopping and doesn't go through to voicemail. I know exactly what that means – he has blocked me.

I ring Eva in a panic.

"Hey! You're calling early," she answers in a sleepy voice.

"He blocked me."

"Huh? What?"

"I've been thinking about the conversation we had yesterday, and I wanted to call him and tell him I'd changed my mind and that I didn't want things to be over between us, but he's blocked me. He blocked me!"

"My brother?"

"No, Santa Claus! Of course, your brother! He doesn't want to talk to me anymore. He blocked me!"

"OK, I think I get it now. What can I do?"

"Tell him I want to talk to him."

Eva lets out a mammoth yawn.

"OK, OK… Give me a couple of minutes and I'll call you back."

When she hangs up, I'm so worked up. He blocked me! I can't believe it.

When Eva calls me back, I'm still holding my phone in my hands.

"So? What did he say?"

"Nothing."

"Nothing?"

"Nope, he's not here."

"Where is he?"

"He went to help clear the snow around the ski school."

"Will he be back soon?"

"How would I know? OK, I can tell you're not going to leave me alone until we sort this out, so let's meet up in an hour in front of my folks' store, and we can go together. What do you think?"

I'm finding it hard to get my breathing back to normal.

"OK. Thank you. See you soon."

There's so much snow, I almost brought my sled. The only reason I didn't is because I didn't want to push Mom over the edge.

When I get to the centre of town, my ski pants are soaked. The snow was up to my knees in some parts. There's not a single vehicle on the streets. It's crazy. I feel like I'm at the North Pole.

Eva's waiting for me in front of her parents' store, and by the look of her, she didn't have a great night. As soon as she sees me show up, she throws her hands up in the air.

"I know, he blocked you!"

"Stop teasing me, it's not funny!"

She rolls her eyes.

"Come on. We'll go to the ski school, you can declare your love for him, the two of you can make out, and then I can go back to bed."

We walk side by side along the cleared sidewalk toward the ski school chalet. My heart leaps in my chest when I see

Augustin. He has just leaned his snow shovel against the wall of the hotel opposite. I come to a standstill.

"What are you doing?" asks Eva. "Go on!"

I shake my head.

"You're kidding me, right? You wanted to see him, and there he is!"

"What if he doesn't want to talk to me?"

She raises an eyebrow.

"That's a risk you'll have to take. Having said that, being the person he is, I can't imagine that's the case."

"Are you sure?"

"No, but we haven't come all this way for nothing. Do it!"

I take a deep breath and walk toward him, with Eva at my side. He turns his head and stops when he sees me.

"Go on, I'll wait for you over there if you want," whispers Eva.

I swallow and walk up to him.

I'm trying to guess what he's thinking, but his face remains blank. I want to turn around and run away. I look back at Eva, who gestures me on. OK…

I stop in front of him and have to tilt my head back to look into his eyes.

"Hi. We didn't end up leaving because of the storm. We'll be here for Christmas. What a huge amount of snow, it's not too much hard work, is it?"

I can't seem to stop the drivel coming out of my mouth, and Augustin doesn't reply.

"Well, anyway," I add, looking around the ski school, "you've done a great job."

Oh man, when did I become a work inspector? I'm so lame. And Augustin still hasn't said a word. I'm mortified. I should never have come.

"Um, well... I don't want to hold you up anymore, I'd better go."

I give him a strained smile, but as I'm turning around, he says, "Why did you come here?"

I turn around and face him again. There's no point beating around the bush. I don't even know how to do that.

"I... I don't want us to break up."

"It's not as simple as all that," he replies coldly.

"I know. I made a mistake."

"And?"

"Maybe you could... ignore it? Forget what I said? Maybe we could talk about it?"

He looks down at me without a smile.

"I don't know."

I blink, my stomach in knots.

"You don't know?"

"I'll think about it."

And he turns on his heels, crosses in front of the little hut in the kids' play area and gets onto the snowmobile parked at the bottom of the ski slope.

With a sinking heart, I see him start it up and drive off on the snow.

"What did he say?" asks Eva.

"That he's going to think about it."

"About what?"

And while I'm standing there like a fool in the middle of the street, with people passing to and fro on the sidewalks and Christmas carols sounding out from loudspeakers, tears start to fall down my cheeks.

"About nothing. I think this time it's really over."

December

22

"April, can you get the door, please? Our hands are covered in dust!"

While my parents are fiddling around doing who knows what in the fireplace, I'm still in my pyjamas, half-asleep after a night spent wide awake because of the howling wind. I drag myself from the kitchen to the living room to see who could possibly be at the door at 8:30 in the morning.

It's Eva. Her face is deathly pale and the shadows under her eyes are so dark it looks as if her night was just as bad as mine.

"Eva?"

"Please tell me you've heard from Augustin…"

I look at her in surprise. Yesterday he told me he was going to think about things and that's all I know. I'm still blocked, and I haven't received any messages from him.

"No, sorry."

Eva brushes the snow off her jacket and comes into the chalet.

"What's going on?" asks Dad.

"We haven't seen him since yesterday. The snowmobile isn't in the garage, and there was an avalanche near the Portes du Soleil mountain pass early this morning. The emergency services have been advised that there were backcountry skiers near there."

"Oh, no," murmurs Mom.

My heart rate shoots up.

"Are Jimmy and Jeff with him?"

"Jimmy isn't, but we can't find Jeff. Margot said he was looking for Augustin yesterday afternoon."

Eva is holding back her tears.

"They're such hotheads, I'm sure they're together."

"Damned fools," mutters Dad. "It must barely have been daylight when they left, and they would have known there was a huge risk. What were they thinking, for Pete's sake?"

Eva runs her hand nervously through her hair. Her eyes are red, and I feel like the room is spinning. I'm well aware of the statistics. In an avalanche, after three or four hours, there's only a ten per cent chance of finding someone buried still alive.

I close my eyes and try to pull myself together.

"Are you sure he went skiing? I know he loves the thrill of it, but I'm sure he wouldn't have taken such a stupid risk. Maybe he just dropped the skiers off, and Jeff wasn't with him? Augustin wouldn't have lent his father's snowmobile so that someone else could drop him off, would he?"

I want her to reassure me. I want it with every cell in my body.

"I don't know, April. This is driving me crazy."

"Maybe he didn't even go anywhere. Yesterday he said he needed to think. Maybe he went to his friend's apartment?"

Eva furrows her brow.

"What apartment? What friend?"

"I don't know his name, but I can go with you. I went to the apartment with Augustin."

I turn to my parents. They exchange looks, but there's no way I'm going to start justifying myself and repeating everything about the night I slept away from home. Not now.

"Do you want us to have a look there?"

"Yes, please. My parents are really upset."

"Go on," Dad says, "I'm going to make a couple of calls and see if I can find out anything else."

"Wait for me," I say to Eva, "I'll be back in a minute."

I run up the stairs to my room, pull on a pair of ski pants and a sweater. All I want is to find out that it's Jeff and not Augustin up there. When I go back down, Dad is still on the phone.

"Yes, OK. I understand, of course we can wait. Thanks for your help, Mike."

He hangs up.

"The avalanche was in the Crosets region, at an altitude of 1,970 metres. The area is 450 metres wide and 1,500 metres long. There were no ski lifts open, so they must have gone by snowmobile. As far as we know, the avalanche took the skiers by surprise before they got to the summit."

I'm sure I'm going to faint. Even imagining something happening to him makes it hard to breathe.

"A Swiss rescue team is on site, and there are already dogs working. All we can do is wait," he finishes. I take Eva's hand. She's about to break down.

"Come on," she says. "Maybe my idiot brother isn't under the snow. And if he is, when he gets out alive, I'll kill him."

It hasn't snowed since yesterday, so when we get to the centre of town, the roads are clearer and it's easier to circulate. There's a big group of tourists a couple of hundred metres below the slopes, waiting for the lifts to open, unaware of the drama taking place only a few kilometres away. I want to scream at them that they're not allowed to be so carefree, while we're so worried.

I speed up until we reach the chalet where the apartment is. On the ground floor there's a butcher's store, and the owner, a guy with a big pepper-and-salt moustache, is clearing the snow from the sidewalk. We go to the main door, but it's locked, of course.

"The skylight opens out onto the street just round the corner. It's not very high up, so maybe if we call out, he'll hear us?"

Eva nods in agreement, follows me, and as soon as I point out the window, she starts yelling her brother's name. I do the same, but no one answers.

"Are you looking for someone?" asks the butcher, who has come round to see what we're doing.

"My brother!" replies Eva. "There's been an avalanche at Les Crosets. We hope he hasn't been caught in it, but we haven't heard from him since yesterday."

The man frowns.

"I have the keys to the main door, I can open it for you."

We nod in thanks, follow him and then run up to the third floor.

"Here it is!"

She doesn't hesitate for a second before knocking on the door and yelling.

"Augustin, Augustin! Open up, it's me!"

The silence deepens, almost suffocating us.

"Damn it, Augustin, open the door!"

Nothing.

"Augustin!"

I touch Eva on the shoulder.

"He's not here."

I'm struggling to stop my voice from shaking. Eva bursts into tears.

"He must be here. He's got to be here."

Then suddenly, we hear the lock turn. We literally stop breathing. The door opens to a tall guy with dark, tousled hair.

"And you are?" he asks, taken aback to find two noisy girls crying on his doorstep.

"I'm Augustin's sister. We're looking for him."

"Oh, sorry, he's not here. I arrived the day before yesterday. I got my keys back from him and haven't seen him since. Is something wrong?"

I can tell Eva can't bear to explain the situation again, so I jump in.

"Can you get him to call us if you hear from him? It's urgent. My name is April."

"Yeah, of course," he replies in a voice that still sounds sleepy.

"I hope it's not serious."

"I hope so too. Thank you and sorry we woke you up."

I put my arm around Eva and take her down the stairs. We're back outside on the sidewalk, more downcast than ever. With a shaking hand, I get my phone out of my pocket.

"I'm going to call Dad and see if he has any more news."

"If he had, he would have called you already," says Eva. "I'm going to flip out if I don't do something to calm myself down. I swear I'm going to poke his eyes out when I next see him! Let's go to the Blue Yeti. I don't know if Jimmy serves hard liquor, but I need at least two litres!"

The bar is about a hundred metres away, and to get there we go past the ski school. Eva doesn't even notice, but I grab her by the arm and stop her.

"Why don't we go and ask them if they've seen Augustin?"

When we go in, an instructor is tidying away some documents.

"Hello, is Augustin Favre working today?"

"No, he starts again tomorrow. At least, we hope so. The snow is very unstable at the moment. There was an avalanche at the Portes du Soleil pass this morning. Do you want me to give him a message?"

"I'm his sister," says Eva. "We haven't heard from him since yesterday, and there's a strong possibility he went back-country skiing. Skiers were reported in the area near where the avalanche occurred."

The instructor turns pale.

"Oh… You don't think he…? Listen, I'm sure that wouldn't have been him. Augustin is always so careful. You know what, I'll go and see whether his skis and snowboard are still in his locker. That'll give you an idea!"

She gets up, disappears into a back room and then comes back. Her expression is serious.

"His skis are there, but not his snowboard."

I close my eyes. Eva wraps her hand around mine. She is trembling. Our hopes keep being raised, only to be dashed one by one…

I pull off a sticky note from the pad on the desk, grab a pen and scribble our telephone numbers down.

"Can you call us if you hear anything?"

"Yes, of course. And listen, I know this doesn't mean much, but I'm sure he wouldn't have taken any stupid risks. If you find out anything, let us know, OK?"

We leave the ski school and head to the Blue Yeti. All I want is to walk through the door and see him there, drinking a coffee with Jimmy. I would wrap both arms around him, ruffle his hair, kiss him in the hollow of his neck and tell him how much I missed him. But right now, there are only three customers in the bar, and none of them is Augustin.

The television is on a news channel; we can see the Air-Glaciers team working at the avalanche site. A red-and-white helicopter is sitting on a stable patch not far from the huge mass of dislodged snow. You can see dogs, rescue people, bags of equipment and stretchers. There is so little time, I feel like vomiting.

"They've found a body," says one of the customers in a loud voice. "You've got to be stupid to go skiing after so much snow. All the tax money we fork out just to save stupid idiots!"

"Don't you have anything better to do?" says Jimmy, coming round the bar and standing next to Eva. "If that's the most intelligent thing you have to say, why don't you go and watch the news at home!"

Then he says to us, "I'm sure it's not him. It's not him. I can just tell."

My heart stops beating. I'm scared I won't be able to stay standing, so I hold onto a table. My legs are only just holding me up.

Jimmy takes Eva in his arms, but she pushes him away gently, picks up her phone and calls her parents. When she hangs up, she's breathing easier. But I'm suffocating.

"It was a Swiss skier. According to the detection beacons, there are still two in there."

The television image switches to an aerial view of a helicopter lifting up a white snowmobile that's in bad shape. It's the same as Augustin's father's. I can feel the bile coming up my esophagus and reaching the edge of my lips. This time I sit down. This is a nightmare and we're all going to wake up from it soon.

I refuse to believe it's him.

I refuse to believe he's up there, buried somewhere under the snow.

I refuse to believe I'll be without him.

I refuse to believe I'll never see him again.

I refuse to believe he is dead.

Eva's telephone starts to ring. It looks like she's empty, unable to cry or speak, but she manages to answer the phone mechanically. While Jimmy is supporting her with an arm around her shoulders, I see Eva literally collapse. She sits down on a chair, and her face is bright red, as if she has been holding her breath.

"It was the instructor at the ski school. She didn't realize, but she was just told that last night Augustin asked if he could leave the snowmobile in their storage building, and it's still there."

My breathing accelerates as on the television I watch the helicopter lift the machine up into the air. It's the same type of snowmobile, but it's not his. It's not his!

"He hadn't taken it…"

"No!" Eva says, laughing nervously.

"But what about his snowboard?"

"It needed a service," says Jimmy.

Eva and I look at each other, then she realizes something and grabs her phone again. It's only when I hear her asking some guy called Pierre to go and look in the workshop to see if Augustin's snowboard is there that I understand she's calling her parents' store.

"It's there! The snowboard is there!"

Eva hangs up, looks at me, then starts laughing hysterically. It's such a release of emotion that she cries, chokes and can't seem to stop. I don't know how to react. I still feel short of breath. I watch her without moving, without saying anything, frozen, as if someone had turned on the light after I had been in the dark for a long time.

Eva gives free rein to her feelings, and Jimmy starts to laugh too. It's contagious. My shoulders start to shake, I give a hiccup, then two, before letting all my emotion out. We can't stop. The customers in the bar don't understand what's going on, but we don't care. Augustin is somewhere out in the world, alive. He's alive!

Eva finally calms down. She wipes her eyes and drinks the big glass of water Jimmy has brought her. It takes her a few more seconds to pull herself together, then a determined expression comes over her face.

"You absolute asshole!" she barks out at an imaginary Augustin. "As soon as I find out where you're hiding, I'm going to give you a piece of my mind!"

With that promise, I go back home. I'm completely empty. I feel like I've run a marathon. My body is so tired, so exhausted. I'm dead on my feet. Mom comes to greet me with a worried look.

"You're all pale."

"I'm all right."

"I guess you've heard the news too," says Dad to reassure me. "It's highly likely that Augustin didn't go out skiing."

I nod. I don't have the strength to tell them I had a front-row seat to all the drama.

"I'm going upstairs to get changed. Can we talk later?"

My parents don't argue, and I shut myself up in my room.

I don't know where Augustin is at the moment, and I want to believe he's safe, even though I'm still worried to death.

I know I'm still blocked, but I write him a long message he won't ever receive.

> I didn't know it was possible to be so scared.
> I didn't realize that the thought of losing you could make my heart stop again. I didn't realize it was possible to love someone so much and at the same time be so disconnected from reality. Maybe you're still thinking, maybe you're going to say I'm not worth it, maybe you'll want to kiss me again. I have no idea what you will decide. I don't even know what you think about me. Today I thought you were dead and I hated you. I hated you for making me love you so much. But what about you, Augustin? Do you love me?

I put my phone down just as Dad knocks at my door. He comes in and sits next to me.

"We had some more news. We've just learned that Jeff was one of the skiers. Augustin wasn't with them."

The relief is so great, I choke back a sob.

"How's Jeff?"

"The knucklehead is alive, but he's in shock. He has a few fractures."

I feel submerged by a wave of emotion, and I start to cry.

"I was so scared."

"Everything is fine now," he says, smoothing my hair away from my face. "Try and rest for a bit, OK? You need it."

I nod and fall asleep quickly. When I open my eyes two hours later, it's midday and Eva has sent me the only message I wanted to receive.

Augustin is back! But don't get too excited cos obviously now I'm going to have to kill him. Farewell. Come and visit me in prison.

PS don't bring me oranges, you can't hide a razor blade in them.

PPS don't contact my brother. Let him marinate for a while. He deserves it.

PPPS oh whoops, that's right, he'll be dead!

I put down my phone and sit on the edge of my bed, almost in a state of shock. Then I burst out sobbing, unable to hold back my tears of relief. I have never in my life prayed, nor called on any higher power, but I find myself thanking the heavens, the universe and the world around me. I know better than anyone how ephemeral and cruel life can be, but for the first time, I realize that this feeling of powerlessness is multiplied tenfold when you think you've lost someone you love. Suddenly I understand my parents.

I get out of bed, go downstairs and find them next to other each preparing dinner.

Without saying a word, I put an arm around each of them.

"Augustin is back home, and I just wanted to say I love you."

"We love you too," says Mom.

She shifts a little, as overcome by emotion as I am, and points to the dish behind her.

"We're having potchons."

I smile. We truly are a family again. This horrendous day is finally over, and all I want is to put it behind me forever.

It's midnight, and I'm exhausted. I pull on my long nightie and a pair of warm socks and snuggle under the duvet. Augustin hasn't written to me, but I can't blame him. Tomorrow I'll go and talk to him. He'll just have to listen to me. I was so frightened that now I've got to tell him how important he is to me. And if he still doesn't want to be with me? I can't bear thinking about it.

I turn off my bedside lamp, close my eyes and quieten the thoughts in my brain.

Just as I'm about to fall asleep, I hear a knock on the bay window. It startles me and I switch on the lamp again, my heart beating fast.

Someone is on my balcony.

"Are you going to keep me waiting out here for long?"

He's whispering so my parents can't hear him. As I hold the French door open, I'm so surprised I can't say a word nor am I able to make any movement. Augustin is standing in front of me, his hair covered in snowflakes and his face illuminated by the light from my room. He seems to find the situation funny.

"I'm freezing, and you probably are too. Can I come in?" he says in a low voice.

I step back so he can come inside.

"I hope you don't mind that I climbed up onto your balcony. It was actually quite difficult, it was really slippery. I did think about just knocking at your front door, but after the last conversation I had with your father, I'm not sure he would have been very happy to see me. Sorry, but I've got to take this off otherwise your bed'll get soaked."

He brushes the rest of the snow off before unzipping his snowsuit and removing his arms from the sleeves, letting it drop to his feet. Underneath he's wearing thermal leggings and a tight, black t-shirt, clearly revealing the outline of every muscle and… bulge. I have to force myself to look him straight in the eye. How in the world can someone have such a perfect body.

"Um… what are you doing here?"

"Apparently you were worried about me. Also you apparently hate me, so I came to talk to you about it!"

"Ah… I hate you?"

"Yeah, that's what you wrote in your message, right?"

"Did you read it?"

"I read it."

"Ah ha…"

He takes a step toward me, and I instinctively step back.

"Are you afraid of me?"

"No, of course not! It's just that…"

"You hate me!"

He gives a little lopsided smile.

"I don't hate you. We were all so worried. I've never seen Eva in such a state."

He sighs.

"I'm so sorry. I needed time on my own, and I disconnected in every sense of the word. For the past few days, I had managed to get out of everyone's way and make sure no one needed anything from me. I had no idea the situation would get so out of hand. I didn't even know there had been an avalanche."

"Where were you?"

"In Montriond, at a friend's place."

I raise an eyebrow.

"Not entirely on your own, then…"

"An invisible friend," he replies, looking amused. "He rents out private rooms, so I tried my luck. And today I went out walking in the forest."

"To think about things?"

He smiles.

"I was upset. You didn't give me the opportunity to say how I felt. It was as if my feelings didn't matter to you. And then when you came and told me you had changed your mind, I wasn't sure. Did that mean at the slightest difficulty you'd tell me it'd be better if you left? Did you truly have feelings for me? Or was I just the person who allowed you to be someone else? The person to help you stand up to your mother, face your fears and your certainties? I wasn't sure."

It's painful to hear him speak like this.

"I wasn't angry, Mrs. Claus, I was just scared I wasn't as important to you as you said I was."

"Oh, but you are… So much more than I could have imagined."

He gives me a smile, when without warning, the noise of the stairs creaking reaches our ears.

We freeze.

"Who's in the room next door? Your father or your mother?"

"Maybe both!"

Augustin can't hide his surprise.

"Are they back together?"

I shrug my shoulders.

"Yeah, something like that."

I'm still standing in the middle of the room, my arms folded over my chest, my hands jammed under my chin. It almost feels as if I'm cold. But it's Augustin who's making me tremble. From nerves. From desire. All at the same time. I want to hold him tightly to me and tell him that right now I couldn't care less about what my parents are doing, but I'm not brave enough.

He studies me carefully. My breathing gets faster.

"Do you really believe everything you wrote to me?"

"Yes."

"What made you change your mind?"

"I never stopped thinking that, it's just… I don't want to be that person anymore, scared and hiding behind her fears. Did you know that I'll need another operation in ten or so years, and then maybe again ten years later?"

He nods.

"That's what I understood, but with everything you're doing to stay healthy, I'm sure it'll be longer than that."

"I'm going to have to be careful until the very end, but I don't want my life to be just a question of survival."

He takes another step toward me, and this time I don't move.

"Your heart doesn't scare me," he murmurs. "I want you to let me get to know it, and when it scares you, to hide behind me and let me look after it."

"Augustin…"

In a movement I can't even control, I throw myself at him and our mouths meet. I kiss him as if my life depended on it, as if he were a well and I had been without water for days. I kiss him as only someone who is entirely determined can, because that's what I am – in love, free and determined. No one will ever separate us again. Augustin's hands tighten about my waist and draw me closer to him. I can tell he's not going to let me leave again. Our kiss is no longer rational, no longer shy. It is beautiful, intense. It is just us.

My eager fingers tug at the bottom of his t-shirt and slide underneath in search of the warmth and softness of his skin.

"Wait a minute," I whisper against his lips. "I'm going to lock the door and close the curtains."

As we stand looking at one another, his burning gaze shines with a light I can't identify.

"April, I don't want you to think this is why I came. I'm here because…"

"You thought I hated you, I get it. As you can see, I really, really hate you."

He smiles and brushes his fingers over my cheek and down my neck. I close my eyes and take a deep breath.

"I don't want to think. I don't want to know if this is good or bad. I just hope you want this as much as I do."

"I want this as much as you," he whispers before kissing me.

I take the edge of his t-shirt and this time he lifts up his arms and removes it. He is even more beautiful than

I imagined, and my breath catches in my throat. Augustin looks at me for a long moment, his breath unsteady, then he puts one arm behind my legs and lifts me up as if I weighed nothing more than a rag doll, tearing a small cry from me as he does so.

"Shh… they'll hear us."

I smother my laugh against his neck and let him place me on the bed.

While continuing to kiss me, he stretches out and removes my socks. His fingers move up my legs and stomach under my nightie, then stop at the exact spot where the raised knot of skin marks the end of my scar. I'm no longer breathing. He looks deep into my eyes, seeking my permission.

In response and without hesitating, I undo the buttons of my nightshirt one by one and pull the two sides apart, laying myself open to his gaze.

Augustin observes the pale line that once bared my heart, then he sweeps his hand over it, as if he had the power to make it disappear. My chest rises, my breathing is slow and deep.

"You are magnificent," he murmurs.

I smile at him, pull him to me and let his large body cover my own.

He is warm, so warm… I'm no longer scared.

I am with him, nothing bad will ever happen to me again.

The sun's rays shine through the thick curtains, bathing my room in a soft light. I open my eyes and see this space, so familiar and comforting, in which I've spent so many years of my life. I remember that something has changed. I turn my head and see Augustin. He is sleeping deeply, his cheek buried in the pillow. He is so handsome, with his face relaxed, his breathing slow and regular. Today is Christmas Eve, and I've already received my gift.

I just had the most wonderful night of my life, and I can't wait for more to come.

He shifts a little, screws up his eyes and stirs.

"Mmm… good morning, Mrs. Claus! What's the time?"

I stretch out and grab my phone from the bedside table.

"Nine o'clock."

Augustin sits up straight.

"Crap! I didn't mean to stay this long. Your parents will be up by now!"

"Yes, they are. I heard them go downstairs."

"Damn it!" he says, trying to find his clothes, which are scattered around the room. "I'm going to have to be extra careful when I leave! I'm so stupid."

He's panicking, but I'm not. My parents, Dad especially, are going to have to face up to the reality and accept it. I think it's the right time. I feel as if I could achieve the impossible.

While Augustin is pulling on his socks, I sit up and wrap my arms around his waist.

"We're both going to go down calmly, like the two responsible adults we are. We're not going to hide."

He turns and looks at me.

"But what about your father?"

"He's going to have to understand. Mom already does."

He raises an eyebrow.

"Really?"

"Yes. Now, get dressed and let's go. I'm hungry."

I drop a kiss onto his lips and then make myself a little more presentable. I have no idea how Dad will react, but once thing I know for sure is that I'm not going to give him the choice. Augustin is "Augustin and I," not "Augustin without April." If he doesn't understand, then that's too bad.

When I open my bedroom door, Augustin looks like a little boy who's been naughty, his shoulders are rounded, his hair is dishevelled, and his gaze is directed downward. He has put his snowsuit on again, leaving the sleeves dangling at his side and revealing his burglar's t-shirt.

"You look good, it'll be fine!" I reassure him with a smile.

"Oh man, I'm not looking forward to this."

We go down to the living room. My parents are in the kitchen, eating their breakfast. When Mom sees us, she almost drops her toast on the floor. I can see Dad stiffen immediately. No need to draw a picture, he knows exactly what's going on and what's already gone on.

"Etienne," says Augustin hesitantly. "Amélie… Good morning."

"Um… hello," says Mom. "Have a seat. Would you like a coffee?"

As Augustin sits down, Dad doesn't take his eyes off him. His nostrils flare. I admit he looks a bit scary, but he's never hurt a fly and remembering that gives me courage.

"Dad, we have decided to get back together, despite all that has happened. I would like you to try and accept this, because I know that what you want most in the world is for me to be happy. Augustin makes me happy."

My approach is a little naive perhaps, but it's to the point at least.

Dad gets up, and Augustin does the same. They even look at each other in a challenging way.

"Into the living room, we need to speak. Man to man."

"No need to be so old-fashioned," says Mom in an attempt to lighten the mood.

But Dad doesn't look as if he's going to smile. He heads out of the kitchen and gestures to Augustin to follow. I intervene.

"Except that this is to do with me, Dad, so I'm coming too."

"You put my daughter's life in danger…" he begins.

"I admit that I didn't have a proper handle on the situation and that I wasn't careful enough," replies Augustin calmly. "I'm sorry."

"Oh, come on, you didn't force me! Dad, if we're going to blame Augustin, we may as well blame you too."

He frowns, not understanding what I mean.

"You invited me here to make the most of the fresh air, to get me away from my feelings of fear and anxiety, but maybe you were wrong from the beginning? If we're working on the basis that I wasn't ready…"

"April, stop right there. That won't work with me."

"You're right. Blaming you is just as ridiculous as blaming Augustin. I am the only person who is responsible for this situation because I am the only one who knows all the ins and outs of the situation. I'm the one who wanted to reach out and claim my right to live. And that's not a crime, for crying out loud. Neither you nor Augustin are in my shoes. I refuse to allow you to hold him responsible, he's not."

"Well, maybe, but Augustin, you're not mature enough to carry such a responsibility. Your parents were looking for you for twenty-four hours without you once thinking of contacting them. They thought you were injured or dead. You're still young, you'll learn, but not at my daughter's expense."

This time it's Augustin who asserts himself.

"Sleeping away from the house without warning is a thing that happens, and my family has never panicked about it before. I'm almost twenty-two, I'm no longer a child. It was the avalanche that caused their understandable fears, not me."

Dad makes a sound of frustration.

"You're trying to take yourself out of the equation, but you're wrong. Every one of your decisions has its consequences, my boy."

"He can't be responsible for everything, Dad!" I say, as I start to lose my cool. "Did you know that yesterday Jeff came and asked if he could drop him at the pass, and that Augustin refused? It's because he is responsible that he would never go out into the backcountry without getting you to check the conditions."

"Well, actually, he already has, and it nearly cost you your life."

Bam. Augustin is visibly shaken.

Dad's expression is both dark and unyielding, but I know that the words I'm about to say will have an effect. I know exactly what it is I want from my life.

"You can't stop us from loving each other, Dad. You can either accept our relationship or choose not to have me in your life."

"OK, guys!" interrupts Mom, coming to stand in the middle of us. "Look at you all getting on your high horses! You know what, tomorrow is Christmas Day, so let's not get carried away, all right? April, I'm sure you and Augustin have something super important to do. Your father and I need to talk. Now."

Dad and I continue to stare each other down for a few seconds, then I grab my stuff from the coat rack and go outside with Augustin.

"Were you serious?" he asks, stopping a few metres down the road.

"Totally."

He shakes his head.

"You can't do that, they're your parents."

I smile at him.

"Hey, it's OK. I'm not about to ask you to marry me, but I'm also not going to live with my parents for the rest of my life."

I turn and look him seriously.

"I know I love you, Augustin, and Dad is going to have to accept that, even if he's worried about me, even if he'd rather I lived under a glass jar."

He slips his arms around my waist and pulls me to him.

"Like the rose in *Beauty and the Beast*."

"There's no way I'm going to wilt! Dad'll come round."

"You think?"

"Yes, because he loves me and because Mom is going to harass him until she convinces him she's right!"

"There's been a big shift between the two of you."

"She was young before me, she experienced love before I did and I'm her only child. I think she's understood that after all these difficult years, maybe it's time for us to be happy – both her and I."

"Do you think your parents will get back together?"

"I really hope so."

With all my heart.

December
24

"So, who's spending Christmas in a hospital room because he wanted to be Ötzi the Iceman 2?"

Jeff pulls a face as he watches Jimmy placing a mini plastic Christmas tree covered in artificial snow on his bedside table.

With his unkempt hair and pale skin, Jeff looks exactly like a cave man. He pulls on the handle above him to try and sit up, and grimaces.

"Ah, shit, that hurts."

Augustin purposely drums his fingers on the plaster cast on Jeff's leg, making him grumble in pain.

"Complain as much as you want, it could have been so much worse."

"Too right," adds Jimmy, "you still have a quarter of the half-brain you initially had!"

Jeff lifts the hand that doesn't have an injury and sticks up his middle finger.

"Thanks for coming, guys. I'm glad you're here."

"And here we go again," says Margot. "There are three girls in this room, half and half, so why do you keep calling us 'guys'?"

"Oh, give it a break, I'm in pain…"

Eva and I smile, we all feel a bit sorry for him. The avalanche that caught them was huge, Jeff was lucky. A few broken ribs, a fractured tibia and a dislocated shoulder. He's sore, but he'll bounce back quickly.

"Can you give me a hand!" Eva asks her brother.

Augustin passes her a huge faux-pine garland with red Christmas balls. She climbs up on a chair and pushes in a few thumb tacks to hang it just above Jeff's bed. Meanwhile, I tie some fake holly branches to the end of the bed.

"Do you have to?" Jeff says. "I don't like Christmas."

"This is your punishment for having scared the shit out of us," says Margot.

Eva gets down from her chair and pulls an extremely ugly snow globe out of her bag and puts it on his bedside table, next to the Christmas tree. Then she flicks the switch on the base and a shrill version of *Jingle Bells* rings out in the room.

Jeff's on his own in the room for the moment, but I can just imagine the look on his future neighbour's face when he moves into the bed next to him. Margot rummages in her bag and shows him a box of Mon Chéri cherry liqueur chocolates.

"Look, if the morphine isn't strong enough, you can drink the alcohol and throw the chocolate out the window for the pigeons!"

"Oh, that's so nice of you."

"But wait, I haven't shown you the best part yet! Mrs. Rosset made you a present to brighten up your Christmas. She hopes you get well soon, she already misses you."

Jeff gets a nauseated look on his face.

"Is she the owner of the hostel?" asks Jimmy. "I told you she liked you, dude!"

Margot picks up a big see-through bag that has a duvet in it. She opens it out and unfolds it under Jeff's horrified eyes. It's green, with stars, snowmen and reindeer with red noses. I've never seen anything so kitsch!

"There is no way you're putting that on my bed!"

"You can whinge as much as you like, but you can't stop me because you can't move!"

Augustin comes up to me and puts an arm around my shoulders.

"And what did you bring for Jeff?"

That was the deal, we each had to bring Jeff a present. Augustin brought the garlands, Jimmy the Christmas tree, Margot the chocolates, Eva the snow globe, and me...

I go up to his bed and kiss him on the cheek.

Jimmy laughs some more.

"A kiss? I bet you he would have preferred it somewhere else!"

I roll my eyes and look at Jeff.

"That's just to say I'm really happy you're OK. We were all so worried about you."

Then I pull out of my pocket the Christmas decoration he had looked at so carefully when he came to my house – the tiny pair of wooden skis.

"Here. And remember that a happy skier is a living skier. No more of these silly escapades, OK?

Jeff looks ten years younger, like a kid in front of his parents.

"Yeah, that's a lesson I'll never forget."

We all sit around him on the edge of his bed to show him our support.

"I don't even know what happened to the two other guys."

"One managed to get himself out without too much damage, and the other is in a similar state to you," answers Augustin. "How do you know them?"

Jeff leans his head back against the bed. He looks exhausted.

"I don't know them. I'd been told that some guys were going out to the pass to try something. I heard they were real pros, who did these incredible tricks. I just wanted to see them ski and maybe film them. After you said you wouldn't take me, I went to see them just before they were leaving, and they agreed to take me for a hundred bucks."

"A hundred bucks to get caught in an avalanche? That's pricey," says Margot. "Damn it, Jeff, you almost died."

"I know."

"You were so lucky, I hope you realize that."

He nods.

The festive atmosphere of just a few minutes ago has completely disappeared.

Jeff looks around at us.

"Thank you for coming. Tonight I'll be eating soup with my folks, but you're all in here," he says, tapping his heart with his fist.

Then he closes his eyes.

"OK, you're completely worn out, it's time for us to go," says Margot getting up. "I'll come back tomorrow with a slice of Yule log. Rest up until then."

"Thanks. See you tomorrow, girls," he manages to say before going out like a light.

It takes us an hour to drive back to Morzine. Augustin drops Margot off first, then parks in front of the Blue Yeti.

"I'll see you tonight?" he asks Jimmy.

"Yep, sure thing. I'll bring the champagne!"

I turn to Eva with a questioning look.

"Jimmy's parents are working tonight, so he's spending Christmas Eve with us!"

"Oh… cool."

How I would love it if Augustin was welcomed so warmly into my house.

"You know what?" says Eva. "I still have a few things to get in town. Take April to hers and I'll walk home. Oh man, look how many people there are out. It's nuts!"

"I'll come too!" says Jimmy, getting out of the car with her. "See you tonight!"

Once we're alone, I look at Augustin, sadder than I would have liked to be.

"Don't worry," he says, without me having to explain. "It'll get better, I promise."

"I don't want to go back to Lyon with the situation like this. In fact, I don't want to go back at all."

"It's not the end of the world, you know. I'll come visit often. And as for your dad, he has always liked me, and it's mutual. He's a good guy, he's just upset, angry and suspicious. He'll get over it."

"I hope so."

"Of course he will! You'll see."

He pulls me toward him, and with my head resting on his shoulder, I close my eyes. I don't know what the future will hold, but for the moment, nothing is more important than being with him.

It's dark outside. The magic of Christmas brings time to a halt, making us feel like children. No matter our age, we want to believe that it's the most beautiful day of the year and that anything is possible.

Mom, who can't sing to save her life, is doing her best with *All I Want for Christmas Is You*. She's just about finished preparing a meal for twelve, even though there are only three of us. Dad is reliving the eighties and has gotten out the old tinsel, which he's hanging on the stair railing. He has an enormous smile on his face. And I'm watching my parents as happy as I've ever seen them. Irrefutable proof that at Christmas, anything is possible.

"Are you going to put your presents under the tree?" cries out Mom from the kitchen.

"Now?" grumbles Dad, getting off his step-ladder. "Can't we just go and get them when it's time to open them?"

"Yes, now! It's much more festive when they're under the tree. Don't argue with me!"

I smile. Happy or not, they're still going to disagree about almost everything, and I've come to accept it. I go upstairs to my room and collect the gifts I bought this week. For Mom I found a pretty red silk scarf, edged with little light green and gold leaves. For Dad I got a wool scarf to replace the one he's been wearing for billions of years and that he'll keep wearing until the end of time unless someone gives him a new one.

While I'm there, I get changed into the only partially acceptable outfit I brought with me, a pair of black jeans, boots and an oversized white shirt with a neckline that isn't too low and doesn't show my scar. I put on a bit of make-up, tie my hair into a ponytail and when I go back down, Mom and Dad are both on the phone, each with an earphone in one ear. Dad is holding the phone.

"Say yes!" Mom whispers to him enunciating the words clearly.

My father looks at me, looks at my mother, then sighs and gives in. I'm not yet sure what he's giving in to, but I'll find out soon enough.

"OK, of course," he says. "We're here and there's plenty of room in our house. See you soon."

And he hangs up.

"Right," Mom says to me. "April, can you put out more plates, please. There's going to be eight of us now!"

"Huh? What?"

"The Favres are coming over. They've had a power cut, and there's no way they'll be able to get the electrician over on Christmas Eve!"

"I'm sure there'd be people on call," mutters Dad to himself.

"What, and we're also going to make them eat uncooked turkey? Come on, Etienne, you're normally much more hospitable than that!" she teases him.

I'm sure I've gone as white as a sheet.

"When will they get here?"

"They're coming over now."

I catch Dad's eye. My heart is racing. Mom goes back into the kitchen, and Dad comes over to me, takes me by the hand and sits down with me on the couch.

"April, I can't stop you from seeing him, because you're so important to me, but also because you're right. Nothing is more important to me than your happiness."

He heaves a great sigh.

"It's hard for a father to let go of something that is so precious and see her in the arms of another. You love him, don't you?"

There's no way I can stop tears from coming to my eyes.

"Yes, Dad. Yes, with all my heart."

"That's life I suppose, and I can't do anything about it."

I throw myself into his arms and hug him tightly.

"He's a good person, and he also likes you."

"I know. Right, go and finish setting the table, otherwise your mother will have our hides."

"Dad… it is official?"

He furrows his brow, perplexed.

"I mean you and Mom. Are we a family again?"

Dad smiles at me.

"We never stopped being a family. Go on, scoot!"

As I add more settings to the table, I feel like I'm on cloud nine. I can't stop smiling, and all of a sudden, Dad's faded Christmas decorations are the most beautiful things I've ever seen. The whole room is filled with the atmosphere from my childhood, with all the things I loved and that made me feel safe, carefree and excited. Tonight, though, those emotions are focused on the incredible evening we're going to have.

My first Christmas with Augustin.

I can't describe how impatient I am. I'm counting down the minutes, and I literally jump when the Favres ring the doorbell. I'm standing at the front of the living room, ready to welcome them and unable to hide the huge grin on my face. Our parents say hello, Jimmy and Eva talk to them without letting go of each other's hand, loved up to the max, but Augustin and I just look at each other without a word. We devour each other with our eyes, and when he comes up to me, I can barely stop myself from grabbing him and showing him exactly how happy I am that their power meter broke down.

"You look stunning," he murmurs as he kisses me on the cheek.

"I just can't believe you're really here!"

"Maybe I'm the one who fiddled with the electrical cables, who knows..."

Then Eva joins us, a happy smile on her face.

"So? Life has a way of working out, doesn't it!"

I burst out laughing.

"I wanted to spend Christmas with my man, and you're with yours. Cool, right?"

"Very!"

I cut off my laugh as I see my father appear, his head held high and a determined look on his face.

"Ooh, I'll be off then!" laughs Eva as she backs away.

"That's right, leave just when I need you!"

Dad pretends to inspect the both of us, then smiles.

"The best way to love someone is to trust them. That's what my mother always used to say. My daughter is the most precious thing I have, so you'd better look after her for as long as she wants to be with you."

"Dad! What kind of a speech is this?"

But he remains stoic. I'm dying of shame.

"He won't break up with you, I forbid him to," he goes on, still in a serious tone. "If one day your relationship comes to an end, it'll be because of you."

I raise my eyes to the heavens. The things we have to listen to...

Augustin is just as tall as my father, so he looks straight into his eyes.

"I will take care of her for as long as she'll have me," he replies steadily.

"In that case, we're in agreement. Welcome to the family."

This is just so ridiculous. I'm almost expecting them to shake hands and seal the deal, but instead, Dad grabs Augustin by the shoulders and gives him a bearhug.

"I like you, but if you let me down..."

The rest of his sentence disappears into Augustin's ear, who bursts out laughing.

"Got it, boss!"

"What did he say to you?" I ask, once Dad is out of earshot.

"You don't want to know, I can assure you! What's for dinner? I'm starving!"

Augustin's parents came bearing as much food as Mom had prepared. We'll need days to work our way through it all. We take our time, we taste each dish, we laugh, we talk about all sorts of things, we sing even, we share and all we think about is how Christmas makes people happy. The wine is good, apparently, and our stomachs will never be able fit in all this food. Dinner continues, so do the laughs, and no one notices time passing. The clock ticks, ticks, ticks, until suddenly the bell for midnight sounds.

"It's Christmas!" cries Eva. "Let's go and get the presents!"

They're under the tree, and we all have something to open. We thank each other, give each other kisses and go into raptures. Champagne starts to flow again, and plates are filled for the hundredth time. Jokes fly thick and fast, Dad starts a karaoke session on the television, Eva starts singing and Mom follows suit.

"Do you want to go outside?" whispers Augustin into my ear.

We pull on our coats and hats, and seek refuge outside without anyone noticing. The night sky is clear, the storm has passed over, and it feels wonderful to be outside.

We walk to the back of the chalet and sit down on the old bench opposite the wood shed. The automatic lights switch on as we go past, and we can see the steam coming out of our mouths when we breathe.

"I have a present for you," begins Augustin.

"Oh… I don't have anything for you. I didn't think you'd want to see me and… now I feel a bit ashamed."

"Here, take this, and we'll call it quits."

Intrigued, I watch him dig into his pocket and then hand me a tiny wool felt pouch. I open it and inside is a heart made from polished wood, flat and smooth. I turn it in my fingers, enjoying its soft touch, and look up at Augustin.

"Keep this heart on you always, and whenever you're scared, it'll remind you that you're stronger than you think, and that my heart is yours."

I blink. I think to myself that the last remaining romantic on Earth is here, sitting right next to me. And he's mine.

"Thank you. It's so pretty."

Augustin leans toward me and places a gentle kiss on my lips.

"Merry Christmas, Mrs. Claus."

"Merry Christmas."

Above our heads shine thousands of stars, encouraging signs of promising times to come. Everything brings me back to the two of us. It's just meant to be and that's all.

I kiss him back, holding his special gift tightly in my hand, the best present I could ever have hoped for.

A heart for Christmas.